More Notes of a
Dirty Old Man

More Notes of a Dirty Old Man

Dirty Old Man

The Uncollected Columns

Charles Bukowski

Edited, with an Afterword,
by David Stephen Calonne

City Lights Books • San Francisco

Library of Congress Cataloging-in-Publication Data

Bukowski, Charles.
 More notes of a dirty old man : the uncollected columns / Charles Bukowski;
edited, with an afterword by David Stephen Calonne.
     p. cm.
This collection gathers previously uncollected entries from the author's autobiographical column.
 ISBN 978-0-87286-543-3
1. Bukowski, Charles. I. Calonne, David Stephen, 1953– II. Title.

PS3552.U4M65 2011
818'.54—dc22

2011017877

City Lights Books are published at the City Lights Bookstore
261 Columbus Avenue, San Francisco, CA 94133

Visit our website: www.citylights.com

MORE NOTES OF A DIRTY OLD MAN

God knows I am not too hippy. Perhaps because I am too much around the hip and I fear fads for, like anybody else, I like something that tends to last. Then, too, the hippy foundation or diving board or resting place or whatever you want to call it does suck in its fair share of fakes, promoters and generally vicious people trying to overcompensate for some heinous psychological defect. But you have these everywhere—hippy and non-hippy. But, like I say, the few people that I know are either a bit on the side of the artistic, the pro-hip or the understanding-hip, so I have been generally getting more of this slice of cake and it has seemed a bit SWEET.

But, lo, the other day I got the OTHER bit and I think I'd rather eat sweet than shit. Being locked into a large building where 4,000 people work at dull and menial tasks has its compensations but it has disadvantages too—for instance, you can never be sure who is going to be assigned to work next to you. A bad soul makes for a worse night. Enough bad souls can kill you.

He was balding, square-jawed, mannish???, with this look of hate-frustration upon his face. For months I had sensed that he had wanted to talk to me. Now I was hooked—he was assigned to the place to my left. He complained about the air-conditioning and a few other things, then worked in a question about my age. I told him that I would be 47 in August. He said he was 49.

"Age is only relative," he said. "It doesn't matter if you are 47 or 49, it doesn't make any difference."

"Umm," I said.

Then the speaker screamed out some announcement: ALL THOSE QUALIFIED ON THE L.S.M. MACHINES REPORT TO . . .

"I thought they were going to say LSD," he said.

"Umm," I said.

"You know," he said, "that LSD has put a lot of people in madhouses—brain damage."

"Everything puts people in madhouses."

"Whatcha mean?"

"I mean the LSD brain damage scare is probably an exaggeration percentage-wise."

"Oh no, leading doctors and laboratories and hospitals say so."

"O.K."

We worked away without conversation for awhile and I thought I had escaped him. He had one of those easy mellow voices that drowned and warbled in its own conviction. But he began again:

"Are you for LSD?"

"I don't use it."

"Don't you think it's a passing fad?"

"Nothing that is against the law ever ceases to exist."

"Whatcha mean?"

"Forget it."

"Whatcha think of the hippies?"

"They don't harm me."

"Their hair stinks," he said. "They don't take baths. They don't work."

"I don't like to work either."

"Anything that is unproductive is not good for society."

"Umm."

"Some college profs say that these kids are our new leaders, that we should listen to them. HOW THE HELL CAN THEY KNOW ANYTHING? THEY DON'T HAVE ANY EXPERIENCE."

"Experience can dull. With most men experience is a series of mistakes; the more experience you have the less you know."

"You mean to say you are going to listen to what some 13-year-old kid tells you?"

"I listen to everything."

"But they aren't mature, they aren't MATURE, don't you see? That's why they're hippies."

"Suppose they got jobs? Suppose they went into industry, went to work turning bolts for General Motors? Wouldn't they still be immature?"

"No, because they'd be working," he said.

"Umm."

"Furthermore, I think a lot of these kids are going to be SORRY that they didn't go to the war. It's going to be an experience they'll wish they hadn't missed. They're going to regret it later on."

"Umm."

There fell again the peaceful silence. Then he said, "you're not a hippy, are you?"

"I'm working, damn it. And I told you I was 47."

"The beard doesn't mean anything then, does it?"

"Sure it does. It means, at the moment, I feel better wearing a beard than I do the other way. Maybe next week it will be different."

Silence, silence. Then he switched his stool, turned his back to me as much as possible and continued working. I got up and walked to the men's crapper and stuck my head out the window for fresh air. The guy was my father all over again: RESPONSIBILITY, SOCIETY, COUNTRY, DUTY, MATURITY, all the dull-sounding hard words. But why were they in such agony? Why did they hate so much? It seemed simply that they were very much afraid that somebody else was having a damn good time or was not unhappy most of the time. It seemed that they wanted everybody to carry the same damn heavy rock they were carrying. It wasn't ENOUGH that I was working beside him like an idiot; it wasn't enough for him that I was wasting the few good hours left in my life—no, he also wanted me to share his own mind-soul, to sniff his dirty stockings, to chew on his angers and hates with him. I was not PAID for that, the fucker. And that's what killed you on the job—not the actual physical work but being closed in with the dead.

I got on back to my stool. He had his back turned to me. Poor, poor fellow. I had let him down. He'd have to look elsewhere. And I was white and he was white and most of them were black. Where ya gonna find a decent white man in a place like this? I could sense him thinking.

I suppose he would have gotten around to the Negro question if I had sent out the proper rays. I had been spared that.

His back was to me. His back was broad, American and hard. But I couldn't see his face and he didn't speak any more. What had hurt him worst was that I had neither agreed with or argued with him. His back was to me. The remainder of the night was peaceful and almost kind.

Tucson, Arizona, 6-29-67

Sitting in a country store that went broke, sitting at last after getting out Henry Miller's *Order and Chaos Chez Hans Reichel*, one year's work, putting the thing together piece by piece, magic by magic, held up by lack of funds and a praying, quivering, shaking 8x12 Chandler & Price, 50 or 60 years old, that fell apart on the last page; sitting there a moment, moulding their next move, hoping there is enough money for a next move are Jon and Louise (Gypsy Lou) Webb, who wrought the miracle of this third book out of LOUJON PRESS—which already has won awards in Typography, Type Direction & Design in TDC's 13th annual awards show in New York City.

Sitting here now behind an abandoned store front of crumbling adobe—they call it their "desert workshop printery"—they are almost broke.

It is Tucson and I am down here interviewing Jon Webb in 105 heat, and you know that Art can come from anywhere: the center of hot hell and the ghosts of old bean cans. I begin the interview:

"Both of you are great editors and bookmakers. Loujon Press is up there with the gods with your books and the Outsider Magazine. Your Miller book is perhaps the most revolutionary piece of bookmaking in the past several hundred years. My question is, do you think that you will be able to survive or will the walls fall in and eliminate you?"

Jon: We'll survive, but the walls suddenly will fall in, they always do, same as they did on Alan Swallow—tho we don't put ourselves up in his area of greatness, we're far from it."

Buk: "O.K., so, well where did the idea ever begin to become editors of this sort?"

Jon: "I gave up writing after two or three million published words because I felt that I'd never make it creatively, that I'd never get published without making compromises of some sort. Of course, that could have been an excuse for laziness or inadequacy—but I'm convinced I made a good move, from writing into publishing. I think I'm a better editor than I was a writer. If I keep going, tho, I'll only get into a morass of rationalizations."

Buk: "Fair enough. Let's leap into something else: the inflation spiral on paper, ink, type, everything from hamburgers to paperclips has, in a sense, become ridiculous. Don't you feel that after finishing one project that the next one has become almost priced out of reach?"

Jon: "I was pretty ignorant at this business when I started but I learned to become an honest con-man, meaning I've given in to developing cordial relationships with businessmen—the ones who sell me these things at such high prices. I simply con them into thinking my small order is only a sampler, the first part of a huge order, and in so doing lay the groundwork for a deal, which in business parlance means getting a cut in price. In other words, I talk in carloads until they quote me carload prices. It's a dirty approach, but the fact I have to wear a starched collar and conservative necktie to put the approach over sort of cancels in my mind the dirtiness out of it."

Buk: "I agree. Now, all of your work is done by the two of you. Breaking down your total profit and dividing the hours worked, what do you judge your hourly wage, per person, to be?"

Jon: "If it turns out there is a profit—we call anything above cost profit—our net income for hours worked so far has never exceeded 8 cents an hour."

Buk: "Is it worth it? Wouldn't you rather be picking beets or selling Fuller brushes door to door? And how about those editing and design offers from New York publishers? Don't you ever get tired of the hard road?"

Jon: "No, we work out of a compulsion, same as I always did when writing. It's a love that's transferred, that's all. Just like when a loved one dies, the idea of writing died too. I simply transferred the love for writing to the love for publishing. I could go on but I would only get increasingly flip. Because the reason any of us are in a work that is economic suicide can't logically be articulated upon without getting into a bragging—like calling oneself an artist. I think we're artists, but it could be everything we're doing that's good is just accidental. We've still a long way to go."

Buk: "All right, fair enough. But now let's talk about 'angels'. Where are the angels? I know that they DO exist. For instance, there is a poet in Europe, an American exile, not overly exceptional who is supported by some rich folk who rarely ask questions or slug him with demands and he is simply not that good. Frankly, I think you deserve an angel or 2 or 3. Do you think that yours will ever appear?

Jon: "Everybody who buys our books are angels. But getting back into the meat of it, you have to go after angels and we haven't had the time. We will eventually put on a big promotion for an angel. A good angel. We've had lots of offers from bad angels, the ones with strings attached. Like the rich widow in Louisiana who owns 4,000 acres of bottom land that's zooming in value because the Northern manufacturers are coming in. She offered us 40 acres plus a plantation house if we published her True Story Magazine style book under our Loujon Press imprint. Book was about her discovery after her husband's death that he once had a mistress. This book she wrote was an unending lambasting of him, hoping to turn him over in his grave. Broke our hearts, but we had to turn her down."

Buk: "Is the Miller book moving?"

Jon: "How could a Miller book not move?"

Buk: "I mean fast. How can we let people know that if they see these books with their eyes they will buy them? How can we let people know that these books you do will be collector's items selling for 5 or 10 times their publication price in 4 or 5 years, or less?"

Jon: "We're not much interested in selling to those people, the ones we have to let know these books we do are eventual collectors' pieces. But a lot of those people buy our books, and without knowing it are angels of a sort. So we love them, they help us keep going."

Buk: "Very true. But these formats you use that scream collectors' item at one look, what's behind them?

Jon: "Behind them is the fact that all rules of book publishing have come to a deadend, especially in design. All we're doing with our mixed-up formats is fumbling for a way out of that deadend, or past it. If we don't get past it we'll get out of this work, same as I got out of writing—and into something else. Like maybe underground filmmaking.

"But getting back to design, I believe with McLuhan that the medium is the message. And it has been our good luck, so far, to publish writers who will let us dress them up in our particular types of format, our packaging. So far, in the books we've done it hasn't hurt either of us."

Buk: "Have basic type styles changed? How do you select your types?"

Jon: "By eye. The more you pore over books of typefaces, type samples, so forth, the more type you might tend to like, and after weeks of studying you end up picking a certain typeface, cable some far-away country and you get a reply that that particular typeface has not been cast for 20 or 30 years, so you begin all over again. This happens mostly because, in our opinion, type design has also come to a deadend. So you start going back into time to find something good. You can't do that with book design, because you can't create new book design by copying the old masters at it. But type is okay to copy. It's merely one of the tools you work with to create."

Buk: "How do you decide on publishing a book?"

Jon: "It's rough, but mostly it's a case of love, of the work to be published, and the writer too. Because around that work, also the writer, you have to work months creating a format which fits that writer. Not one that fits us, that's silly. The whole format has to be an extension of both the writer's personality and the work of his we're publishing. And you'd get nowhere there without a love involved for the writer embodied in his talent. People say we must love our work. We don't. Work always is pretty drab, if it isn't just plain hell. But we love what comes out of the work. And when it's done, there's another hell in which we have to transfer the love for a book just done to the next one in line. To the next writer in line. Queer, eh?"

Buk: "Hell, no. But go on, what is the ultimate you would like to do in book design?"

Jon: "Well, if I'm constantly mulling over an elusive idea, Gypsy is too. It's to put out a book of great beauty and original design with which the buyer immediately falls in love and which is certain to become a top value collector's item, but which on opening and reading to the last page suddenly falls apart in the reader's hands, virtually disintegrates, and can in no way be put back together again."

Buk: "I get you. The buyer will buy another book at once to see if the same thing happens with the second copy."

Jon: "That isn't the reason for it, no. But you've given me an idea—thanks."

Buk: "Whatever the reason, seems like a dirty trick on the writer. All his work and yours too shot to hell forever."

Jon: "Oh, I'd first find a writer who didn't mind, be sure of that. Like you maybe."

Buk: "Come to think of it, I probably wouldn't mind. Might be fun writing for a posterity that disintegrated in the reader's hands instead of his brain. But space is running out. Any final good word to the reader of this column or any readers anywhere?"

Jon: "Well, even the broadside announcement on the Miller book, printed on Parchment paper, 19 by 25 inches, is now a collector's item. But we'll mail one to anybody who sends us a postcard, and we'll go the postage. Our address is 1009 East Elm, Tucson, Arizona 85719. LOUJON PRESS."

Buk: "How come it's so damned hot down here in June and July?"

Jon: "I don't know, but it's the next best thing to hell. That's probably why we're here."

Buk: "I think this interview is over."

Jon: "Me, too."

Buk: "You got anymore beer?"

Jon: "We knew you were coming by."

Bukowski goes out into the kitchen of the Desert Workshop Printery and gets one. The interview is over. The great poet Bukowski and the great editor Webb sit across from each other, looking in and out and over with glazed and perhaps? immortal spirits. Life goes on anyhow.

I was going over my old *Racing Forms*, having a beer and a smoke, really hungover, shaky, depressed; gently thinking suicide but still hoping for a lucky angel when there was a knock on the door, a very light knock, I barely heard it. I listened and there it was again. I hid my bag of Chesterfields under the fireplace and opened the door just a slit. "Bukowski?" said the voice. "Charles Bukowski?" and there was this woman standing out in a light rain, in the 9 p.m. rain between 2 dying plants on the front porch of the front court in which I lived, badly, among beer, and mouse-shadows, and old copies of Upton Sinclair and Thomas Wolfe and Sinclair Lewis, and I looked out looked out looked out and IT WAS A WOMAN and WHAT a woman in that 9 p.m. rain—long red hair all down the back, jesus: tons of red miracle. And the face, open with passion, like a flower ripped open with the fingers from the bud, a kind of fire-cheating, and the body, the body was nothing but SEX, sex standing still jumping singing looking flowing humming in the 9 p.m. rain saying, "Bukowski, Charles Bukowski?" and I said, "Come on in," and she did, she came in and sat on the chair in front of the fireplace and the walls of the room began to weave in and out like on a trip, and the rug said, what the hell oh my god oooh ooooooooooooh, and she CROSSED HER LEGS and the skirt was high and I looked up the thighs, boldly, jesus, I was out of my skull, thighs knees high heels long tight stockings flow and flesh oh lord and she kicked her foot, turned on ankle, ow ow ow, mercy! And the red hair the red hair flocked all along the back of the chair, the red hair on fire in the lamplight, I could barely hold on I could barely understand, I did not deserve to even LOOK, and I knew it.

"Care for a beer?" I asked.

"All right," she said.

I got up and I could hardly walk. I had enough hose to put out a forest fire of napalm.

I came back with the beer, didn't give her a glass, watched her drink it from the bottle, that stuff going into her, into her red hair into her body into her everywhere and I peered up her legs not getting enough and I drank out of the bottle.

She put down her bottle. "You are a great writer," she said.

"That's no reason for coming to see me."

"Yes it is, yes it is. You see you fascinate me, you write this way and you look like, you look like—"

"The trashman?"

"Yes, or a diseased gorilla, an undergrown aged gorilla dying of cancer. And those goddamn eyes, slits of eyes but when you finally OPEN them for just that second—shit, I never saw eyes LIKE THAT, that COLOR, that VICIOUS FIRE—"

"And you came here to see what I was, see what I am, oh?"

"I guess so. I don't know. I don't know why I'm here. I don't. I only know that I'm here. I can't help it. You're a gorilla. You're some kind of snake. You're anything filthy. You stink. I don't know you. I know that you're not the guy at Bryan's staff meetings, threatening cripples, staggering about the room, cursing everybody and looking for more to drink more to drink more to drink. Such a swine you are!"

"A woman always wants to find the core, tame it, mold

it; a wise man never shows the core to a woman. He just gives her a shot of light, shuts it off, becomes himself again. A woman practices rearing the child by taming the man first. I've got no use for women except to fuck them. I won't be trapped in. Love is a form of selfishness. Love is an excuse for cowards to quit."

"Nicely spoken. Sounds all right, bastard, but what does it mean?"

She lifted her beerbottle again, recrossed her legs, the skirt going HIGHER, jesus have mercy, the skirt going HIGHER, all that leg, all that thigh, all that red HAIR, god.

I got up and pulled the beerbottle from her mouth and put my dirty bearded face to hers, my lips sucking and twisting at hers, hard full crazy, she did not push me away, I grabbed her under the back, I had her back arched, I had her head rolling on the back of the chair, our lips splashed together spliced together crazy, my hand under the back of that BIG body, god, the beerbottle knocked over and spewing on the floor, and I reached down with the other hand and ripped her skirt all the way UP, lord lord lord then I had her standing, I was walking, pushing her all over the room, feeling that red hair around my ears across my face, feeling miracle and madness, and then I worked the pants down and then I HAD HER, I HAD HER, I HAD HER, and I worked, I grabbed that long red hair and I yanked down on it. I had her back arched arched hurting her and I HAD HER I worked and holding the hair still in my hands in back I got the cheeks and spread them, I had her nailed in the center of the rug, I had her on the cross, it was too late for her, she was on the spike, ripped ripped and the yellow light from the lamps bathed us and all that could be heard was our breathing and our grappling. Who would have guessed? Who? And then BANG the walls shook, a man on the street stepped on a grease spot, fell and broke his ankle and we slid apart like worms going in different directions, and she stood there and said, "ooooh ooooh ooooh I liked it, I liked it I liked it, you filthy greasy pig," and then she turned and walked into the bathroom and closed the door. I went into the kitchen, took a dishtowel, wiped off. Got out 2 more beers. Lit a smoke.

She came on out, looking better than ever, she glowed all over burning, she was really beautiful, I could say it easy, she was really beautiful. I drank my beer and looked at her, neither of us saying anything. I lit her a cigarette. Then I had to piss. I went to the bathroom, closed the door, pissed, flushed, washed my hands, came out, and she was . . . gone. Fast like that. No goodbye. Nothing. I looked at the chair she had sat in. At the beerbottle on the floor. No, it had happened. Yes, I found one of her earrings. A green earring. Just one. It's always ONE earring. What the hell? But never an earring like this.

I drank my beer straight down, walked outside. It was cold. All up and down DeLongpre it was the same. People locked in tight. Behind doors, behind windows. Everybody with their possessions, their people, their madness, their bank accounts, their car keys, their walnut faces, their constipation.

I looked north where I figured she lived with some fine intellectual chap who spoke the big words and the big meaning; some guys got these dolls automatically, I was lucky to see a photo in a newspaper. I took the earring the green earring and threw it north, hard, high in the dark sky, it flew out of sight in the neon mash of light from Sunset Boulevard a block north and I said, "Here, baby, your earring back and your life and all the rest, baby baby. But thanks for the splendid grade-AAA fuck."

Then I went back inside, found her still untouched beer, picked it up, drank drank drank. Found the *Racing Form*, sat down in HER chair and began checking out my plays for the Santa Anita meet, and then I found one long red hair, one very long red hair along the arm of my chair and I picked it up and touched the end of it to my cigarette; it sizzled and shriveled and smoked ever so slightly. I moved the cigarette right up along the hair until it was all burned except to the smallest bit in my fingers and then I put that in the ashtray and burned that.

Charles Bukowski. Immortal writer. Immortal lover. You can't go home again. It's all too late.

I worked at the beer.

I'm not feeling good. Jesus, man, throw those beercans in the trashbag. Fuck, I got no old lady to pick up the shit, and thank god for that. Maybe that's why I'm a peepfreak and a jackoff artist. I can't stand pussy around all the time. I mean sitting around terrorizing me with her up and down emotions and crazy head. Another beer? Right at your foot there, half a six-pack. More in the box. Here in America a man ain't a man unless he's got three or four whores and a late model car. All right, I'm a little drunk. Maybe that's why I mock myself. But put a new car and 3 women on my back and I'm fucked. I don't have a t.v. I don't even have a radio. A big Brazilian cunt who wants to put that thing on me, calls me the last of the monsters. A monster-angel, whatever that means. But I'm running from *her* too, tho she'd be a beautiful fuck, a tremendous fuck. There's something inside of me grown a little wiser. After that walk back from the bathroom you start sharing a little two person hell. Yes, I've got a story, but wait, let me get another beer. Sure, I'm a degenerate peepfreak. I'd rather look at it. I don't want to get on top of it. Understand? So, I got this funny story. For peepfreaks. All right, Frank, I know you ain't a peepfreak. But pretend you're one. No, I ain't a homo, goddamn, why does *that* always come up?

I *said* I wasn't feeling good, so don't give me any shit. Sometimes I feel so bad I think I'm going nuts. You ever felt that way, Frank? No? Well, you're just a nice American beerdrunk with standard American feelings. You like to feel like a MAN. Doesn't that make you feel good to feel like a MAN, Franky boy? No, I don't want to fight. Suppose I won the fight? Your whole life would be ruined. Why do you interrupt me? I'm trying to get over and tell this funny peepfreak story, and I'll bet you've done some peeping too—on buses or with the ladies climbing out of cars or bending over garbage cans. No, I don't have a dirty mind; I just enjoy myself the way I am. Fuck off. I told you I'm not feeling good. Throw me another beer. Shit. I can't even go get my laundry. I'm going nuts. I even forgot where I TOOK my laundry! And when I find *that*, there'll be another chickenshit thing I'll have to do that is driving me crazy. What's that? I have to get a HAIRCUT! Look, dentists are nothing, but barbers TERRORIZE me! They are such ASSHOLES, that's why, Frank. That's why! You know the most TERRIBLE thing?? Eh? Frank, when they finish, they've just got to SPIN me in that chair, right BLAM in front of that MIRROR and I've got to look at my FACE, *pretend* to look at my HAIR, as if I gave a damn whether there was a piece of hair sticking up here or there! Who cares? Shit, man, I just want to get OUT of there! And there's that asshole barber standing behind me, I see him in the mirror, he's yawning and I'm on fire, and then I'm supposed to say "fine" or "o.k." I don't know where hell is, but it's gotta be in a barbershop. It's such smucky vain finky shit, jesus, who built men this way? Give me a dentist putting his elbow on my chest, sweating, with liquor on his breath. He gets the thing—"narrrrr, that didn't hurt, did it?" and then you spit out the blood and half of your jaw: "narrrrrb, narrrrrb, o.k., bloooooop . . ." You're not indebted—spiritually—and he begins whistling. Dentists always have this wonderful lack of faith in their ability that barbers don't have, no matter how lousy barbers are. And most of them are, not that it matters. So then the son of a bitch of a barber unfrocks you and you are supposed to get up real calm, like the whole thing was so lovely and sweet and you are now a new man, and then you have to pay and TIP the son of a bitch! "Goodbye, now," he says, "see you later." "Goodbye," you say. Goodbye, goodbye, goodbye.

I'm trying to tell this peepfreak story. What? Yeah. I know, I KNOW! I know that many men *like* barbers. Many men sit in barbershops for *hours* and they don't even *need* haircuts. They don't need *anything*. They just play cribbage and talk about sports. They can look upon that dirty linoleum floor with dead sad hair upon it and they don't feel anything. They are the *sane* men of the universe. They have nothing to do with their time except watch it die. They are goldfish. I'm *not* sane. They are always fucking with me. By they, I mean the must-do people. Shit, just thinking about getting a new driver's license almost made me cut my throat. All those people in there taking their shitty little tests. Questions so simple that they are terrifying. People rubbing their heads—"psst, hey buddy, what'd de answ to the question number 3? Hey, I don't unnerstan that one a tall . . ." Lines,

lines, lines, lines, lines—lonely ladies in their late forties talking to the clerks, asking them question after silly question just to have somebody to TALK to . . . holding up the line for 15 minutes and the clerk, also lonely and lazy and with a hard dick, smiling, answering question after silly question. Dick hard, hot in there, everybody sweating and on the cross. FOR CHRIST'S SAKE, EVERYTHING'S SO HARD AND STUPID! Dicks, barbers, cops, landlords, income tax; fried eggs for breakfast . . . it's looney. Give me another beer, shit, almighty, man. I'll never tell this funny peepfreak story. I can't pay my gas and light bills, my phone bill. It's like trying to lift 4,000 pounds. It just doesn't make sense. It's just this chickenshit GNAWING, all these little snotty bills, again and again and again, no sense. You take a breather, say fuck it, look at the clouds for a couple of weeks. You come to your rented hole one night—the gas is off, the lights are out, the phone yanked out—what for? You owe them *all* a total, combined, of $39; they couldn't wait. Shit, you've got $80 in your wallet. You just couldn't go to the post-office and ask for 3 stupid money orders—the lines are long, the girls are suffering or stupid, and there's always some idiot stepping on the backs of your shoes or trying to squeeze around in *front* of you. Madmen, dolts! A PISS UNIVERSE, I tell you! THERE ARE SO MANY STUPID THINGS TO DO THAT THERE ISN'T ANY TIME LEFT TO DO ANYTHING THAT ISN'T STUPID. And then you're driving along and a cop gives you a ticket because you haven't had TIME to get the motherfucking taillight fixed that somebody bashed while you were parked. And while he stops you he finds eight or ten things wrong—there's *never* enough brake, the headlights are out of line, the brake light doesn't work, the windshield wipers are *worn* and you only have one windshield wiper, on and on. Man, you're trying to *kill* yourself, here, good thing I came along. Here, take this ticket. Sign. Thank you, sir. Oh, thank you, officer. I don't have brains enough to know whether I can drive this car safely or not—I really want to kill myself, you know.

Throw me another beer, Frank. Everything drags me down. That's why I can't have any cunt around here chopping me down with her yak and demands. The whole thing is a war, Frank, can't you see? And I'm weakening. I've got a week's worth of newspapers on the floor. I can't pick them up. I can't even put a roll of toilet paper on a roller. That's work. Springs and twisting. More work. I just sit the roll on the floor. My guts are shot, my soul is shot. You must believe me, friend—just to set my soul *halfway* straight is a monstrous and impossible task.

You say I need LOVE? Horseshit! All right, I'm a loner and a loner usually hangs himself; a lover needs help and usually gets it; it all ends up in hanging. Sure I'm sick. Dizzy spells, and these white blisters on the hands; boils on the ass; inflamed throat, heart flutter, glass in the feet, neuritis and bursitis, toothache, headache, ulcers, ingrown hair and toenails, broken fingers, insomnia, anxiety—what the fuck. Name it, I'll trot it out. And a peepfreak. Hell, yeah. Which brings us to *that*. Goddamn it, I been trying to get to this peepfreak thing!

So I'm in the doctor's office. What was it for? I hate to tell you, but there's this thin line along my ass, very thin, indented, like I been sitting in a slab chair and it won't go away, this thin indented line. It's stupid, sure. I once saw a pigeon lying on the sidewalk. It was sick or something. Its wings wouldn't work. I could see it breathing. And on its still alive body the ants were already crawling. The top eye was open and looking at me. There were ants crawling across that *eye*. I didn't know what to do. I stepped over the bird and walked on down the street. 2 hours later I had forgotten about it. Now I had this line on my ass.

There were 3 of us waiting. Guy with crutch next to me. Girl with impossibly short skirt and fine nyloned legs all stilted up with very high heels. Holy, ummm, ummm. So I get a hard-on. I can't help looking. I want to look. Wow, it's all free. It's like walking into a closet full of gold. Such crazy things happen. And those broads are so off-hand about it. Real cinchy cool, which only makes it worse, and hotter. Oh my god. I am a peeper since the age of 6, 8, 10, 12, 48. When I was a kid we used to go under the slatted grandstands, crawl under there and peek up the women's legs, me and my buddy Harry. We used to go to the air races and do it. There was a lot of wind there and it was summertime. We saw some things. "Think of it," Harry said, "THOUSANDS OF PUSSIES!" "Jesus," I said, "you're making me a little sick." Harry is now a municipal court judge.

Well, anyhow, there I am in the doc's office with the line on my ass and there aren't thousands of pussies or millions, which is terrifying, but just one, and I can't *quite* see it and it's best that way. Of course, you imagine there might be something else there, some crazy kind of miracle.

Like a dick? There you *go*, Frank. I'm trying to tell this funny peepfreak story and you've got to come on like some dumb American lonely hero on the barstool of the good old neighborhood bar. Fuck you. This is the funny story. Listen. I told you I was a peepfreak. O.K. Listen, will you?

Right in the MIDDLE of my beautiful hard-on, I have to think, you KNOW what I HAVE to think? After all, she IS in a doctor's office. Christ, she might have the gon or the siff, right? AND THE THING DROPS RIGHT ON DOWN AND I ALMOST BEGIN HATING HER.

You think I'm nuts? The guy with the crutch must be

thinking the same thing for he has been staring straight ahead for ten minutes at one of the paintings of a castle on the Rhine that the good German doctor has hung all about the waiting room. He must have 5 or 6 paintings of castles on the Rhine in that waiting room.

Me, I reach out and get a magazine, a dull one. *Newsweek* or such.

I had to read all about the Russian tanks in Prague so long after it happened. More mad shit like getting a driver's license. Hardly ever occurred with reason. Just more waste and waiting and bullshit. So I read it all again to keep from looking at those siff legs. The magazine account seemed no different than the newspaper version. God drab yawn insanity. More barbershop. That's what's so terrible about doctors' waiting rooms. All the warmed-over cón. You had to *read* it and wait wait wait, or else it was sit and look at each other's FACES and *that* couldn't be done, obviously. So, everybody turning pages, everybody reading these dull magazines and sitting there THINKING: I wonder why I feel so bad?—"Some of the Hungarians riding tanks were asked by the Czechs why they had helped do this thing when Hungary was the same victim of the same Russian tanks not so long ago. The Hungarians turned away."—I wonder why I feel so bad the people in the waiting room think, reading magazines. Do I have the clap, cancer, acidosis, hepatitis, catalepsy, pyemia, seborrhea or scarlet fever? Flip, flip, the pages go, thinking, thinking.

So, you find *another* magazine, and wait.

So, there I was, and then an old woman walked out, chirping chirping to the GIRL in the short short skirt: "Ooooh, he put a stitch in my eye! Ooooh, I feel so much *better* now! Ooooh, honey, I feel so much better now! The stitch will have to come out later but I feel so much *better* now!"

"Well, sit down a moment, mama, and then we'll go home," says the girl in the short short short skirt with the nyloned legs of magic on the high high black tight heels. God.

My mind got at me good: Idiot idiot peepfreak lost lost. Fool, you WASTED all this time! She's the DAUGHTER! No CLAP! No nothing! Just the miracle of all those legs looking at you FREE, oh god have mercy, those clean miracle legs. WUNDERBAR!!!!

I began to leer over the top of a 4-week-old copy of LOOK.

I just got something GOING when mama and daughter rise and LEAVE. The daughter has on this short black slip, red dress, green panties, and after mama leaves out the doorway, she rather pulls the red dress down, stretches, bringing up the breasts, out the ass, then she is gone after mama and I am left with a shaft of pale sunlight in the doorway.

Then what happened? What could happen? The doc called in the guy with the crutch and I took down one of the paintings of a castle on the Rhine, took it down the elevator. Hit floor one, carried the castle on the Rhine to my car, threw it in the back seat and drove off.

What did I do that for? I don't know. Maybe it was all I had left of the nylon legs, the green panties, I don't know. Rather like taking one ant out of the eye of a living pigeon. Not much. Throw me a beer. I told you it was a funny peepfreak story. Why aren't you laughing?

What? The line in my ass. It went away. I'd like to phone the doc and find out when the old lady is going to have the stitch out of her eye. But if I can't hang up a simple roll of toilet paper then you know that I can't do that either. Listen, Frank, I said THROW ME A BEER. I'm not feeling well, I told you so . . .

Going east. In the barcar. They had sent me money for the barcar. Of course, I'd had a pint getting on, and had stopped for a pint at El Paso. I was the world's greatest poet and he was the world's greatest editor and bookmaker (and I'm not talking about horses).

2,000 people in America read poetry and 900 of them bought books of poetry if they could be conned into it by word or format. The old boy took care of the format and I took care of the word. I spoke the language of the people through the mind of something else. "Charles Bukowski and the Savage Surfaces": *Northwest Review*. I wasn't supposed to have a mind. What I believed in was the clarity of the word. If I wanted to scream I screamed. Fuck them.

The old man bought paper that would last for 2,000 years. Put my words on the paper, but I wasn't going to last any 2,000 years. I knew I didn't have that much; I began late and would have spit it out 5 years back, but the others, the famed and the fancied, wrote so badly they made it difficult for me to quit.

So balls, the first book had sold out, all 750 copies—now the things went for 25 bucks and up at rare book dealers and I had one pair of old shoes and a long haul to Valhalla. The old man had a backer, a New York publisher. They were going for 3,000 copies and I wrote the stuff straight into the press, didn't even send it off to the mags. The old man had sent back 5 for every one I wrote but he'd finally got enough, and I threw the others away.

I looked out that barcar window and remembered all

my days on the bum, seeing that same dry dull frightening endless brown yellow yawning zero of land—travelling with track gangs, back and forth on hot stupid buses—all that senseless land—they told me the world was overpopulated? Nothing, nothing, nothing. And here, at last, I was in a barcar, playing poet. How odd it is, really, I thought, what a bunch of horseshit. I am no different than I ever was. I might have even been a better man then, though I doubt it. The older I got the better I got. What a crazy elixir! Elixir? What was that? It sounded good, but not a savage word.

"Bukowski is a beast," said the woman at the party. "He's horrible!"

"Oh come now," said the professor, "do you *really* think that?"

(Dear old Dr. Corrington, he always said I was a "savage," not a "beast.")

But I couldn't get a drink in the barcar. All those picture windows, and no drink. All that dry desert, wanting my bones and my ass; snakes to crawl through my eyesockets, and no drink.

2 porters or waiters or whatever they were, they were standing in the vestibule (how's that for a word?) talking to each other about the stockmarket and pussy and the stupidity of the white man. It had gone on for about 10 minutes and I had sat at the table, waiting. I always felt inferior around those neatly white-jacketed black men, as if they knew something that I didn't. But they really *didn't* know anything that I didn't know, so I finally got up and weaved toward them, stood there a foot from them and listened to them talk. They ignored me. Finally their talk bored me so much that I broke into it:

"Pardon me, please. Pardon me."

"Yes?" one of them asked.

He would have said "yes sir" but I was already a bit drunk.

"Can one of you gentlemen tell me where I can find the bartender or just who *is* the bartender?"

"Oh," said the other one, "I am the bartender."

"Would it be possible to get a scotch and water fairly soon or is the bar closed?"

"Oh no, the bar is open."

"Then, please, I'd like a scotch and water. Beer chaser."

"Beer chaser, sir?"

"Yes, please, if you will."

"Any kinda beer?"

"No and yes. The best."

The savage went over and sat down. The s & w and beer arrived. The bill was atrocious, of course, and I also tipped atrociously. The other people in the barcar were well-dressed; I was the only poorly-dressed one, my shoes, in particular, being badly scuffed and worn. But now that I had found the bartender, everybody wanted him. I had spoiled his day. But the day of the train was over. The rich rode the jets and crashed to their deaths in planeloads totaling 186, or ended in Cuba, hijacked, pissed and scared. Only the poor rode the trains. The Mexicans, the Indians, the Negroes, the poets. The porters sniffed and lifted their noses at us. They remembered the better days. When everybody was laughing and throwing money. Now it was over.

I ordered again. The same. I liked the picture window. It was a horror show. I kept imagining myself out there with the snakes and toads and cacti, and it was horrible. And then I imagined myself back on the train with the white-jacketed aristocratic blacks and the poor blacks and the starving Mexicans and Indians and it was still horrible, in or out, up or down; I drank it down. There wasn't a woman on the train under 40. It was a shitty trip. Even on the first trip traveling toward that first book I had picked up a looker; all right, she had 2 small children, but what a body and legs, and we'd sat ass to ass, one of the kids in her lap, one in mine, both asleep, and she'd run that tongue down my throat while our flanks were together, and I'd felt her all over. Hardly a fuck, but it helped time go. And during the day I'd felt like a married man, but I allowed myself to drink all I wished and it was rather funny. Then helping her off at the New Orleans station and then skipping off to the great editor and his wife. "Bye bye, dear." I'd bet she'd thought she'd hooked a damn fool. Well, she would have, I suppose. Thank god for the great editor and his pages that last 2,000 years.

Now there was nobody. Not a cunt under 40 within 400 miles. Life could be bitter. Even for a mindless savage.

I stayed on in the barcar, through the afternoon and into the night. Everything looked better at night because you couldn't see it as well. That's why it's best to screw in the dark if you can't go grade A. The less you can see of a human being, for screwing or even for looking, the more you can forgive.

Anyway, by the time I made New Orleans this second time I was further drunk and further flung apart than ever before. Poet? What the hell was that? I didn't play freak games.

The great editor and his wife were there to meet me.

"Hello, Buke," the great editor said with a tiny smile. He was the kool one.

"What do they call you?" people would ask me.

"Buke to rhyme with Puke," I always told the people. This satisfied them.

We got into a cab and they took me to my chosen room. Their own place was stacked high with pages of Bukowski poems, page one, 3500 high, standing there. Page two, 3500 high standing there. Pages in the bathtub, in trunks, pages everywhere. You couldn't shit for pages. They even put the bed on stilts high up in the air. Bukowski under the bed. Bukowski in the shitter. Bukowski in the kitchen.

"Bukowski, Bukowski, Bukowski, Bukowski EVERYWHERE! Sometimes I think I'll go mad! I can't stand it!"

He was the kool one. She was *Italiano*—the fire. I loved her. Everybody did. No bullshit about her.

"But we love you, Bukowski."

"Thank you, Louise."

"Even though you are a bastard most of the time."

"I know. But sincerely, I don't try to be."

"You don't have to try, Buke," said the old man.

I made them stop for a pint somewhere. I hadn't eaten in a couple of days but I wasn't hungry. We got to the room, Louise paid the cabbie and we went on in.

Now, me, I'm crazy. I like solitude. I've never been lonely. There is something wrong with me. I have never been lonely. So when I saw this place, I saw it wasn't for me, because look, the whole place ran long, front to back. I mean you came in through the shuttered doors, and here was the front room and you just walked straight on down through to the rooms. It was like one long hall, kitchen in the back, get it, only the shitter was a little off to the side but everything was lined-up like a long snake and you had to pass through one room to get to another, no doors. Shit, for a monk of solitude it shook me—I mean, I'll take a whore for a one-night stand but who wants the whole world forever?

So, we all went in back, to the kitchen, and here was my landlady. They had arranged it. Nice clean place. Sure, and she was fat, very fat, my landlady was very fat in a big pink and white housegown and we all sat at the table and I opened the pint and the landlady got out some beers.

"This is Charles Bukowski, the great poet," said the great editor.

"This is Shirley."

"Poor and savage," I said, "pleased ta."

"Pleased ta," said big sad fat Shirley. Lonely.

(Oh, god have mercy upon my spare and worn parts.)

Well, the beer got around and I didn't let anybody touch my pint. I was worried about my solitude. I guess Shirley had gotten up early. Maybe worried about meeting Charles Bukowski. They had probably given her a bit of a line, not a line to them. The old man had once told me, "you've ruined me for all other poets. You lay it down so hard, like a rail-road track straight through hell."

Well, I wasn't that good, but he got the message.

So, Shirley was drooping with me. Shirley in her big fat housegown, and me, a bum, playing the role of Charles Bukowski. The world is full of literary-hustlers and the less talent they have the more they hustle; me, I didn't have to hustle very much. I didn't have to hustle very hard. But there was Shirley. And when people figure they are around a writer, especially a poet, they just have to open their soul-pores. Shirley opened up.

Well, really, tho, it's nice talking in kitchens, esp. if you have a lot to drink. Kitchens are where you can really talk. It's harder to lie in a kitchen or while you are taking a shit, than in a fancy front room. However, it can still get itchy, sticky. I was only an emotional man when it concerned my own problems. I was still growing, but very slowly, and I knew it. I knew I'd have to hit 50 before I got a bit of sense, got a bit objective, and then I'd be too tired to make it interesting. In short, I was fucked.

So Shirley started dropping these tears down her fat, materialistic face, human still, real still, she was an old gal who'd been there, the mill. I'd met dozens of them, but they could be as cruel as the rest. It was a hard slam. She was talking about a good Jewish boxer she'd known, married. I wasn't Jewish, but I knew my boxing. When a Jew laced on those gloves he'd show you a battleship full of guts. In those days, there were quite a few good Jewish fighters.

"Jackie," she said, "he beat everybody. But the champs wouldn't get into the ring with him. He was too good. And he never trained. All he did was drink. That was his training. But they locked him out. The championship went from one man to another. He blew all his purses. Bought drinks all up and down the bar, all up and down the street. He loaned money and they never paid him back. He died one night fast, just died in bed. He just let out this loud moan and died. Everybody was at his funeral, everybody. He was such a great man."

The tears were rolling.

I was finally quite drunk. "What the hell," I said, "he can't do you any good in the grave! He can't fuck you from the grave. I can lay it to you. I'm right here! I can shove you ten inches!"

Then she really started to cry.

I lifted my drink: "Ten inches. Solid."

Everybody started acting rather peculiar, so I took my bottle and went to the place they said was going to be my bedroom, stripped down to my shorts, and sat there drinking from my pint.

"Hey," I screamed, "you sons of bitches rolled me! Which one of you rolled me?"

I kept screaming for my money until I found I had hidden it under the pillow. Then I had another drink, crawled into bed and went to sleep. Shirley was frightened of me and didn't want to let me stay but the great editor said I was all right—long train ride, too much to drink. When they told me the scene the next day I didn't remember any of it. Shirley owned an eating place in the French Quarter. When she went to work I went out and bought two dozen red roses and put them on the kitchen table. She kept those roses until they fell to pieces. And she kept the card. And pressed one rose in a book.

Meanwhile, the old man had me signing pages. 3500 pages to make sure that we got 3000 good ones. I had to sign them with a silver pen, mostly, and various different colored pens, a kind of thick ink paint. It was slow. It took each page 8 minutes to dry. I had pages spread all over the bed and on chairs and dressers. When Shirley got in from work, there I'd be, all covered with pages and drunk on beer. I got tired of straight signings. I'd sign my name, then say something, and then draw a picture, any kind of picture. This slowed up the process but it took the dullness out of it. Shirley wasn't frightened of me anymore. On the beer, I was just mellow. She'd cook me a good dinner and then tell me about the store, the café.

"Jesus, I burned two pots of strawberries today, two whole pots! It was awful."

"No shit."

"Yeah. I was in the other room talking to a friend a mine and she said, 'I smell something burning!' and I ran into the kitchen and there were burned strawberries boiled over everywhere! God!"

"You oughta keep your mind on your business."

"I like you Buke. You remind me of Jackie."

"I can't fight a lick."

"No, I mean you don't come on with a lot of phony talk the way most people do."

After dinner I go back to the bedroom and sign more

pages. Then around ten I'd take my beer into the kitchen and Shirley and I would watch television together until midnight, sometimes one or two a.m. All the time she was making these little dolls which she sold at her place. She was very good at it. And she made hats. The hats were good too. Very unusual.

"Business ain't what it used to be. People don't even carry money anymore. Everything is credit and travelers checks. I can barely make it. Want a little nip of whiskey?"

"O.K. Shirley, thanks."

It was the same every night. I could lay around and play poet. I'd never have to leave. All I had to do was lay it into her. But she was so fat. So fat. I didn't have the desire.

"Have another little nip."

"O.K., Shirley, thanks."

"Do you ever hear them people next door?"

"No."

"Oh, that's right, they're on vacation. Wait until they get back. The minute he gets home he starts hollering at her, calling her a whore, all sorts of things. Then he beats her. Then he fucks the shit outa her. You can hear the whole walls shake."

"Jesus."

"Every night, the same thing."

"Ummm, ummm. Well, Shirley, I have to go to bed now. See you tomorrow."

"Sure, baby."

Then I'd go to bed. Alone. About noon I'd go over and take the editor the pages I'd signed. When I finally got finished the stack of pages was 7 feet high. But I didn't finish until my last night in town. Sometimes I'd drink over at the editors and tell them some bullshit stories. They liked them. The roaches ran up and down the walls and Bukowski was everywhere.

I met their fiction editor in a bar one night in the Quarter. They introduced me. He was deaf and dumb. We wrote messages on paper napkins all night. He came on good. We wrote messages on those napkins until I drank him under, then I made my way back to Shirley's place. Another night, I am sitting in a bar with a guy at the piano playing and clowning, then he grabbed the mike and said, "Ladies and gentlemen, we have with us tonight, the poet, Charles Bukowski."

I waved and the bastards applauded. I'm sure they never heard of me. Later, back in the crapper while taking a leak, some guy walked up to me.

"Are you the Charles Bukowski they announced up front?"

"Yeah."

"Well, would you mind telling me where you have been published and when?"

"Fuck you, buddy!" I zipped up, washed my hands and walked out.

I never stuck it into Shirley. Night after night, I never. It looked like back to Los Angeles for me. At least in the Quarter I was a half-celebrity. Back in L.A. I was just another guy without money. Louise stood on a corner trying to sell paintings while the great editor rolled Bukowski off the press. And the roaches lazed in the sun. It was a quiet and easy time. I signed the last of the pages while drinking at their place and when I was done, we had a stack seven feet tall. 3500 Bukowski signatures and drawings. I had done it. The book was going to go for $7.50. CRUCIFIX IN A DEATH-HAND. And how.

I said goodbye to Shirley the next day in her shop. She looked genuinely sad. The long t.v. nights of drinking while she made the dolls and hats in the kitchen were over. The good dinners were over. The easy New Orleans life was shot for me. I couldn't stick it in. "I'll never forget the roses and you," she said. "I'll write about you some day, Shirley," I threatened her. I squeezed her hand and left her there with her boiling strawberries and some rich bitch trying on one of her 25 dollar hats that cost her a dollar to make. The rich bitch looked good, but she was for somebody else.

The great editor and his wife took me down to the train station. In the baggage room they had this long wooden partition. It looked like a bar. I hit the wood and hollered, "I wanna buy drinks for everybody in the house!"

Two young girls there started laughing.

"That was really funny," one of them said.

Balls.

I packed into the train and the great editor and his wife waved to me through the window. I blew a kiss and the train pulled out. I broke the cellophane on the pint and had the first one. I'd find the barcar later. So here we were. Louisiana. And thinking of the long ride through Texas that broke your back. I found the barcar anyhow. I didn't like trains, trapped in there with the people. It was sometime next day, sitting in the barcar, I seemed to hear a porter hollering "Charles Bukowski! Charles Bukowski!" Maybe I was going mad at last. He walked up to my table. "You must be Charles Bukowski," he said.

"Yes. Poet, and lover," I answered.

"Telegram, Mr. Bukowski."

I gave him a quarter, opened the telegram.

"Dear Buke. We miss you terribly. Our world is not the same without you. Please be careful and take care of yourself.

        love,
        Jon and Lou Webb."

I ordered a drink and looked out the picture window. "California here I come, right back where I started from . . ." The trainride was just one long drunk. Days later, dead and torn, I opened the cab door and got out. There was the old front court, my little girl saw me. "Hank! Hank!" I was hooked. I carried her inside. There was the woman.

"Well, how was it?"

"Hard to describe. I'm tired."

"You go to bed, Hank," said the little girl, "you go to bed."

"First I gotta peepee."

"O.K., you peepee, then you go to bed. When you wake up, we'll play."

"O.K."

The woman made a bacon and egg sandwich. I laid in bed and read the L.A. Times and then I knew I was back. There were ten or fifteen letters. I read them. Everybody was lonely. Everybody was in agony. I threw the letters on the floor and in ten minutes I was asleep at 2 in the afternoon. Outside the cats played, the butterflies flew, the sun kept working. The party was over. Charles Bukowski was Hank again. Rent was needed. Food. Gasoline. Luck. CRUCIFIX IN A DEATHHAND. Finished.

It's a world, it's a world of potential suicides, well, I speak mostly of the United States, I don't know the rest, but it's a place of potential and actual suicides and hundreds and thousands of lonely women, women just aching for companionship, and then there are the men, going mad, masturbating, dreaming, hundreds and thousands of men going mad for sex or love or anything, and meanwhile, all these people, the love-lost, the sex-lost, the suicide-driven, they're all working these dull soul-sucking jobs that twist their faces like rotten lemons and pinch their spirits, out, out, out . . . Somewhere in the structure of our society it is impossible for these people to contact each other. Churches, dances, parties only seem to push them further apart, and the dating clubs, the Computer Love Machines only destroy more and more a naturalness that should have been; a naturalness that has somehow been crushed and seems to remain crushed forever in our present method of living (dying). See them put on their bright clothes and get into their new cars and roar off to NOWHERE. It's all an outside maneuver and the contact is missed.

The other night—at somebody else's suggestion—we drove down Hollywood Boulevard. I have lived in Los Angeles, off and on, since 1922 and I don't believe I have driven down Hollywood Boulevard more than half a dozen times (I am eaten by my own kind of madness). It was a Friday night and here they drove slowly, the street was jammed. The people in the cars were watching the people on the sidewalks and the people on the sidewalks were walking along looking in the closed store windows. Here and there was a movie house showing movies of people supposedly living. Further on were a few clubs and bars but nobody went in. Nobody was spending any money. Nobody was doing anything. They just watched and drove and walked. I suppose there was action enough somewhere, but hardly there and hardly for the masses. Here they worked all week on jobs they hated, and now given the slightest bit of leisure time they wasted it, they murdered it. It was more than I cared to have a lengthy view of.

I turned off the boulevard, found Fountain Ave. and drove back toward Los Angeles.

I sit here playing writer each day and my typer faces the street. I live in a front court, and I don't consciously work. Wait, that's a mistake—I *do* consciously work—but I don't consciously *watch*, but toward evening I see them coming in—walking and driving—most of them are young ladies who live alone in all these high rise apartments which surround me. Some of them are fairly attractive and most of them are well-dressed, but something has been beaten out of them. That 8-hour job of doing an obnoxious thing for their own survival and for somebody else's profit had worked them over well.

These ladies immediately disappear into the high-rise walls, close the apartment door and vanish forever. From the cubicle of the job to the cubicle of resting and waiting to return to the job. The job is the center. The job is the sun. The job is the mother's breast. To be jobless is the sin; to be lifeless doesn't matter. Of course, one must consider their side—a job is money and to be moneyless is not comfortable. I know enough about this. And every person can't be an artist; that is, a painter, a musician, a composer, a writer, whatever. Many lack the talent, many lack the courage; most lack both. Even artists can't remain artists forever, especially good artists who can earn enough to survive within their craft. The talent goes, the courage goes, something goes. What's left for the average person but an occupation that must, finally, kill the spirit? I am very sorry, for instance, for my own doctor. Now certainly here is a person who could afford a training that might put him into a profession more enlightening than a punch press operator. But I sit in his packed waiting room and see that he too is caught. He hustles his patients in and out, barely asking them what is wrong with them. He weighs them, gives them a pill and now and then sticks a snake up their ass. If something further goes wrong he might suggest a hospital, an operation. He must pay office rent, receptionist rent, and have a wife in his home, an acceptable doctor's wife in an acceptable doctor's home. His life is simply a durable hell. His children, too, might become doctors if he can educate them.

Very well, I watch my ladies vanish into their high-rise walls to shower and eat and watch tv, read the paper, phone Joyce, then smear themselves with cream, set the alarm and sleep. I am not a woman but I must imagine that some of them have sexual drives and a wish for male companionship and love. It must be so. But there's the job. And there's nobody down there, my god. There's the weekend. What to do with the weekend? Those sons of bitches just want to get in my panties, that's all. Hit and run, goodbye. Who wants to be part of a cunt pile?

Everybody's blocked off from each other. Finally, out of desperation and advancing age, a man is chosen, first, perhaps for sexual pleasure and then later for marriage, a marriage that never works, a marriage that becomes dull and desperate, another durable hell or maybe an unendurable one. Marriage is a contract to live in dullness until death do us part. What else then? Prostitution? Ugggg.

Hundreds of thousands of lonely and frustrated men and women living mostly without sex and certainly without love, working at jobs they hate, running red lights, crashing into fire plugs and store windows, gambling, drinking, taking dope, smoking 2 packs a day, masturbating, going crazy, going crazier and crazier, getting religious, buying goldfish and cats and monkeys ...

Hundreds of thousands of lonely and frustrated men and women who settle for Disneyland instead of love, who settle for a baseball game instead of sex . . . Hundreds of thousands of lonely and frustrated men and women who'll pass each other on the sidewalk and be afraid to look at each other's faces, at each other's eyes for fear they'll be accused of being on the make. Blocks and walls of horror-movie magazines, girly magazines, nudey magazines, nude movies, vibrators, dirty jokes—everything but contact and real action. I must guess that the United States must be the loneliest place in the world with England not far behind. Too often I'd heard the guys talk on the job about the wild times they had in the army, the drunks, the whores . . . When I asked them, "What are you doing now? Why did you stop?" I got these strange looks. It's simple. They are afraid here now in civilian life. Have to keep the job. Have to pay off the car. Have to—No army to take care of them now. No 3 square meals. No bunk. No sure payday. No Uncle Sam to cure their clap . . . Their wildness, their courage was regulated and safe enough.

I tell you, we must be the most backward nation on earth. In our prisons we do not believe in allowing the men even limited sexual relationships with the opposite sex, yet we wonder why the men molest and ravage each other in desperation. You say they made a mistake? Crime is in the definition of it. Suppose you made a mistake? Would you like to be beaten by a dozen men and made into a sexual idiot? What judge passed that sentence? It's strange that in one of the most backward states, Mississippi, certain inmates are allowed to have limited sexual relationships with women—even though most of them are or pose as wives—from the outside.

We murder ourselves with sex and occupation; the madhouses crawl with sexually maladjusted and occupationally-destroyed people.

Answers? Who knows? We're structured in. The bars are heavy.

The other day I stopped for gas. I don't know how it got around to the subject, I think a woman walked by and that started it, but the attendant said, "I haven't had a piece of ass in 5 years." I laughed. "You're kidding, man." "No, I'm serious. 5 years now." He was in his 20's. I drove away thinking about what a friend of mine had said, "Where *are* the women? Tell me, where *are* they? Where's the *action?*" There's none. It's a desert.

My friend drives from Los Angeles to Mexico each weekend to fulfill his sexual desires in a whorehouse.

I don't know, my friends. Look at these walls, look at these people, look at these faces, these streets . . . We've all locked ourselves up. The rapists come out at night and the murderers, and the ladies lock themselves in and wait for the big one, the dream man, the money and soul man, the man of brilliant conversation, the man that mama might like. Set the alarm. He may walk in on the job . . . tomorrow, next week, next month, next year . . . surely he's out there . . . These sons of bitches just want to get into my panties . . . I wonder what Bukowski's like?

Monday afternoon was my day to see the girl. She was 7.

The hangover wasn't too bad and I drove down to Santa Monica via Pico Boulevard. When I got there the door was open. I pushed in. She was writing a note. The mother of my child. Her name was Vicki.

"I was just going to leave you this note. Louise is at Cindy's."

"O.K."

"Look. Could I have some money?"

"How much?"

"Well, I could use $45 now."

"I can only let you have 20."

"All right."

She lived in an unfurnished one-bedroom Synanon apt., $130 a month. Vicki was one of those who had to always belong to some organization . . . she had gone from poetry reading workshops to the communist party to Synanon. Whenever she became insulated she went to a new organization. Well, that was as sensible as anything else.

We walked over to Cindy's. Cindy was black. The 2 girls played with their paper dolls on the floor. Her mother was white, fat and in bed.

"She's got asthma," Vicki said to me.

"Hello," I said to Cindy's mother.

Cindy's father wasn't about. He was on the cure and working a gas station.

"Will you drive me to Synanon?" Vicki asked. "Or I can take the bus."

(Synanon had a bus line too.)

"All right," I said, "I'll drive you down."

"Come on, Louise," she said, "pick up your stuff and let's go."

"But, Mommy, I just want to get this last dress on the doll."

"All right, but hurry up" . . .

I left Vicki off in front of the building. Then we drove east.

"Where we going, Hank?"

"To the beach, I guess."

"But I wanted to go to the Synanon beach . . ."

"The beaches are all alike . . . there's dirty water and dirty sand."

Louise began sobbing. "But I wanted the Synanon beach! They don't like war! They don't kill people!"

"Look, little one, we're almost at the other beach. Let's try it anyhow."

"But people don't carry guns at Synanon!"

"You're probably right, but I'm afraid that sometimes we still need guns just like we need knives and forks."

"Silly," she said, "you can't eat with a gun!"

"A lot of people do," I said.

It was winter and cold and there weren't many cars about or people either. Louise had had lunch at noon but I hadn't eaten yet. We walked into the little Jewish grocery store next to the candleshop. I got a hotdog, some chips and a 7-UP. Louise got some kind of candy cracker and a 7-UP. We walked to the last cement table near the water.

"It's cold," I said. "Let's turn our backs to the sea."

So we sat there facing the boardwalk. There were 14 or 15 people about but they had the strange tranquility of the seagulls, the winter seagulls. No, it wasn't a tranquility but a deadness. They were like bugs. They simply stood or sat together, motionless, not talking.

"It's too bad I have to look at those people," I said, biting into my hotdog.

"Why don't you want to look at them?"

"They have no desire."

"What's 'Desire'?"

"Well, let's see. 'Desire' is wanting something you usually can't get right when you want it, but if you have enough 'Desire' you can sometimes get it anyhow . . . Oh, hell—that sounds like 'Ambition' which is something you're trained to do instead of something you want to do . . . Let's just say that those people don't want anything."

"Those people don't want anything?"

"Right. In a sense, nothing affects them so they don't want anything, they aren't anything. Especially in Western Civilization."

"But that's the way they are. Maybe that's a good way to be."

"Some wise men say so. I guess all of everything is how you work at it. A direction. I still don't like to look at those people while I'm eating."

"Hank! You're not nice! There's nothing wrong with those people! I ought to slap you across the face with this cracker!"

She picked up the cracker as if to hit me with it. I thought that was very funny. I laughed. She laughed too. We both felt good together, at last.

We finished eating and walked down toward the water. I sat down on a little cliff above the water and wet shore, and Louise built a sand castle . . .

It was then that I noticed the two men walking along the waterfront from the east. And the one man walking along the waterfront from the west. They all appeared to be in their mid-twenties. The man walking from the west had a large bag and seemed to be stopping and picking things up and dropping them into this bag. He didn't seem to sense the two men approaching him from the east, but there was still quite a football field between them. 2 football fields.

The two walking from the east had on heavy boots and

kicked at things along the shore. The one from the west almost swayed in the wind, bending over, picking up things for his paper sack. And I thought, it's too bad, but the poor guy with the paper sack doesn't realize that the other two guys are going to jump on him and beat him up. Can't he realize that? It was a surety. And since I sensed it, I couldn't understand how the guy with the bag couldn't sense it. And the lifeguard in his little white shack on stilts . . . couldn't he see?

It almost happened in front of me. All the men had beards but the 2 from the east had shorter beards; their beards almost looked angry . . . The guy with the paper sack just had hair all over his face and neck and back and front and everywhere. Then he looked up and saw the other two . . . He tried to walk around them, on the side toward the sea. Just then a wave rolled in and the guy nearest him pushed him into the water. His paper sack went out with the tide.

As he got up, the other guy hit him and he went down again and then they were kicking at his body and his face with their boots. At first he held his hands over his face, then his hands fell away, but they kept kicking at his face.

Then they rolled him over and took something out of his pocket. A wallet. They took something out of the wallet and then threw the wallet far out into the sea.

Then they looked around and saw me sitting there. They looked at me. It was a kind of zoo thing—the way monkeys looked at you. They could see that I was old but they could see that I was big too, and I looked bigger in that black lumberjack my landlord had given me.

I looked at their faces and noticed that they were not particularly brave faces. I turned to the kid and told her, "You stay up here on the sand . . ."

Then I leaped from the cliff and hit the wet sand and

walked toward them. I pulled the switchblade, hit the button and the blade jumped out.

They didn't move. Their game. I moved forward.

Then one guy started running and the other guy moved after him. They ran down the shore, around the pile of searocks and were gone. The lifeguard still stared out at sea . . .

I walked over to the guy and turned him over. Sand was mixed in with blood and hair. I took the sea water as it came in and splashed it over his face. Hair grew upon his face where it wasn't supposed to grow. It grew right in near the nose. I don't mean under it, I mean right around the edges of the nose. Up by the eyes. There was a bird-like thing about him, an inhuman thing about him. I disliked him. I helped him up.

"You o.k.?"

"Yeah. Yeah. But they took my money. 3 dollars. My money's gone."

I picked him up and walked him over to a small cliff, away from Louise and sat him down.

"I live under the pier," he said.

"Are you serious?"

"5 years now. I think it's been 5 years."

"I can only give you a dollar."

"Will you?"

"Here."

The dollar seemed to bring him out of it.

"Do you live around here?" he asked.

"No. Los Angeles."

"How do you make it?"

"Luck, I guess."

Then Louise waved from her sand castle. I waved back.

My friend and I looked out at sea. A small ugly boat of some sort was slowly passing by out there, doing something.

Then my friend said, "Yesterday 2 guys were sucking each other off under the pier and some plain-clothes cops caught them and locked them up. Do you think that's right?"

"Well, I don't know," I said.

"I mean," he said, "if 2 guys want to suck each other off, that's their business, isn't it?"

"Well, looking at it from that angle, I suppose you're right . . . But look, I've got to check on my little girl right now."

I walked over and sat down by Louise.

My friend walked up the sand toward the boardwalk.

She smiled at me:

"You like my castle?" she asked.

I looked.

"It's beautiful," I said, "but better than that, it's very nice."

"What's the difference between 'Beautiful' and 'Very nice'?"

"Well, 'Beautiful' is usually what people say when they don't mean it and 'it's very nice' is usually what they way when they really mean it."

"Oh."

It was a very nice sand castle. We both hated to leave it there like that, so we smashed it down with our feet. Then she held my hand as we walked across the sand toward the parking lot. There were quite some hours left in our Monday together and we needed something different to do.

I have lost some of the letters or I am too lazy to look for them but the first one was something about him being in a motel, in Sunland maybe, no, that doesn't sound right, maybe it was the Sunland Motel, no, that isn't it either, anyhow, I let the letter lay around three or four days and then I phoned, and the phone number given was one digit short, so I looked up the motel, whatever it was, and I phoned in and asked for a Jack M—, and Jack M— was out, and I left the message, and then I got lost, either at the track or in some other way and one day I was home (home?) and the phone rang and it was Jack M— and he said he had been trying to reach me and would Friday night be all right? I said yes. And he said, about 8, I gotta catch a plane at the International at 10:30, it's a shame I couldn't a gotten you earlier.

So that Friday Neeli and Liza happened to be around and we were drinking beer in the breakfastnook and I warned them that this professor from this eastern university was coming around and that they'd better brace up, you know, for anything.

We weren't to be denied. The doorbell rang and Neeli and Liza began laughing. "It's the professor," I said.

I went to the door.

"ARE YOU CHARLES BUKOWSKI?" he asked with great pompous and sonorous force.

"Yeh," I said, "Come on in."

He followed me to the breakfastnook. He had a briefcase and a six-pack of beer. He had heard the legend: you go see Bukowski, you better bring a six-pack. I made the introductions and opened the beers. The prof sat down. He looked more like 1940 than anything else. Very straight back. Tie. Tweed jacket.

He began to interview. But he didn't have a tape recorder. And he didn't take shorthand. It was evident he couldn't interview me. The questions were harmless and I suggested that we go into the other room. I still attempted to answer Jack M—'s questions the best I could. We finished his beer and then I brought out my own. But he was nervous. Neeli and Liza were goading him a bit and I don't think they realized that he knew it, so I tried to treat him with a bit more civility. But then he had to leap up to use the phone.

It was the time of the protests of Nixon's move to blockade the harbors in N. Vietnam. Jack M— had heard that protestors were down at the airport, and they were, but he found out over the phone that flights were still leaving, but it was obvious that he was very nervous about it, and we agreed with him that it was best that he left soon.

A week or so later I received a letter from the professor explaining that here were some questions he had really meant to ask (but in all the confusion . . .) and would I mind? The questions sat about a week or so and then I sat down and answered them. It went like this:

1) Why is your phone unlisted?

Simple. Two years ago, that is before I quit my job, I didn't have as much laying around time as I do now. The little free time I had then was needed toward creation. A ringing phone is a hazard. People have a way of inviting themselves over. At one time I didn't answer the door, the phone or the mail. I feel that I was justified. I feel that what I created during that time proves it. Now I murder my own time. But I feel that what I create now also justifies that.

2) Have you ever written, or thought about writing, a film scenario?

Excuse me, what is a film scenario? Does it have anything to do with movies? Then the answer is no. I have never seen a movie that didn't make me a bit sick. I don't want to make anybody sick.

3) Do you have anything like an aesthetic theory?

What does "aesthetic" mean? I don't have any theories. I simply DO. Or is that a theory, uh? Uh.

4) How about a philosophy of history?

I don't like history. History is a terrible weight which proves nothing except the treachery of man and I am aware of that by walking down the street NOW. History is dull and doubtful and I don't know how much of it is true. History is the memory of victory and defeat, and I've got enough on my mind now.

5) How about the common belief that all poems are political?

No, I think that most poems are cows with big sagging empty tits. I presume that by "political" you mean poems that move something toward the ultimate betterment of Man and the Government of Man. That's all too perfect and coy. A poem is often something that is only necessary toward one man—the writer. It's often a perfect form of selfishness. Let's not credit ourselves with too much. Garage mechanics are more human than we are.

6) Have you written music?

Uhuh. I never liked those notes and lines and things they tried to teach me in school, I hated the teacher, so I deliberately didn't learn the notes. Now it seems too late and too silly. Music affects me much more than writing or painting, though, and I seem to be listening to it continually—classical, rock, jazz, anything. It's awfully good shit.

7) Other writers you admire (besides Jeffers and Aiken—I'm thinking of Anthony Burgess, for example, whose *Enderby* is somewhat Bukowskian . . . & as a matter of fact, Burgess used to be a composer)?

Never heard of Burgess, which doesn't mean he isn't any good. I don't read much anymore. I like Artaud, Céline, Dostoyevsky, Kafka and the STYLE of the early Saroyan without the content. Then maybe Eugene O'Neill or somebody like that. Most writers simply don't have it and never will. There's hardly any looking around, up, down, before and before that. A pack of shameful fakes. If I ever go to hell there will be all writers down there. There could be nothing worse.

8) Several times during our "interview" you said, sardonically, "I'm immortal"; now I'm no depth psychologist or mystic-of-the-word ... but the thought occurs to me that maybe you sometimes brood on what sort of trace you'll leave as an artist, a writer ... and also on human perishability. (There's a question somewhere in that preceding sentence.)

There is? Well, about the "immortal," I hope I said it "sardonically." The only good thing about writing is the writing itself—that is, to bring me closer to what is necessary NOW and to keep me from becoming anything like the first face I pass on a sidewalk on any given day. When I die they can take my work and wipe a cat's ass with it. It will be of no earthly use to me. The only trace I want to leave, after death, is upon myself, and that isn't important to you. Incidentally, one of the best things I like about humans is that they do perish.

9) Anything in astrology or Zen or any of the popular cults you believe in?

I don't have time for cults. That business is for the large gang of people who need toe-tickling. For them, it's all right. It might even be helpful. But I build the IDEA of myself from myself and my experience. I will have my blind sides, true. And I might have much to learn from other men. But, basically, I am not a learner from other men. I am headstrong and prejudiced but it's good to live without too much instruction from other men. I've found the most learned men to be bores and the dumbest seem to be the most profound and uncluttered. Who wants to be many voices when there is only one voice trying to get out?

10) You told me you stopped writing when you were 24 (incidentally, have you written an account of this episode with your father? If you haven't we'd like to see it for THE ____REVIEW—we pay something like $50.00 for stories and essays) . . . but you didn't tell me when you started writing before that, and why you started writing.

I'd much rather you paid me $50 for answering these questions. I'm not sure that thing I told you about my father is quite true, although there is a partial truth. Sometimes when I'm talking I improve on things to make them better. Some people might call it lying; I call it an art-form, and, uh uh, no, I didn't tell you when I started writing or why, but I was drinking, wasn't I? And also, you didn't ask. And also, I'm glad you didn't ask.

11) Is there anything, other than booze and women (I presume), that stimulates you creative lust? (Smell of horses, faces in the crowd at the track?) (You sort of answered this, but I'd like to hear more if you'd like to say it.)

Everything, of course, stimulates my creative lust. Faces in the crowd do it plenty. I can look at faces and become disgusted and terrorized and sickened. Others can find beauty in them like large fields of flowers. I guess I ain't much of a man for that. I am narrow. I can't see the horizons or the reasons or the excuses or the glories. The average face to me is a total nightmare.

Well, shit, I guess I don't look so good to others either. I've been told I'm a very ugly man by more than one. So there's your joke. Let's get off these faces. I know that I haven't answered your question properly, but I got into a passion and started yelling. Sorry.

12) What do you think of "confessional" poetry? How do you see your own work fitting and resisting that label?

Confessional poetry, of course, depends upon who does it. I think that most brag too much on themselves or don't know how to laugh properly. Does that sound bitchy? Well, I mean, examine it and see. Even Whitman.

I really do think that most of my confessional stuff relieves itself as a form of entertainment. Meaning, look, I lost my balls or my love, ha ha ha. So forth. But the ha ha ha must be fairly relevant and real, I mean no Bob Hope stuff, so forth.

I find that when the pain gets bad enough there are only three things to do—get drunk, kill yourself or laugh. I usually get drunk and laugh.

Yeh. I don't always do the confessional stuff but I suppose I am hooked on it, it comes easy because much has happened, I almost MAKE much happen—as if to create a life to create an art. I don't think this is the true way to do things, it is probably a weakness, but I am a dreamer and maybe a dramatist and I like more things to happen than happen—so I push them a bit. I suppose it's not right. I don't claim to be.

13) What do you think of college kids reading poetry? Why do they do it? Do they read you? Do they read poetry for what you consider valid reasons? (That last verges on being an asinine question, but you might be able to redeem it with a clever answer.)

Now you know I don't think of college kids reading poetry. I don't know if they do or if they read me. There's no clever way to answer this without making up something I don't know and which I can't get away with, so I'm being more clever this way.

14) What's so great about living in L.A.?

I'm here to begin with and then you build around that. Or I build around it. I've lived most of my life here and I've simply gotten used to the place. I can't even get lost, sober. And just the other day I found out where the L.A. Zoo was. And the women here seem to love old men. I've never seen women like that. At the same time, I'm suicidal and there's the smog to help me out. So, what do you got in *****Ohio?

15) What are you reading now? What are your reading habits?

I'm not reading anything. Well, I write my own things and I read them. I suppose that's a habit.

16) If you were suddenly to become wealthy, how would your life change?

I would become wiser, more profound and more lovely.

17) Do you have any children?

I have a girl aged 7. She's all right.

I mailed the questions and answers in and I didn't expect much but I got, in the return mail, a letter from Jack M—

Dear Buk:

All right! That was good medicine (your response to my questions). I don't think it'll be right for the REVIEW, though. That isn't what I had in mind, and my questions didn't lead into the sort of literary (prosodic & technical) matters that we like for our Interviews with Poets series. (These would have been questions about your sense of the line, your opinion of other poets—specifically, and other matters that I suspect you might consider pure crap.)

Anyway, I've forwarded the interview thing to the editors, and they'll of course give it the eye. (One other thing: we're filled up with interviews already, through next year.)

My reason was, as I explained, to get information for

my own article on you and your work—something that I can peddle elsewhere. I've already written this article, and I think it's a dandy. When it comes out, wherever that is, it'll help you somewhat, surely . . . but of course, my motive isn't altruistic—I simply like your poems a great deal, and think they should be better known than they are.

Enough of that. Now I WOULD like to ask you, specifically and formally, to send us some poems for the ****RE-VIEW. We pay something like $10.00 to $15.00 a poem.

I've ordered HUMMINGBIRD and have read the broadsheet sent out by Black Sparrow Press.

Did I tell you that I enjoyed my brief visit there? I did, and indeed, as you'll guess when you read the essay that came of it.

Cheers,
Jack M—

Dear Jack M—;
Well, & ( ) (therefore) &

(do you understand)?
(your visit was hardly wasted)
(at this end) (either) &

Cheers to you,
Charlie B.

Pete was 13, a difficult age they say, but any age is, and Pete had parents of German extraction, strict, very. "A child should be seen and not heard," was one of their dictums, and that was all right with Pete. He disliked his parents immensely. His father beat him regularly with a razor strop for minor infractions of rules while his mother stood by and said, "The father is always right."

At times, at night, sometimes when his parents were fucking, Pete would be thinking, alone in his bedroom, "These can't be my parents. I must have been adopted. I must have been kidnapped."

Actually Pete had been the reason for the marriage. His father had gotten his mother pregnant and the old man had always held the marriage against him, but Pete thought, with some repugnance, that *he* hadn't stuck that thing in there. And he thought, with further repugnance, can it be that I was once partly jissom in that man's cock? The thought sickened him.

Pete had to mow the lawn twice a week, front and back, once in one direction and once in another each time. In other words he mowed the lawn over *four* times a week, trimmed the edges and watered. The neighbors remarked what a nice lawn his parents had.

It was after his lawn-mowing sessions that his father would get down on the grass and "inspect for hairs." His father would put his eye level to the grass and if he found one grassblade standing taller than the others that was the reason for a razor stropping in the bathroom. And his father would always find a hair. "Ah, I see it! A hair!" And his mother would come to the back window and say, "Your father found a hair, you bad boy!" And Pete would walk to the bathroom where his father would be waiting, sitting on the edge of the tub, strop ready, his face working into a red fury.

After the age of 12 Pete no longer screamed when he was whipped; it was an admission of pain and he didn't want to admit pain to his father, he refused. The beatings became so brutal that he was unable to sit on an ordinary chair for dinner, he had to sit on two pillows and listen to his father recount the day at work, which was always very similar:

"I told that son of a bitch Cranston off today. He let his station go unnoticed while he talked to this blonde. It must have gone on for 20 minutes. I walked over and told him, 'Listen, Cranston, your job isn't to talk to blondes, it's to guard the museum facilities. You straighten out or I'll report you to Mr. Henderson!' Then I walked off. That blonde got out of there.

"Cranston kept giving me dirty looks all day. You know, they robbed his area two weeks ago, got right under a glass case while he was there and lifted out all the coins. They dated way back, must have been worth three or four thousand dollars. Why they dug those coins out of there while his ass was turned. He's asleep on his feet.

"Also I put a suggestion in the suggestion box—that those World War I planes be taken out of the cellar and put on a higher floor. There's a dampness down there and the dampness causes a mildew that is beginning to eat into the fabric of the planes. They need a drier area . . ."

His father talked for hours about the job, he only talked about his job. He went to bed at 8 p.m. every night so that he would be "fresh and ready for the job." That meant lights out for everybody else and bed. But his father always talked on about the job and his mother would answer, "Oh, yes. Oh, yes, I think you're right. Oh, I'm glad you told him! He said *that*? And what did you say?"

The only thing that interrupted them was their once-a-week fuck and Pete would have to listen to the bed squeaking, the walls being thin. Pete would envision his father mounted, going through the motions, and it would sicken him, that he belonged to these people, that there wasn't any escape . . . wouldn't be, for years.

It was after this particular night, after a stropping for missing a "hair," and after listening to their automatic love-making that he had a dream. His mother and his father were sitting in the breakfast nook eating their dinner when a huge spider, blackish-brown, with most powerful fangs and two large yellow-green eyes walked into the breakfast nook. The spider was a good three feet in circumference, very hairy and gave off the odor of distant blood. While his father was talking about the job the spider got up on the ceiling, then dropped down on a single thread of its web and began to spin a net about his mother. His father failed to notice. When the spider had his mother completely in his web he moved down and sunk his fangs into her breasts, then lifted her high into his web and left her dangling above the table. Then the spider simply leaped from his web, grabbed his father with his spider legs and sunk his fangs home. The spider then lifted his father from the chair to the table and sat there above him, sucking the blood from his body.

Pete awakened then. He walked down the hall and looked into his parents' bedroom. They were each asleep in their twin beds. He went back to bed and slept and had no further dreams that he could remember.

The next day was Monday and a day, finally, of no duties. Pete stayed after school and got into a baseball game. He didn't get much practice but he was a good athlete. He got a homer and a triple and made three great catches in the outfield. Then he went home. When he got there his mother was angry. "Go to your bedroom. Your father will talk to you when he gets home."

An hour later he heard his mother talking to his father. Then his father entered the bedroom and closed the door.

His father had a different look on his face than he had

ever seen before, more furious, more brutal, less understanding. Pete sat on the bed and waited. His father sat on a chair, facing him.

"Peter."

"Yes?"

"What have you been doing?"

"Playing baseball."

"What have you *really* been doing, Peter?"

"I don't understand."

"*You* understand."

"I don't know what you mean."

"You son of a bitch, I'll kill you! You ever do that again and I'll kill you!"

"What? Do what?"

"Here! Your mother showed me *these*! Look! Look!"

His father showed him a pair of pajama pants, the ones Pete had slept in last night. Pete still didn't understand.

"Look! Look!" His father pointed to a place on the pajamas on the upper front. There was a small and faded spot of blood.

"What have you been doing, Peter?"

"What do you mean?"

"I mean, if you ever do that again, I'll kill you!"

His father got up from his chair, walked to the door, slammed it violently and then Pete was alone. He looked down at the blood spot on the pajamas. Then he realized that the pajama pants were an old pair of his father's. And that the blood spot was an old one that had failed to wash out properly. He sat there slightly amazed. They had conceived the blood spot to be something evil when actually it had been put there by his father or his mother. But what had they thought it had meant? Did they think that one bled during masturbation? It must have been their thought. For the first time he began to believe that his parents were crazy, or if not crazy, then ignorant beyond belief.

He was made to go without dinner that night and the next morning over breakfast they neither spoke to him or looked at him. After his father had gone to work his mother did mention that God might forgive him if he were good and repented for the rest of his life . . .

That night, after dinner, Pete was made to go immediately to his room and to bed. He turned out the lights and listened to his father talking about the job. God. His mother and God. His father and God. They believed in God. Is that what happened to people who believed in God? His mind flattened and turned, drifted. He slept and awakened. He still heard the voices of his parents.

Then Pete spoke: "God, you have given me such parents! How can You give me such parents? What type of God are you? God, I hate you! If You come down here in this room, God, I'll punch you right in the nose!"

It seemed to Pete that he slept again then. When he awakened there appeared to be a figure looking at him over his knees. Pete's legs were bent, the knees and blankets forming a small hill over which the figure peered back at him. The figure appeared dressed in black, all black, hooded, with a peaked cap similar to those worn by the Ku Klux Klan.

Pete was frightened, he looked back in disbelief. Could that be God? That hooded figure? Was God evil? The figure remained and remained and remained, looking at him. It must have stayed ten minutes, fifteen minutes, then it vanished.

Pete gathered himself and turned on the light. He kept wondering about the figure. He walked over to his dresser, opened the top drawer and took out the small box his grandmother had given him. She called it The Answer Box. Whenever you wanted to know anything you asked a question to God and He answered through The Answer Box. The box contained little scrolls of paper rolled up and set next to each other. There were many tiny rolls.

Pete asked the question. What happened then. . . ? He reached in and pulled out one of the rolls, unrolled it and read: "God has forsaken you." He rolled up the paper, placed in back in the box, put the box back in the drawer and then went to bed.

He could still hear his parents talking in the breakfast nook. Then Pete got up and opened the dresser drawer again. He took The Answer Box out again and unrolled the little slips one by one. He couldn't find the slip that had said "God has forsaken you." He put all the slips back, closed the box and returned it to the drawer. He could no longer hear his parents talking. It was unusual.

Pete slowly opened his bedroom door and listened. The light was on in the breakfast nook but there was no sound. He walked down the hall in his pajamas and his bare feet. He walked into the kitchen. Still there was no sound. Then he walked into the breakfast nook.

The spider was there, that huge blackish-brown spider, huge fangs and two large yellow-green eyes . . . the blood sack was hairy and pulsating and full with blood and the spider was upon his father on the tabletop. His mother was in a large web above the table, dead.

Pete walked back to his bedroom, closed the door and got dressed in his day clothes. Then he climbed through the back bedroom window and dropped into the yard. The grass was neatly-mowed and well-kept. He walked into the garage and found a gallon can of turpentine. His father used it to clean his paint brushes in. Pete took the can in through the back porch. Then he opened it and let the liquid run in under the door and into the kitchen. He emptied a remainder of the can about the back porch. Then he took a loose piece of newspaper, slightly rolled, and lit it with a match. He threw it into the center of the back porch. He saw the flames rise up, he saw the flames run under the door and light up the kitchen.

Then he walked up the driveway and out onto the street. He walked north along the street and up the long hill to the boulevard. Then he turned and looked back. He could see the flames, the flames were very high down there. Then he walked east. He walked three blocks east until he got to the movie. He looked in his pockets. He had enough for a movie. It was a Western. A real good shoot-'em-up. Pete loved Westerns. He paid the girl and walked in. He had enough for a bag of popcorn. He bought a bag of popcorn and walked down the dark aisle. He found a seat about three-fourths of the way in the back, near the center, sat down and began to eat the popcorn. Two guys were about to shoot it out, right in front of a saloon. They were good actors. Pete liked popcorn, popcorn with plenty of salt. At last, he was happy.

Robert had 29 cans of food in the closet and a five gallon jug of Sparkletts. Also, candles and a .32 with plenty of shells. The water had been cut off the second day but the power was still on.

What had started as a series of spontaneous riots had evolved into something that nobody quite understood. All stores, gas stations—supplies of every sort had been looted in the first days.

In a sense, it was a nationwide revolution but exactly who was revolting and who wasn't—the matter wasn't clear. The fire department, after numerous casualties, had ceased to put out fires. Half of Los Angeles was on fire—people were homeless—men, women, children—hiding where they could. They were not roaming, but hiding, trying to hide, trying to exist.

The police, the National Guard and the U.S. Army attempted to control the streets—and control meant killing all others who were upon them. Basically it had become a war between the uniformed and the non-uniformed; and worse, through fear, had evolved into a war between black and white and a war between white and white and black and black and all the colors in between. Each man seemed a unit divided until something happened. The revolution had no central leadership, and so its demands and ambitions were hazy. There seemed no way it could surrender; there also seemed no way it could win.

Robert could understand neither the revolutionaries or the government; both left him with more than a bad taste. But he had always been an odd guy, not fitting anywhere. Now it had broken down into Man against Man, which it had always been, but now it was clear—they were back to the caves, and every man, beast, every weather was the enemy. The centuries had burned back down.

Luckily, Robert had three fifths of Scotch and three-fourths of a lid of grass and ten packs of Bull Durham and plenty of Zig Zag, all of which helped the spirit. Also, he was a natural loner and, all in all, the situation which existed was not far from the one he had existed in before the revolution. His greatest joy had always been solitude, albeit cut with an occasional piece of ass, a bit of Mahler or Stravinsky, a joint or two and a good night's drunk.

The gas and water were shut off and he had all the windows nailed closed and kept the night latch on the door. Late at night he would open the door and throw out his excretia and urine, all the garbage. It was more dangerous to go out and attempt to bury it.

Constant firing was heard in the streets. Bodies were left where they fell. Rats, dogs, cats prowled the streets, ripping pieces of flesh off dead bodies. Maggots and flies were everywhere.

Robert knew it wouldn't be long before the electricity went. He turned on the radio. (He had never purchased a t.v. set.) Some of the radio stations were replaying the President's message over and over. For all he knew the President was dead, but he still heard the message over and over:

"My fellow Americans: Never has this great nation been in such agony and fear and chaos, but we will come through, and after this is over we will cleanse our ranks of the cowards and back-stabbers who have weakened us. We will be a greater nation than ever before.

"Growth is oftentimes accompanied by pain. At this moment we are feeling this pain, we are feeling it very much. But, listen, we will grow to an even greater Manhood. We will rid our land of this pestilence and of these pests. We will rid our land of the insects that have sucked our blood.

"Have faith: God and Country will prevail. Have faith, I beg of you, and this hour will not be our death but our rebirth into greater freedom, a greater freedom than any ever known to Man in the history of the world.

"Meanwhile, it is my duty to inform you that two nations, Russian and China, have banded together and given us an ultimatum. This ultimatum being that we will have until Oct. 25 to surrender all our governmental powers over to them. The United States of America has never surrendered and we do not intend to do so now. Should Russia or China, either or both, attempt any invasion or any move at all which we shall consider hostile we will release immediately upon them our nuclear force, which at this time is four times greater than all the combined nuclear power of all the nations on earth.

"The United States of America, troubled from within and without, will persevere. Don't doubt Her unless you doubt your very own soul. God, Might and Freedom will shine throughout the World tonight, tomorrow and forever."

Robert turned the dial.

". . . and this station is still in control of the rebels! Brothers, this hour is ours! This is Truth, at last, come face to face with the imprisonment of Man, with the materialistic and spiritual degradation of Man. This Revolution, this effort of ours, cannot be compared to any revolution in the history of the world. For, at last, Man has awakened to what he wants, and what he really wants is the freedom to form and live his life in any damned way he pleases—to wear the clothes he wishes to, to fuck in the streets, to smoke pot, to paint, to do nothing or something or everything. We demand materialistic needs if we need them and we demand spiritualistic needs, which are forever needed. The eight-hour job be damned! Our job, and it isn't a job at all—is to enjoy life as we wish it. But some of us must die first, many of us must, so those of us who are left will be able to live as humans instead of as driven beasts. The spirit of Man has risen at last to swallow his subnormal keeper! Damn the President of the United States, and damn and break this torture chamber which has enslaved us all too long! Right on!"

Robert turned off the radio. He walked into the bedroom, stretched out on the bed and jacked-off. He wiped off on the sheet, got up, decided that he was hungry, but he was strictly rationing himself. He decided upon a can of cold beans. He walked to the refrigerator and opened the door. The inside light didn't go on. He walked over to a lightswitch and flipped it to on. No overhead light. Back in the front room the radio didn't work. The power was off. He had four boxes containing 12 candles each. But darkness was better and it was night. He forgot the beans and sat down, rolled a smoke. He listened to the shooting. He sat there perhaps an hour when he heard a knock on the door.

"Brother," Robert heard a voice, "brother, help me!"

He sat still.

"Brother, brother help me! Mercy! God o' mighty, isn't there any mercy in your soul? Oh, Jesus!"

It sounded like an old man. Robert took the latch off the .32 and walked up behind the door.

"Yeah?"

"Brother, please! God o' mighty!"

Robert opened a small side panel near the door. It was an old white-haired guy, maybe in his late 60's or early 70's. He was in rags, flat upon his belly on the porch.

"Brother! I'm dying! A cup of water! I beg you! Only a cup of water and I'll go!"

"Will you go then?"

"Yes, yes! Believe me!"

Robert opened the door. The old guy began to crawl forward. The door was only open a notch. The old guy tried to push the door open wide with his arm. Robert looked up in time to see three young guys rush from around a hedge. He fired. The leading guy screamed, grabbed his belly and fell forward. Then Robert kicked the old guy in the mouth, pushed his head out the door and got the latch on just before the other two guys, who had paused a moment, hit the door. Robert's door had been glass, but he had braced it partially with boards. The shade was down. Robert pulled the shade up, dropped to his belly, saw a piece of one of the guys through the boards and glass, fired. He got him in the chest. The other guy leaped off the porch. Robert couldn't see the old man. The phone rang. Robert walked over and picked it up.

"Robert Grissom?" somebody asked.

"Grissom isn't here," Robert said.

"Come on, Bobby, we've got you by the balls."

"What?"

"CIA, Bobby, your game is up."

"I don't understand. I thought the power was off. How can you phone me?"

"Don't worry your ass, Bobby. We've got you by the balls."

"I've always been apolitical."

"There's no such thing as 'apolitical,' Bobby baby, there's only such a thing as facing it or not facing it."

"You're wrong," Robert said. "I don't think a man has to be a registered Democrat in order to go to hell."

"We've found some things in your writings, Bobby."

"Shit."

"Yeah, there's a lot of that, too. You didn't think we were watching you, eh Bobby? You thought you could feed us that 'apolitical' bullshit, huh? Well, we happen to know who you're pulling for, kid."

"'Kid'? I'm 55. In fact, today is my . . . "

"We know, Bobby, we're coming right over with your birthday cake."

Robert hung up.

He pulled down all the shades except for a small peek-through area at the bottom of each, got down flat on his belly with the .32 and with all his shells around him. Then he got up and got the can of urine out of the bathroom and put several rags next to it. He'd learned an old trick—urinate on a handkerchief, hold it over the nose and you strain out a great deal of poisonous gas.

"GRISSOM, COME ON OUT! YOU HAVE 60 SECONDS!"

Robert lifted the .32 and shot out of the side window. He heard a scream. The impossible had happened. He had hit somebody.

The first canister of gas came lobbing into the room. Robert picked up his shells and the rags and the can of urine, ran into the bedroom, closed the door and climbed under his bed. He dipped the rag into the can of urine and put it over his nose and mouth. The ultraviolet ray glasses were already taped around his skull. It was an attempt to seal the eyes from any possible tear gas.

And there under the bed he grinned just a bit and watched the bedroom door for whoever wanted to be an immediate part of chapter one in the History of the Second American Revolution.

Down there under the bed he noticed that he wasn't a very good housekeeper: several missing stockings, an undershirt, various gatherings of dust. It was one hell of a way to end a literary career: not one pair of panties, a love letter or a box of Tampax about. And the Pulitzer Prize looked more impossible than ever . . .

We were both in handcuffs. The cops led us down the stairway between them and sat us in back. My hands were bleeding onto the upholstery, but they didn't seem to care about the upholstery.

The kid's name was Albert and Albert sat there and said, "Jesus, you guys mean you're going to take me and lock me up where I can't get candy and cigarettes and beer, where I can't listen to my record player?"

"Stop your sniveling, will you?" I asked the kid.

I hadn't made the drunk tank for six or eight years. I was due, I was overdue. It was just like driving that long without a traffic ticket—they were just going to get you finally if you drove and they were going to get you finally if you drank. On drunk tank trips vs. traffic tickets the drunk tank led by 18 to seven. Which shows I'm a better driver than I am a drinker.

It was the city jail and Albert and I got separated in the booking. The routine hadn't changed except the doctor asked how my hands got cut.

"A lady locked me out," I said, "so I smashed the door in, a glass door."

The doctor put one band-aid on the worst cut and I was led to the tank.

It was the same. No bunks. Thirty-five men laying on the floor. There were a couple of urinals and a couple of toilets. Ta, ta, ta.

Most of the men were Mexican and most of the Mexicans were between 40 and 68. There were two blacks. No Chinese. I have never seen a Chinese in a drunk tank. Albert was over in the corner talking but nobody was listening, or maybe they were because once in a while somebody would say, "Jesus Christ, shut up, man!"

I was the only one standing up. I walked over to one

of the urinals. A guy was asleep with his head against the urinal. The guys were all around the urinals and crappers, not using them but sitting crowded around them. I didn't want to step over them so I awakened the guy by the urinal.

"Listen, man, I want to piss and your head is right up against the urinal."

You can never tell when that will mean a fight so I watched him closely. He slid over and I pissed. Then I walked to within three feet of Albert.

"Got a cigarette, kid?"

The kid had a cigarette. He took it out of the pack and threw it at me. It rolled along the floor and I picked it up.

"Anybody got a match?" I asked.

"Here." It was a skid row white. I took the matchbook, struck up a smoke and handed it back.

"What's the matter with your friend?" he asked.

"He's just a kid. Everything's new to him."

"You better keep him quiet or I'm going to punch him out, so help me, I can't stand his babble."

I walked over to the kid and kneeled down beside him.

"Albert, give it a rest. I don't know what kind of shit you were on before you met me tonight but all your sentences are fragmented, you're making bad sense. Give it a rest."

I walked back to the center of the tank and looked around. A big guy in grey pants was laying on his side. His pants were ripped up the crotch and the shorts were showing through. They'd taken our belts so we couldn't hang ourselves.

The cell door of the tank opened and a Mexican in his mid-forties staggered in. He was, as the saying goes, built like a bull. And gored like one. He walked into the tank and did some shadow boxing. He threw some good ones.

Both of his cheeks, up high, near the bone had raw red

gashes. His mouth was just a blot of blood. When he opened it all you could see was red. It was a mouth to remember.

He threw a couple more, seemed to miss a hard one, lost balance and fell over backwards. As he fell he arched his back so when he hit the cement the ball of his back took the blow, but he couldn't hold his head back up, it snapped back from the neck, the neck almost acted as a lever and the rear of his head was hurled against the cement. There was the sound, then the head bounced back up, then fell down again. He was still.

I walked over to the tank door. The cops were walking around with papers, doing things. They were all very nice-looking fellows, young, their uniforms very clean.

"Hey, you guys!" I yelled. "There's a guy in here needs medical attention, bad!"

They just kept walking around doing their duties.

"Listen, do you guys hear me? There's a man in here needs medical attention, bad, real bad!"

They just kept walking around and sitting, writing on pieces of paper or talking to each other. I walked back into the cell. A guy called to me from the floor.

"Hey, man!"

I walked over. He handed me his property slip. It was pink. They were all pink.

"How much I got in property?"

"I hate to tell you this friend, but it says 'nothing.'"

I handed his slip back.

"Hey, man, how much I got?" another guy asked me.

I read his and handed it back.

"You're the same; you've got nothing."

"What do you mean, nothing? They took my belt. Isn't my belt something?"

"Not unless you can get a drink for it."

"You're right."

"Doesn't anybody have a cigarette?" I asked.

"Can you roll one?"

"Yeah."

"I got the makings."

I walked over and he handed me the papers and some Bugler. His papers were all stuck together.

"Friend, you've spilled wine all over your papers."

"Good, roll us a couple. Maybe we can get drunk."

I rolled two, we lit up and then I walked over and stood against the tank door and smoked. I looked at them all laying there motionless upon the cement floor.

"Listen, gentlemen, let's talk," I said. "There's no use just laying there. Anybody can lay there. Tell me about it. Let's find something out. Let me hear from you."

There wasn't a sound. I began to walk around.

"Look, we're all waiting for the next drink. We can taste the first one now. To hell with the wine. We want a cold beer, one cold beer to start it out with, to wash the dust out of the throat."

"Yeah," said somebody.

I kept walking around.

"Everybody's talking about liberation now, that's the thing, you know. Do you know that?"

No response. They didn't know that.

"All right, I say let's liberate the roaches and the alcoholics. What's wrong with a roach? Can anybody tell me what's wrong with a roach?"

"Well, they stink and they're ugly," said some guy.

"So's an alcoholic. They sell us the stuff to drink, don't they? Then we drink it and they throw us in jail. I don't understand. Does anybody understand this?"

No response. They didn't understand.

The tank door opened up and a cop stepped in.

"Everybody up. We're moving to another cell."

They got to their feet and walked toward the door. All except the bull. Me and another guy walked over and picked the bull up. We walked him out the door and down the aisle. The cops just watched us. When we got to the next tank we laid the bull down in the center of the floor. The cell door shut.

"As I was saying . . . well, what was I saying? O.K., those of us who have money, we bail out, we get fined. The money we pay is used to pay those who arrested us and kept us confined, and the money is used to enable them to arrest us again. Now, I mean, if you want to call that justice you can call it justice. I call it shit down the throat."

"Alcoholism is a disease," said some guy from flat on his back.

"That's a cliché," I said.

"What's a cliché?"

"Almost everything. O.K., it's a disease but we know they don't know it. They don't throw people with cancer in jail and make them lay on the floor. They don't fine them and beat them. We're the roaches. We need liberation. We should go on parades: 'FREE THE ALCOHOLIC.'"

"Alcoholism is a disease," said the same guy from flat on his back.

"Everything's a disease," I said. "Eating's a disease, sleeping's a disease, fucking's a disease, scratching your ass is a disease, don't you get it?"

"You don't know what a disease is," said somebody.

"A disease is something that's usually infectious, something that's hard to get rid of, something that can kill you. Money is a disease. Bathing is a disease, catching fish is a disease, calendars are a disease, the city of Santa Monica is a disease, bubblegum is a disease."

"How about thumbtacks?"

"Yeah, thumbtacks too."

"What isn't a disease?"

"Now," I said, "now we got something to think about. Now we got something to help us pass the night."

The cell door opened and three cops came in. Two of them walked over and picked up the bull. They walked him out. That broke our conversation somehow. The guys just laid there.

"Come on, come on," I said, "let's keep it going. We'll all have that drink in our hand soon. Some sooner than others. Can't you taste it now? This isn't the end. Think of that first drink."

Some of them laid there thinking about that first drink and some of them laid there thinking about nothing. They were resigned to whatever happened. In about five minutes they brought the bull back in. If he had gotten medical attention it wasn't noticeable. He fell again but this time on his side. Then he was quiet.

"Look, gentlemen, cheer up, for Christ's sake, or for my sake. I know they treat a murderer better than a drunk. A murderer gets a nice cell, a bunk, he gets attention. He's treated like a first-class citizen. He's really done something. All we've done is empty a few bottles. But cheer up, we'll empty some more . . ."

Somebody cheered. I laughed.

"That's better. Look up, look up! God's up there with a couple of six packs of *Tuborg*. Cold and chilled they are with tiny icy bubbles glistening on the side . . . think of it . . ."

"You're killing me, man . . ."

"You'll be out, we'll be out, some sooner than others. And we won't rush out to an AA meeting and take the 12 great steps back to infancy! Your *mother* will get you out!

Somebody loves you! Now which mother's boy of us will get out of here first? That's something to think about . . ."

"Hey, man . . ."

"Yeah?"

"Come here."

I walked over.

"How much I got?" he asked. He handed me his property slip. I handed it back.

"Brother," I said, "I hate to tell you . . ."

"Yes?"

"It says 'nothing,' a very neatly typed 'nothing.'"

I walked back to the center of the tank.

"Now look, fellows, I'll tell you what I'll do. Everybody take out your property slips and throw them in a pile in the center of the floor. I'll pay a quarter for each pink slip . . . I'll own your souls . . ."

The door opened. It was a cop.

"Bukowski," he announced, "Henry C. Bukowski."

"Be seeing you fellows. It's my mother."

I followed the cop on out. The checkout was fairly efficient. They simply extracted $50 for bail (I'd had a good day at the track) and gave me the rest, plus my belt. I thanked the doctor for his band-aid and followed the cop into the waiting room. I'd made two calls out while being booked. I was told I had a ride. I sat for ten minutes and then a door opened and I was told I could go. My mother was sitting on a bench outside. It was Karen, the 32-year-old woman I lived with. She was trying her damnedest not to be angry but she was. I followed her on out. We got to the car and got in and started off. I looked in the glove compartment for a cigarette.

Even the city hall looks good when you get out of the tank. Everything looks good. The billboards, the stoplights, the parking lots, the bus stop benches.

"Well," said Karen, "now I suppose you'll have something to write about."

"Oh, yeah. And I gave the fellows a good show. The fellows are going to miss me. I'll bet it's like a tomb in there . . ."

Karen didn't appear to be impressed. The sun was about to come up and the lady on the billboard, one strap down on her bathing suit, smiled at me as she advertised a sun tan lotion.

Walden, shit, well I'm writing this in King's Pasture, Utah, no transport, no racetrack, no beer, no Cal Worthington, no love letters from insane ladies in Michigan, Louisiana, New Jersey . . . no poetry readings, no nudie bars . . . My few aficionados who expect tales of drunken nights, child-rape, woman rape, jail, murder—the general calm madness of Hollywood and Los Angeles, will have to wait.

As I write this I fight off a few mosquitoes but, by comparison to the average person, they don't contact me too often. The alcoholic content of my blood gives them pause, but the few who get a nip of me whir off singing.

I stare right off into 40,000 trees and not a toteboard in sight. But I gather no mental clarity or insight.

I suppose that I am terribly inbred to my prejudices. I find my prejudices comforting; I find my ignorances comforting. I have no desire to be an intelligent man and I have succeeded. Intelligent men bore me with their understanding, with their deep-set knowledgeable eyes, with their vocabularies, with all and everything they know. I prefer a slower seasoning.

So many people are doomed by their ambition and their gathered intelligence, their bank account and savings and loan intelligence. If there is any secret to life, that secret is not to try. Let it come to you: women, dogs, death, and creation.

In writing, especially, there are many fast starters. All men are born artists but most of them are quickly mutilated. Ambition is bad enough but when an obscene ambition gets connected with a commercial recognition it's not long before the shit backs up in the sewer. Creation means creation without attachment; too many imagine it means a house in Beverly Hills, a red sports car, talk shows, and going to bed with all offers . . .

One could write such a thing without staring at 40,000 trees. I came up here because my woman said there were wildmen in the forest with Wilt Chamberlain peckers who hadn't been laid for years. I have no idea how many wildmen she has met . . .

There was a party in Escalante before we got up here. I furnished the beer and the cowboy-ranchers furnished the dancing. Those boys are in good shape. They lift their women (and mine) over their heads and whirl them about. They are pitiful drinkers but they can dance for hours. They can start a fire with wet wood, hitch and shod a horse, kill and skin deer, trap, fish, fight, and fuck. Their conversation isn't too bad either.

I'm no dancer. I'm a hermit who has spent most of his life in a tiny room with a bottle and a typewriter and an occasional woman. I admit to disliking crowds, crowds anywhere, and parties. I suppose there should be a meeting ground for most people, and a party, a dancing party, could be the place. But I've seldom been to a party that didn't generate bad feelings. Basically the men are in too much of a rush to be on the make instead of allowing it to happen. Things become ugly, a contest, a push, a joust, a sham.

I got up and kicked my arms and my legs but I soon tired. I am in horrible shape. Also, I am a man who appreciates symphony music. When the ear and the mind become accustomed to classical music then the steady and almost invariable beat of the sound of popular music, turned top volume on the stereo, does dehydrate the inner gut. The very limitation and persistency of the sound is an insult to the senses.

So I found myself sitting on a rock in the desert, getting at the cans of beer I had brought out with me. I had been drinking for days and my stomach was raw. My jumping about and the sound of the music had made me ill. I stood up and started vomiting.

Carl, the owner of the ranch, was coming in from his car which was parked out on the road.

"Having trouble, man?" he asked me.

"I'm all right, Carl."

I let go another load.

"I'm staying right here with you," he said.

"It's all right, Carl, I've been through this a thousand times before."

I let go another batch.

"I'm standing over you," said Carl. "I'm standing over you tall and true until you're finished."

Carl stood over me tall and true until I was finished. Then we walked on inside where I opened another beer and I walked back into the front room where the full-blast stereo gutted the walls with the same limited notes. They danced and they leaped and I stood there with my can of beer and I watched, just to let them know that I knew what a good time was . . .

(I have just watched something murder something here

on the ground. Ah, nature, beautiful nature, the beautiful animals and bugs, the beautiful people.)

My first night out in nature, down in lower camp, I had to go.

"What'll I do?" I asked my woman.

"You just shit in the bushes."

It was a more crowded camp, one of those roadside machinations, tourists abounding, so I had to put on my clothing. I wasn't entirely sober. I walked along and looked at the bushes.

I selected some. I got out of my bluejeans, hung them on a bush but before I could squat the beershit began; waterfalls began rolling down my legs—wetwash of stinking beer mildewed with improperly chewed and improperly digested food. I grabbed at a bush and squatted, pissed on my feet, and eliminated a few very soft turds.

My pants fell off the bush and onto the ground. I leaped up, worried about my wallet. And, of course, it had fallen out of my pants. I staggered about the brush looking for it and managed to step right into my excretia, me who had stolen the land from the Indians.

I found the wallet, put it back in my pants, hung it all very securely upon a bush and began to wipe myself. I wiped and I wiped. I wiped myself for 5 minutes, put my pants back on and walked back.

I undressed and got into the sleeping bag with my woman. She was asleep but not for long.

"Jesus Christ, what's that?" she asked.

"What?"

"That stink!"

"I shit in the bushes."

"Did you wipe yourself?"

"For 5 minutes."

"What happened? You smell god-awful! What happened?"

"I'll tell you in the morning."

Then we slept. At least, I did. And to my few aficionados, don't worry; I'll soon be back in Los Angeles.

Linda was down. We'd left a zipper open in the tent flap and the mosquitoes had been on us all night. She was reading a book on sex. I had given her enough sex, grade-A, oral, spiritual and standard, but she was in an off mood. We were in the middle of 160 acres of mountain, trees, and pasture owned by five sisters. Linda was one of the sisters and Linda was down and I was far away from Hollywood Boulevard and Western. "Come on," I said, "let's take a dip in the beaver pond." "You go ahead," she said, not looking up, "I'll be along later."

Downs disturb me, especially when I can't understand why. I took my red notebook and a fountain pen and began walking. I got up to the beaver pond, sat on a rock, opened the notebook, but nothing came. I took off my clothes and stepped into the pond. It was like icewater. My body looked white and ridiculous. I stepped forward into a two-foot hole and I was in up to my arm pits, chilled in swirling muddy water. I stepped out over rocks that cut my feet. I found a spot and bathed with the small bar of soap. Then I gave myself a shampoo. When I stepped out of the water the flies were on me. Mountain flies are not like city flies; mountain flies are energetic and angry, very angry. I got my clothing and shoes on and walked off with my red notebook, the flies following me, while I thought, "I wonder what's wrong with Linda? I love her, doesn't she know that? How can she cut her feelings off? Love is not something you flip about like a TV dial."

I walked up over a hill of trees and looked back and

saw the beaver pond. Then I was over the hill and into a bit of shade. I found a rock and sat down and opened the red notebook. I didn't have stockings on. As I began to write I felt this stinging pain on my right foot. There was a cut across my feet and a huge fly had landed and was sucking into the cut. I reached down and brushed him off. I got up and the flies followed me.

Why in the hell can't a woman love a man even if he makes mistakes? Being together is the miracle, being together and caring. Sleeping together, feet touching, legs touching. Being asleep and together. Only the strong can live alone, the strong and the selfish.

It's good to eat with somebody, to listen to the rain with somebody, to get through Christmas and New Year's and Labor Day with somebody, to see their ring of dirt in the bathtub, to look at a toilet they forgot to flush. And to have the sex get better and better . . . For Christ's sake, what was wrong with that woman? Didn't she understand?

I walked some distance and found another rock under another tree. I opened the notebook and began to write something. I just let the flies have me and I wrote. I wrote something very bitter about humanity and love and the human race. Sometimes such things work, especially if they jell up fundamental truths instead of various self-pities. It didn't work. I tore the pages out. Even when I wrote about unhappy things I usually had to be happy when I wrote.

Then I heard a sound of water; it sounded like a waterfall. I got up and moved toward the sound. As I walked I heard Linda's voice. She was hollering for me: "BUKOWS-KI!" I kept walking. I decided not to answer. If she calls once more, I'll answer. She didn't call again. I moved toward the water. Then I saw it. The water was coming out of a spring and spilling down over a row of rocks that came down a high cliff. It was a good sight. I sat down and watched it. Then I got down into the stream and had a drink.

I decided, on going back, not to go up over the hill but to go around the easy way. I took my notebook and began. It would bring me right back to camp. I walked along and the ground was soaked with many little streams. I had to change course to get around them. There seemed to be very much brush. The brush got thicker. I pushed through, often stepping into mudholes up to my ankles.

Then very quietly a voice entered into my brain:

You're lost . . .

Oh, no, that would be too damned silly.

Silly or not, you're lost.

I looked around and I was lost. It was that simple. A tiny emptiness entered through my bellybutton.

You're lost and you're a coward and a fool and this proves it. You don't deserve to live. Linda's right.

I pushed on through the brush, downhill, stepping into streams . . . I threw my red notebook away. A lost man doesn't care about a red notebook. I was the man who had once wanted isolation; I was the man who had once fattened on isolation. Now I had it: mountains and trees and brush; nobody around.

I walked on. I climbed a barbwire fence. I felt it was not the thing to do. I did it. I walked on. I climbed another fence. I was more into nowhere. I was in the center of 160 acres. Mountains, trees.

At first there is panic, a rather clubbing sickness inside. Then one says, I'm lost. One says it several times. Then one adjusts to being lost. One says, I am lost. Well. I might die. Well. But the conclusion is hardly joyous. I began to think of Linda. If I ever get out of this, I will treat her so good, oh I will treat her so good.

I climbed another barbwire fence. I kept following a stream down the hill. Looking ahead I could see a large body of water. I left the stream and walked toward it. I found a road. The road had tire tracks on it. There was a small pier built over the water. I got under the pier and took my shoes off and bathed them in the water. I drank the water. Somebody had built that pier, some humans. They might return, those efficient humans, those humans I had once as much resented. They were clever sons of bitches and strong. I wasn't. That's why I wrote poems. And, shit, I hadn't finished my second novel yet. It was laying back in a drawer in Los Angeles. I could see the bit in *The Garfield County News*:

The minor poet Charles Bukowski, who had come to Utah to visit the King sisters, was found perished under the reservoir pier by Dale Barney, Bruce Wilson, and Pole Griffith. Mr. Bukowski was 52 years old and wrote a column, Notes of a Dirty Old Man, *which was published in Communist newspapers. He is survived by an eight-year-old daughter, Marina Louise Bukowski. Mr. Bukowski's red notebook was found, empty, 175 yards north and east of the campsite. Evidently the state of Utah did not inspire Mr. Bukowski.*

I put my shoes back on and walked out from under the pier and got on top of it and walked out toward the end. There were a couple of box-like contraptions which were locked and made of steel or a high-grade tin. Might be a telephone in there, I thought. I walked on to the road and found a large rock. I brought the rock back and smashed it against the lock. I skinned the knuckles of both hands, but I kept smashing the rock down. I really didn't expect the lock to open but it was something to do. I was most surprised when the lock snapped open. I opened the compartment and stuck my hand in. I immediately got an electric shock.

There was a loose wire sticking up from what appeared to be some type of transformer.

I stood and looked into the box. The sun beat upon me and my feet were covered with blisters. It was the end of my sanity. Alone and lost in the world, unloved by my love . . . demented, appalled, the shit of my very soul stuck into my ears, I stood there and looked. A needle moved very slowly back and forth across a semi-circle of cardboard. There were four numbers written upon the cardboard:

One, two, three, four.

The needle moved very slowly back and forth across the numbers:

One, two, three, four.

I decided not to flood the reservoir. I put the lock back on and got down under the pier and bathed my feet again. Having finished that I put my shoes back on and walked down the road a bit. I came to a gate, walked through the curving side entrance and found a picnic ground. But it was a Tuesday. There was nobody there. There were pits for cooking but I had no matches and no food. But civilization had been there, my beloved mankind.

I found a half loaf of stale French bread in the dirt. It was grey and mouldy. I walked over to a garbage can and dug out the cellophane bag inside and wrapped my bread inside of it . . . Garbage cans . . . meant garbage men . . . Where were they? Sons of bitches were probably on strike. I took my bread and my cellophane bag and began walking back toward the reservoir. It occurred to me that in spite of the general nearness of humanity that it was still possible that I *could* die up there—exposure, panic, madness . . . The thought disgusted me. I was like any other dreamer— I wanted to die while being sucked-off by the 15-year-old neighbor girl while her parents were at Mass.

I walked back to the pier, hung my bread from a railing, went out to the road, and piled boulders in the way so that anybody who might drive by would have to stop. I had left camp about 10 a.m. I figured it to be about 1 p.m. The most difficult thing is waiting, especially when waiting is useless. They figured I was hidden in the mountains writing immortal poetry. I decided to walk inward on the road. Perhaps it led to camp, although it hardly seemed the road we had driven in on. We didn't have a car; we had been driven up and left. They were to return at a later date.

I began walking down the road. It was very hot. I walked slowly. I walked several miles. Then I screamed out, "Linda!" It was such a sad sound, bouncing and echoing.

For a moment I had the feeling of running off into the trees, screaming, crashing my head against tree trunks and boulders. But that hardly seemed very manly so I decided against it. A poem began to from in my mind as I walked along:

> *Imperfection breeds Charley*
> *While other men love*
> *Crack-wise*
> *Ride broncos*
> *Imperfection breeds Charley*
> *While other men light fires*
> *On vistas*
> *Study Shakespeare*
> *Discover uranium, oil,*
> *Sex. . . .*
> *Imperfection breeds Charley*
> *While other men hit*
> *600 home runs*
> *shoot deer and panther*

shoot lion, elephant and
man. . . . imperfection breeds
Charley

Then I decided, to hell with that poem, I'm not that bad. And I kept walking. I don't know how long I walked, two hours perhaps, but there was nothing but road and road and road. I saw three or four deer. My energy was getting very low and my city shoes were blistering my feet. I had made another bad move. I turned and had a two-hour walk back to help consume me. One does reflect at such times. One thinks of the city, of walking about in a room and listening to the radio, reading the race results. I thought about the poet Jeffers who said there were traps everywhere, that they'd even trapped God when He came to earth.

But my trap had been so inane, without glory or purpose. The sun was very hot and I should have sat in the shade and rested but I was disgusted with my stupidity and wouldn't allow myself that. Then I thought, it really isn't death that matters: it's dying in some sort of minor comfort that matters . . . where people can sign little papers and keep the flies off your body. I walked on. Then ahead of me in the road stood a small doe. It was just a little larger than a large dog. As I slowly approached, it just stood there and looked at me. I was so tired, so low-keyed, my soul in such a pissed-off state against itself that I gave off no rays at all. The doe just remained in the road looking at me and I moved closer and closer. It isn't going to move, I thought. What will I do? Then as I was almost upon it, it turned and ran, the rear end bounding up and down. I remembered one time I had been very near suicide when I was sitting on a high cliff over the water near San Diego. As I sat there, four squirrels slowly—well, not slowly but in their swift darts—yet it seemed slow—they approached me and they came right up to my feet as I sat there and I looked into their large brown eyes and they looked into mine. They didn't fear me and I wondered at them. It seemed to last many minutes; then I moved a bit and they ran back down the rocks.

Finally I was under my pier again, my feet in the water. My thirst didn't seem to end. I kept drinking water. I tried to sleep. It wasn't any good. I put my shoes back on and walked back to the other end of the road, the picnic grounds. There was nobody about. I tried to remember how far it was back to the nearest town. The drive up had been a long one, very long, over a hot narrow mountain road. If I made it, there wouldn't be much left of me. If I didn't make it at least it would be a form of action. I decided to stay another night and a day and start out the next night. I walked back and got under the pier again. But the inaction got to me. I hardly felt very clever under that pier. I put my shoes back on and walked back toward the picnic grounds again.

Then I saw a little girl walking along the road toward me. "HEY!" I yelled at her, "HEY!" She seemed frightened. I walked toward her, then stopped. "I won't hurt you! I'm lost! I'm lost!" I felt very foolish, for how can one get lost near a picnic grounds with signs around that say NO SMOKING and PLEASE PUT OUT ALL FIRES? "Where's your mother and father?" "Oh, they're in a red and white camper on the picnic grounds." I walked toward the picnic grounds. I saw the camper but I didn't see the people. "HEY!" I yelled. "HEY!"

Then I saw Linda standing there with blue curlers in her hair. Then I saw a man and a woman by the camper.

"Hi," Linda said to me.

"My god I'm glad to see you!" I said. "Did these people bring you up?" "No, I just got here."

The people at the camper were watching us. "He's a city boy," said Linda. "He got lost in the woods. I just found him."

I laughed. "I'm a city boy. I'm a city boy."

"Well, I'm glad you found your man," said the woman.

"Come on," said Linda. "Follow me."

She had her dog with her. She was a good 15 yards ahead of me. "Listen," I said, "I've been lost in the woods for eight hours. Don't I even get a kiss?" She waited and I walked up. She turned her cheek and I kissed her on the cheek. Then she walked on ahead. "I'm mad at you. I been thinking about a lot of the things you've done and said and I got mad at you."

I walked along behind her, stumbling into holes, over rocks and fallen tree branches, into mudholes. "I thought I might die," I said, "and I thought, well, at least I ate her pussy the last two nights we were together. It was the only comforting thought I had."

"I think you got lost on purpose. I found your notebook a couple of blocks from camp. You didn't even leave a note. You always leave a note. I thought, well, he's really mad. All you had to do was look up and you could have seen the camp. You never look up."

"Usually when I look up I don't like what I see."

"You're always so negative," she said, "always so negative."

I followed along 15 yards behind. "I point things out to you, landmarks, but you don't listen. You don't listen to things, you don't participate, you're always so far off. Why didn't you leave a note in your notebook?"

"I didn't get lost on purpose."

"I believe you did."

"No, not at all."

"Or I thought maybe you went over the mountain to get a drink. I thought maybe you'd gone mad for a drink.

"Look, you've found me now, we're back together, Jesus Christ . . ."

We had to climb between and over old barbwire fences. I got stuck in one, three or four barbs stuck into the back of my shirt. My arm was too tired to reach up and pluck myself free. I just stood there between the strands. Linda waited. I couldn't move. She walked back and lifted the top strand off my back and I got out and followed her.

She was always just a little too far ahead and gaining. The dog bounded ahead of her. I followed Linda's ass. I'd followed that beautiful ass for three years; I figured another mile and one half through the wilderness wouldn't be entirely impossible. "Now you'll have something to write about," she said looking back.

"Oh shit yes," I said.

The mountains and the trees and the mudholes and the rocks and the barbs and the ass and the dog and me were everywhere.

I took Patricia to the fights at the Olympic, we were eight or nine rows back and began drinking beer. The opening amateur fights were the best, as usual, and it was hot in there and the beer was good. Patricia and I bet 50 cents each fight and let our loyalties be known, better and better known with each new beer.

By the time the six-rounder came around we were screaming things like, *"Kill 'im!" "Send 'im back to Japan! Re-*

member Pearl Harbor!" "He couldn't beat his grandmother's wet panties with a fly swatter!"

We screamed all through the six-rounder and through both 10-round feature matches. When it was over I was 50 cents ahead. I lit two cigars, gave one to Patricia and we walked out to her car.

On the way in we got into an argument of some sort. What it was about I have since forgotten but I think it was something about which was the greater invention, the elevator or the escalator? She let me out in front of my place and I wandered back through the banana trees and the polluted fishpond and went up the back stairway to Apt. #24 where I found a pint of Grand-Dad in the refrig and lucked onto some Stravinsky on KFAC and sat about drinking and listening.

Halfway through the bottle I remembered a lady in town who was reading the life story of Virginia Woolf. Now not everybody in Los Angeles sits around reading the life story of Virginia Woolf, especially an attractive lady with an eight-room apartment, good French wine and $400 a month alimony. I finished the Grand-Dad and decided to find out more about Virginia Woolf.

The lady was in and we sat and talked for 10 minutes and she didn't bring out any French wine so I suggested that I might go to the liquor store. She said that might be fine, so I went. The small liquor store to the north was closed but the lady lived on a large boulevard so I went on down to the supermarket. The lady's name was Nina. I mean the one who read the life of Virginia Woolf. Nina had told me that Virginia Woolf had led a very tragic life and she also told me of her suicide. I think that she told me that Virginia Woolf had walked into a river naked and drowned herself.

Anyhow, I came back with two six-packs in the bottle and

a pint of Grand-Dad. I walked back up the boulevard and as I got near Nina's place I noticed Patricia's car parked outside. I thought, fine, I'll take Patricia up and introduce her to Nina. Patricia might like to hear about Virginia Woolf. As I got near Patricia's car, the door opened and she leaped out. She began swinging her purse at me. Her purse was a large furry contraption with very long straps. She whirled it around and around, banging it against my head and shoulders and sides screaming, "You S.O.B.! You S.O.B.! You S.O.B.!"

"So help me now," I said, "you just keep it up and I'll have to give you one! Men's lib, you know."

Patricia kept it up and I set the bag down. Just as I did she gave me a good one along the side of the head. It spun me off to one side and she made for the bag. She got hold of a beer bottle and crashed it down against the sidewalk. It exploded! A good cold beer. She got another one. POW! Another one. POW! In the bar across the street they were lined up against the blinds, peering out. POW!

I was too drunk to grab her.

"You bitch! I'll have to put you back in the madhouse!"

I couldn't catch her. She kept circling back to the bag. POW! POW! The moon was high. There wasn't a cruise car within two miles and nobody was phoning in. I rushed the paper sack, picked it up, hugged it to my chest and she gave me one against the back of the head. I dropped the bag and Patricia was upon it. She found the Grand-Dad and held it up in the air.

"Ah ha! You were going to drink this with her and then . . ."

She didn't let me answer. POW! There went Grand-Dad. Nina's door was open and she was standing halfway up the stairway and began swinging her purse at Nina, saying over and over, "He's *my* man! He's *my* man! He's *my* man!"

Then she came running out. She found another beer in the sack. "POW!" Then she leaped into her car and drove off.

I walked up the stairway. Nina was at the top of it. "That was Patricia," I said.

"My god, what's wrong with her?"

"I don't know. Do you have a broom?"

I took the broom outside and began sweeping up the glass. Well, Patricia had been in the madhouse but Nina had been in the madhouse, too. Almost every woman I knew had been in the madhouse. It didn't prove anything. I seemed to hear a sound near me. I looked around. Patricia had gotten her car up on the sidewalk and it was coming down upon me. I leaped up against the wall and the right fender scraped across my leg. Then she bounced off the sidewalk, into the street, made a left turn against a red light up on Los Feliz Boulevard and was gone.

I began sweeping up more glass. I gathered little piles of glass into my hands and carried them up the stairway to Nina who took them off somewhere. Then I went back down and swept up more glass.

Then as I was sweeping I heard breathing sounds. I looked up and Patricia was standing before me. She grabbed the broom out of my hand and broke it into three pieces. Then she ran inside the door and found two bottles of beer on the bottom step.

"Ha! You saved these to drink them, didn't you, ha?"

She took both bottles and ran outside. "POW!" There went one. I walked over and closed Nina's door. Patricia took the other bottle and threw it at the door. It went right through the glass window. It made a neat, round hole. I opened the door, walked in, closed it. I found the bottle one-third of the way up the stairway. It was unbroken. I unscrewed the cap and took a good drain. Nina was at the top of the stairway. "For god's sake, Bukowski, go *with* her! Go *with* her before she kills us all!"

"Ah, she's gone. I wanna hear about Virginia Woolf."

"Don't worry, she's out there."

"You think so?"

"I know so."

I finished the beer and walked down the stairway. I opened the door, closed it. Patricia was out there. She was sitting in her orange car. I opened the door and got in. She turned the key and the car started.

"You know," I said, "she's really a nice woman. She didn't deserve all that. She didn't deserve me and she didn't deserve you."

She pressed the pedal to the floor.

"Bukowski . . . ," she said.

"O.K.," I said, "let's die together."

She had it to the floor and even a Volks will gather speed after a while.

"Bukowski . . . ," she said.

"Yes?"

"You should never take me to the fights. All those guys fighting . . . it gets me too much in the mood."

We did, somehow, arrive at her place. We were too drunk for anything. We slept in each other's arms.

Ralph awakened to the sound of his wife's voice. It was two a.m. and dark, and quiet except for the sound of Judy's voice.

"Tommy," she said, "oh, Tommy, slam that big thing to me! Oh my god, Tommy, slam that thing to me!"

Ralph propped himself up on one elbow and looked at her. She had on a thin pink negligee and had kicked all the covers off.

"Oh! It's so *big*! And purple! Oh, Tommy!"

Tommy Carstairs was Ralph's best friend.

"Oh, Tommy! It's in, it's in! Move that goddamned thing! Put that snake to me, Tommy!"

Ralph put a hand on his wife's arm.

"Listen, Judy, for Christ's sake . . ."

"Oh, Tommy! Oh, my god, I LOVE YOU!"

Her legs were pulled back and up and then she began to have spasms.

"Oh, oh, oh, oh, oh, oh . . ." Then she was still and stretched out her legs. She turned her head toward Ralph and with a little smile on her face she began to snore ever so gently.

"Judy," he said.

"Hey, listen, Judy . . ."

He reached over and shook his wife. Then he took her by the shoulder and twisted it.

"Ouch," she said. "For Christ's sake, what's the matter with you, you going crazy?"

Judy got out of bed and went to the bathroom. She flushed the toilet, lingered a moment and came out. Her hair was almost as pink as her nightgown and one long strand came down over the left eye, crossed the nose and hung there. She brushed it up and away and it fell back to the same location. She climbed back into bed, put the pillow up against her back and lit a cigarette.

"Judy," he said, "you were dreaming."

"So shit," she said, "that don't give you no right to break my shoulder."

"Do you remember your dream?"

"No, no frankly I don't."

"You were taking cock."

"Taking cock?" she laughed.

"From Tommy Carstairs."

"You're crazy."

"I didn't know he had a big purple cock."

"Does he? Who told you?"

"You did. In the dream."

"Look, Ralph, it's 2:30. Let's get some sleep."

"Some sleep, hell. I want to know what's going on."

"Nothing's going on."

"Nothing's going on, eh? 'Oh, Tommy! Oh, oh, Tommy, slam that big purple thing to me! It's in! It's in! Move it! Move it! Oh my God, I'm coming . . . ooooh, ooooooh, oooooh!'"

"Look, Ralph, I don't want to hear that shit. Have you been drinking?"

"Have I been drinking? You know I haven't been."

"You talk like a sick man."

"I'm telling you what I heard."

"All right, I don't know what you heard. A dream isn't reality."

"It can be a tipoff on reality."

"Well, I don't know about you, but I'm going to sleep."

Judy put out her cigarette, rebunched her pillow, turned her back to Ralph. It was a doublebed and the bedlight was still on.

"Listen, Judy . . ."

"Ralph, for Christ's sake . . ."

"I want to tell you something . . ."

"All right. Go ahead."

"If you want this Carstairs guy, go ahead."

"What do you mean?"

"I mean, I'll get out of the marriage."

"Listen, I'm not even *fond* of Carstairs . . . in fact, I hate him . . ."

"Hate and love are very close."

Judy sat up in bed quickly, both arms pressed down at her sides, the palms of her hands flat on the sheets.

"Listen, Ralph, what do you WANT? Are you trying to drive me crazy too? Just what do you WANT? I WANT TO KNOW WHAT YOU WANT!"

"Listening to that dream was very ugly to me, Judy, I love you . . . I did love you. I just wonder how you'd feel if I dreamt something like that and *you* heard it."

"You make too much of everything, you always did. You're the most jealous man I ever *did* meet! By god, now you're even jealous of my dreams! Can I help it what I dream?"

"Then you *did* dream it?"

"I said I didn't remember."

"How do I know it's something that didn't happen? How do I know it's something that you might want to happen?"

"Oh Ralph, I'm so sick of all of this! I'm your *wife*, I'm living with you!"

"If this Carstairs had anything at all I'd understand. Course, I don't know about his cock."

"I don't know about his cock either."

"I'll bet."

"Goddamn his cock."

Ralph reached up and turned the light off. He stretched out. Then he heard Judy stretch out. It was summer and one could hear the crickets. Usually the crickets brought a sense of peace. The police helicopter circled above looking for muggers and rapists. Minutes went by. Ten. Fifteen. Ralph was on his back. He felt Judy's hand. It crawled up over his leg like some small animal, then her fingers closed about his cock. He reached down and took her hand and moved it off. The hand crawled back and grabbed his cock again.

"Ralph," she said.

"Yeah," he said, "what the hell is it?"

"I love you."

"Oh shit," he said.

"I mean it. I love you."

"Women can really throw that word."

She began to massage his cock.

"Don't," he said. "Christ, I need a drink."

"There's a pint in the cupboard."

"There is?"

"Yes, I'll get it."

He heard Judy moving in the dark and reached up and turned on the light. While she was in the kitchen he remembered he had had some dreams too. And it hadn't always been Judy. Sex feelings were something that didn't always stay confined. It was fairly normal to like others. Judy came back with the drinks. They sat up in bed and sipped at them.

"Judy," he said.

"Yes?"

"Forget it. Forget everything I said. I got nervous. That goddamned job is killing me. My eyes hurt, my back hurts, my brain hurts. It's a drain. I get jumpy."

"All right," she said, "forget it. I understand."

They sat there and finished their drinks. Then Ralph got up and mixed two more. He came back with the drinks and got in bed with her.

"You know," he said, "I had a horrible dream once. I dreamt I had a sexual relationship with my mother. I kept trying to draw back in the dream but I finally went ahead. It was one of the hottest dreams I ever had."

"The shrinks probably have something quite unnerving to say about that dream."

"Yes, but the shrinks are almost always wrong."

"I know."

"Give me a cigarette, Judy."

"Sure."

She put the ashtray between them and they both smoked.

"Here we are, talking at 3 a.m. in the morning," he said.

"It's good," she answered, "it breaks things up."

"Sure. Hear the crickets?"

"Yes, I like them."

"I like them too"

"Ralph, if that job is killing you, give it up. We'll make it."

"No, it's all right. It was just a real rough day today. There aren't any good jobs. Everybody is fucked."

They finished their smokes and their drinks and Ralph turned the light out again. This time when Judy's hand arrived like a small animal he didn't push it away. His penis began to grow. He turned and kissed her, lifted her nightgown and gently ran a middle finger across the hairs down there. Something opened and he felt the wetness. Jesus, he thought, we are all so mixed up. It's all so sad and so wonderful.

Then they could still hear the crickets. Then they heard the siren of an ambulance. Then they heard the police helicopter again. Then they heard three dogs barking. Then they heard each other.

belles-lettres?

Dear Mr. B: How come they save all the typos for YOUR column?

Hello Martha K: It is done by a bunch of rancorous old drunks in smelly stockings who hit me over the head with empty wine bottles of white California wine at the conclusion of their staff meetings. The reason is pure old American jealousy because I write so well, plus the fact that I ball everything female (or anything that looks female) which wanders within arm's (?) reach.

Dear Mr. B: I don't believe that a great poet like you works in a post office.

Hello Tilla A: A great poet works at a typewriter. I have more trouble with supervisors than with editors.

Dear Mr. B: I read your article about horseracing. If you know so much about the horses, why ain't you rich?

Hello Karl L: I can't read your handwriting. I had trouble that way once. (I mean a shaky hand.) I was born left-handed and my parents bent my slop spoon so if I put it to my jaw with my left hand all I got was this frustration thing and a slap across the mouth for failing. Besides, riches ain't everything—especially after you've gotten away from parents like that.

Dear Mr. B: How cum they give a column to a prick like you and leave a talented guy like me holding a bag of shit?

Hello Marty E: I keep thinking the same thing. X-factor vs. Y-factor. You take Beethoven. In his time he was not even the most highly-regarded musician. You just can't tell. So keep holding that bag of shit. I have more fan letters to answer.

Dear Mr. B: I am worried about the Hippy invasion of Los Angeles this summer. I am a widow of 39. Suppose 6 young men arrive at my door, covered with hair and spouting Dylan Thomas?

Dear Mrs. Clark J: If you're worried about crabs, always keep a little blue ointment on hand.

Dear Mr. B: I read your column on suicide. That photo of the man hanging from the home-made noose in the attic: is he dead or is it you posing? And why are the creases in his pants so neat?

Hello Mary W: The man is dead. I don't look that good. And he doesn't know why the creases in his pants are so neat.

End of letters . . .

Getting more serious, it is wondrous how much a man can suffer and endure, and I guess there will never be an end to that Bitch, Pain. The simple problem of staying alive in a society of no sense or heart—the totality of hardness every-where. Most of us live on the edge of starvation and insecu-rity all of our lives. The mind and the spirit should go mad with sorrow—they sometimes do. They've built a house filled with half-men and the half-men control us. If the devil ran for mayor of Los Angeles, he'd win by a landslide.

To be casual in the midst of shitfire, that's cool but unreal. We need something to go by. What do we have? Hardly a damn thing. The waste of days and lives is the automatic atrocity. One thing that is needed is leadership but it simply hasn't arrived. We live on luck and guts and that can grow tiring.

Perhaps it is this dark day as I write this, a Sunday, and all around me I can hear the babble of their TV sets. It is a kind of sound vibration that intermixes in the air, a jibberish. The average man stuffs himself with junk and garbage during his leisure. He doesn't have a chance to recover from his job. He is slugged with ready-made commercial contrivances until he becomes another faceless and unfeeling creature—just another of those many you pass on the streets continually.

I'll be glad when the sun comes up, won't you? What a dark stinking day. Like being locked inside a sardine tin. I wish I could make you laugh. Nothing to go by. The police patrolling the dead street. The dirty old man drops a pale blue tear. They ought to make a button for me to wear: AGONY. Then maybe I could laugh.

1.

I missed last week's column because I am a lush, and I looked around and bottles were everywhere and the deadline was past. I live in a rather modern apartment on Oxford Avenue, it's all very quiet, and I sneak my bottles down the stairway, play my radio at low key, and I bathe, modestly, under the arms. The problem with being a drunk is that one usually knows other drunks. One group will arrive one night, another the next. The conversation at these gatherings is hardly noteworthy—it hinges mostly upon gossip, bitching, lying and exaggeration. And when I run these people out on the street after being sickened by their petty musings, they then consider me anti-social (which I am), fat-headed (which I am) and over the hill (which I am not).

Any person into living and creativity must discourage a certain number of visitors, if not most of them. It can be done as Jeffers did by building a fortress of rocks and sending an old aunt to the door to gather messages. I simply tell people *why*. For instance, yesterday I got a phone call: "Are you Charles Bukowski?" "Yes?" "Charles Bukowski, the poet?" "I am *sometimes* Charles Bukowski, the poet." "Well, I'm a young man from New York just got into town, and I've always *loved* your work. I'd like to come by and talk to you." "Kid, just what does *talk* have to do with *poetry*?"

"I don't understand." "I'm not your corner priest. We have nothing to talk about, don't you understand?" I said good-bye and hung up. He'll find another poet, the phone book is full of them.

2.

I've been informed by the Department of Water and Power that I've been allowed 184 units per billing. That's not very much. I have a friend who is allowed 1600 units and we both think alike and eat about alike and live about alike. I don't know why the DWP didn't shut me off entirely. What am I going to do with 184 units? I'll have to boil my weenies and then take them out and used the soiled water for my coffee. Maybe this *is* the way to do it. If they want a

10 percent reduction, just cut off one person in 10 and let the others go on living. Greece and Rome knew how to do this. There are really only two types of people in this world: the noble and the fucked.

I notice the DWP reasoning upon allotments is that they are based upon a percentage reduction of past usage at the same residence over a given period. So a blind woman with a parrot lived here before me and her hobby was braille. Now I'm supposed to wear her pantaloons.

Actually, the way it works is that people who *have* been wasting energy are given larger allotments to waste than those who have not. They are rewarding the wasters with more waste.

I think a more stable measurement should be used, to wit so many units for one person living in a one-bedroom apartment, so many units for so and so many people living in a house of a certain size. In a sense, this would still be giving some tolerance to the wealthy, but it would actually come closer to a general fairness.

Let's break it down more rationally. The way they have it now it's like two men each owning a horse and one is allowed to feed his horse five bales of hay a month while the other is allowed 10. If Mayor Bradley wants to come and live at my place under 184 units to test the validity of things, fine, and I'll come to his place and test the validity of his allotment. And he needn't throw in his wife . . . I've got enough troubles already.

I suppose that when they get into gas rationing it will be another distortion of actuality. Americans have cheated and lied for so long, have become so decayed under this great moral Bob Hope front that I wonder why justice hasn't arrived and all our streets and boulevards do not have Chinese names. We, babies you and I, have been saved by our atomic stockpiles, not our ingeniousness, our guts, our souls, or our courage.

Gas rationing people will make exorbitant claims upon entirely unnecessary travel needs. Some people will become two people with two cars, some people will become three people with three cars. Some people will find need (seemingly) to travel from San Diego to Washington, D.C. three times a week. Everything will happen. More fucking fuel will become consumed, joggled and wasted and resold than if they just left the damn thing alone. The black market for gas and oil will be there for those who can afford it.

Who could have believed that the Arabs and their near-monopoly on oil could have caused massive layoffs here: 55 m.p.h. speed limits, perpetual daylight saving time, grins upon the faces of rapists, muggers and murderers, fear of running the TV too long . . . and over a 50 percent profit-rise for American oil companies . . . while in the long hot summer ahead a man or a woman will have to think five or six times whether to turn on the air conditioner or whether to sweat and stink.

It seems as if there are no shortages of certain commodities: cigarettes, alcohol, speed, cops, smog, bars, McDonald's hamburger stands, bums on skid row, cancer, hydrogen bombs, Lucille Ball, football games, basketball games, poets, politicians, dishes in the sink, infidelity, clap, sparrows, shit, vomit, bad breath, urine, stopped sinks, traffic lights, lines, garbage, roaches, rats, unreason, opera, hangnails, screaming women, rapists, lost laundry tickets and Bukowski.

It was Saturday, July 20, 1974, hot. I'd put ice cubes into the air cooler. I was on the bed sweating out the beer. It got to be 1 p.m., 1:30. I got up, scratched my hemorrhoids, took a bath and got dressed. It was no use. I was trying to stay away, but it was the last Saturday of the Hollypark meet and weekdays were bad enough but Saturdays at the track were nightmares to the vision and the feelings. I decided to go anyhow.

The sixth race was a match race between the two greatest 3-year-old fillies in America, Miss Musket from the west and Chris Evert from the east. It was billed as The Match Race of the Century, $350,000, winner take all. Each stable was putting up $150,000. Match races are very rare. I had only seen one other: Convenience vs. Typecast in 1972. I drove down to Carl Jr's and had a hamburger, fries and a large coke.

There was another reason for going out there. She was there each Saturday, showing leg. She wore very high-heeled shoes, and when she sat down she pulled her dress back and showed all this leg. She wore long hose, no pantyhose for her, and although she didn't go the garter belt route, she wore garters and was continually standing up, lifting her dress and pulling the hose tight. 1937 all over again and I was hardly the only man affected. Still, it was mainly the match race. I had no column in mind and I could report the affair for the *L.A. Free Press*. It would feel good to be a journalist; one didn't need a mind to be a journalist.

I drove out slowly. After you've seen as many races as I have you can miss a few. Match races come about as often as minor and major wars: Man O' War vs. Sir Barton, 1920. Zev vs. Papyrus, 1923. Seabiscuit vs. Ligaroti, 1938. Aisab vs. Whirlaway, 1942. Armed vs. Assault, 1947. Swaps vs. Nashua, 1955. Convenience vs. Typecast, 1972.

I arrived in time for the fourth race. The crowd was large, hot, and by that time—surly and depressed, walking into each other blindly, pushing dazed and dulled. When you see humanity like that, you know there's not much chance. If you want to find what a person is like inside, take them to a racetrack and watch how they react to defeat.

I walked over to the bench where she always sat, my lady with the long glorious legs. There she was—she had on thick, flat, low-heeled shoes. I turned away in disgust. Well, I still had the Match Race of the Century.

I went the No. 3 horse, Grape Juice, in the fourth, and lost in a three-horse photo. The photos weren't coming my way this meet. Some meets they give you all the photos; others they take them all away. It's usually decided for you in the opening days of any meet. Take your cue from there. Also, when you're going hot you bet heavy and go more often; when you're cold you go less and bet less. Never fight the tide.

In the fifth my preference was Afirmado with Tom Landry a close second. The last-minute action on the tote swung to Tom Landry and I got down on him at 8/5 but Afirmado breezed by him in the stretch at 7/2. It wasn't my meet.

The sixth race was the match race. I really wanted Chris Evert to win because Miss Musket was the western horse and I am a rebel by nature. I like to see the crowd murdered, they deserve it. But I also wanted to bet on the winner. I would have to watch the toteboard and do some thinking. All the boys in the local newspapers were picking Miss Musket—inside post, the great Laffit Pincay as jock, and the higher speed ratings. They each carried 121 pounds. Miss Musket was 3/5 on the morning line and Chris Evert 4/5. The betting began. They both opened at 3/5. Then Miss

Musket hit 1/2, then 2/5. At 1/2 or 2/5 I knew Musket had it wrapped but I did want to bet Evert. Musket was Florida-bred and Evert was Kentucky-bred, and the Kentucky-breds are usually horses of greater heart.

The betting windows were empty. The crowd didn't know what to do. A guy leaning up against a girder looked at me and gave me a silly grin: "I wouldn't bet this kind of race, it's stupid." "You're not forced to bet," I answered him. An old woman walked up to me: "How can you bet a race like this?" she asked me. "Lady," I said, "this race is the same as any other race. The track extracts 16 per cent and gives the remainder of the money back to the winning ticket holders. This way it's more obvious to you. In a 12-horse field you don't notice the bite, but it's still there."

With two minutes to go, Musket rose from 1/2 to 3/5. As they were putting them in the gate, Evert dropped from 4/5 to 3/5. Underlays win 75 per cent of the races at any track. I only had one bet: Evert, 20 win. Before the race some children had come by carrying a long banner on poles: "MISS MUSKET CAN'T MISS!" Although Miss Musket was the favorite in money bet to win, Evert had gotten the late action and was the underlay.

Musket on the inside broke out of the gate with a slight lead, but Evert with a lunge quickly had a length and a half. That move right there showed the power. Musket was supposed to have the lick but Evert had outbroken her clearly. Right there, the race was over. Pincay knew that Jorge Velasquez had a hell of a lot of horse under him. Evert took the rail and had two lengths around the first turn, and right there you noticed that Evert's legs were longer, her stride longer, easier. Miss Musket seemed to diminish in size, her strides seemed sloppy and confused.

On the backstretch, halfway down, Miss Musket made

her last effort, she pulled out and came almost alongside Evert, only you noticed that Velasquez had the hold and that Pincay was praying, his horse was laboring, giving away its stretch run on the backstretch. Then Velasquez let go his hold and Evert began to draw clear: one and one-half lengths, two lengths, four lengths, eight lengths on the turn . . . it was pure murder. At the top of the stretch Chris Evert had 30 lengths. One-half way down the stretch Evert had 40 lengths and had never seen the whip.

I had never seen such a defeating defeat. No war, no assassination, no treachery of love could match it. Pincay eased his horse. Evert breezed across the finish line 50 lengths in front and had so much run left in her Jorge had trouble keeping her from going down to the curve and going the distance once more. The Californians booed their Miss Musket and their Laffit Pincay as they finally crossed the finish line in a gentle canter. Shit, Pincay wanted to win, he'd just been on the wrong horse. The rider's share of the purse was 10 per cent, or $35,000. Pincay felt much worse than the $2 bettors.

Evert paid $3.50, which means $34 for $20, or $14 profit. As I came from the collection window, she was waiting. I had seen her at the track for several meets but we had never spoken. She looked frightened, her eyes were a pale blue, a very pale blue. She put her body right in front of me. I had to stop. "You won, didn't you?" she asked. "Yeh," I said and then stepped around her. Her and her flat white shoes. With high heels I might have taken her over to the bar for a drink, and then all things flowing, I would have taken her home and eaten her pussy. Her and her flat heels.

I didn't watch the other races. I had to go home and write about the match race for the *Free Press*. There was never anything about horse racing in the *Free Press*. I found my car in the parking lot and drove slowly back. I knew that that race would go down in history, something to be talked about for a long time—like the Tunney-Dempsey fights, the Dempsey-Firpo fight, the Zale-Graziano fights, the Dempsey-Willard, the battle of Stalingrad, Burton vs. Taylor, but I was glad I had seen it with my own eyes because things have a way of getting turned sometimes, they are not gotten down like they should be gotten down, something enters afterwards that destroys or distorts.

I got home, sat down to the typer and began my journalistic account of the two 3-year-old fillies. The phone rang.

"Hello," I answered.

"Hello," she said. "I was just thinking about you."

"Oh, yes, how you doing?" I asked.

Women have this trick of not saying who they are and they disguise their voices. I got trapped the other night. This one voice sounded like the other and I said, "Oh, did you get your car out of the garage?" And she answered, "Yes, but my oil pan is still dripping all over my pussy." Then I recognized the voice and I said "Oh, I'm sorry. I thought you were . . ." "Who?" she asked. "Oh . . . a friend." So this time I was careful. "I'm doing fine," she said. "I was thinking of you too," I said. The conversation went on and then I said something and she laughed and I recognized the laugh. "Say, that was one hell of an afternoon," I said, "you've got a great piano." "And I didn't know you could play the drums," she said. "Yeh," I said. "And you dance, you dance like you're wearing a hoola-hoop." "Yeh," I said. "Well, I'm just sitting here," she said, "and I'm alone and I just wrote a poem and I look out the window and I see all the lovers walking arm in arm and I thought of you and I thought, well, he's probably alone and writing a poem too." "No, I'm writing about a match race." "What's that?" "Two matches race." "Oh?" "Marion, phone me when you're in town. I've got to get this thing down." "All right," she said and hung up. She'll phone again.

Now, you see, this is the way you write about a match race, future students of journalism take note. And when you answer a telephone, feel your way along. Don't just presume that the last female you were with is the one who is phoning you now. Learn to eat pussy, take your vitamins, especially E, and when in doubt go for the long-legged filly, Kentucky-bred, wearing the tallest cleats possible.

If you think being a matchmaker is easy you're wrong. I average 14 hours a day in that office on a straight salary. It's mostly telephone calls and checking all the fight results, trying to get a couple of good boys in together at the lowest cost possible.

And the heavyweights are the biggest ache of them all. And they make the worst fights. They can't move and they don't have any guts. Just give them a fair tag and they quit.

Heavyweight fights are almost always dull and most of them leave a pretty good stink after it's over, but the fans still demand them. And that's what makes it hard. There aren't eight good heavies in the U.S. In fact, there aren't 30 heavies fighting in the U.S. And those that are only get a fight every year or two.

Here I was trying to find an opponent for Young Sharkey. 12-1-1, 12 k.o.'s. I finally go to Manilla and get Big Baby Herodima. Herodima is 4-6-2 but he weighs 276 pounds and I figure it will be a lot of fun to hear him fall. I phone the papers and tell them it's a match, write it up. Sharkey and Herodima, coming up in two weeks. I'm finally caught up on my matches. I lean back and feel peaceful for the first time in some days. The phone rings. It's Gerda. She's drunk.

"Listen, Gerda, I've asked you not to call me at work."

"Listen, Shithead, you *owe* me something."

"I don't owe you a damned thing. I've told you it's over between you and me. I've had it."

"Who is it? Suzy? Are you back with Suzy?"

"No, I've dumped her too."

"Listen, Doug, you just can't go around dumping women like that at *your* age. Pretty soon there won't be any left."

"When that happens it will be the happiest day of my life." I hung up. The phone rang again.

"Listen, Shithead, I'm not through talking to you. You're the biggest fraud of the ages. It's Suzy, isn't it? You're back with her again, you *always* go back to her."

"Not this time. She's been screwing everything that walks. It's like sticking your cock in a garbage disposal unit."

"Listen, Shithead, I want to tell you about my goldfish . . ." I hung up. The phone started to ring. I put on my coat, locked the door and got out of there . . .

When I got home I had a beer and a sandwich, showered and went to bed. I was just about asleep when the phone rang.

"Listen, Shithead—"

"Gerda, please. I've told you it's over, don't you understand? For Christ's sake, leave me alone!"

"I can *hear* her breathing!"

"What?"

"I can hear her *breathing*! You've got some woman in bed with you eating cheese crackers and olives! She's got her hand around your balls! I can hear her breathing!"

"You're crazy, that's what's wrong with you, you're completely crazy."

"Put her on the phone. I want to talk to her."

I hung up. The phone rang again. I picked it up, hung up, then lifted the receiver and let it hang from the wire. I went to sleep . . .

At the office the next day I got a call from the Commission saying that Herodima wouldn't be allowed to fight Young Sharkey, because he couldn't see out of one eye. I suggested that maybe a guy who weighed 276 pounds only deserved one eye, but they still said no. So there I was. I had to make the top card over again. I got on the phone. I tried to get Hymie Stringer out of Philly but his manager told me Hymie broke his leg when he fell out of a tree trying to untangle a kite for some neighborhood kid. I tried Mexicali. I tried Canada. Nothing. The phone rang.

"Listen, Shithead, I want to tell you about my goldfish. I got up early this morning and went out to the garden. It was about 6:30 and there was this light fog. And there they were floating near the top, mystified by this shroud of leaves that had fallen over them. I thought you'd like to hear."

"Yes, that's a nice story. Thanks."

"Listen, Shithead, was it good, was it *good* last night?"

"Gerda, I'm trying to line up a card. Herodima can only see out of one eye. Stringer fell out of a tree and broke his leg."

"Did you eat her box? Did you give her the treatment? Did she like it?"

I hung up and went outside and walked around the block twice. When I got back I had some luck. I got Frankie Tanada out of New York. Frankie's 2-14-3 but he's been knocked out by the best, been kayoed by 4 former champions. A little class there. I had some trouble with his manager but we finally settled on $1,250.00. I phoned the papers and told them the bout was on. Young Sharkey and Frankie Tanada. The phone rang.

"Listen, Shithead, I've got too many goldfish, there's not enough oxygen. Can I bring you some of my goldfish?"

"No, I'd rather you didn't."

"Do you still have that woman at your place?"

"What woman?"

"The one I heard breathing. I hope she cleans the ring out of your bathtub like I did. I hope she gets the shit stains out of your crapper like I did. I hope she bites off the end of your cock!" . . .

Tanada got out the next day and began working out right away. I went down and watched him. He didn't look too bad. I figured he could last 3 or 4 rounds with Young Sharkey. That's all I could hope for.

On Wednesday I got a call from the gym. Frankie Tanada had broken his hand trying to get a coke bottle out of the vending machine. I got on the phone again. Nothing out of Trenton. Nothing from Texas. The phone rang.

"Listen, Shithead, are you fucking my sister?"

"No."

"Listen, I'm funny, you can fuck anybody you want but I don't want you fucking my sister. I won't *tolerate* that!"

"All right, Gerda."

"I've got this thing about sisters. I don't even want you phoning her. Have you been phoning her?"

"No."

"Well, *don't*," she said, and hung up.

I finally got Gorilla Gibson out of Detroit. Same price: $1, 250.00. Gorilla was 3-11-2 and had been kayoed by 2 former champions. I phoned the papers and told them about the new match . . .

The fight really went off. I was there. When the bell rang Gibson turned and crossed himself in his corner, then scowled and came toward the center of the ring. He looked good. Young Sharky met him in ring center and hit him with a medium left cross to the body. Gibson dropped, stretched on his back and took the ten count. When he got up and walked back to his corner he still looked good. The fans booed and started throwing things into the ring, everything but money. I got up and walked out looking down at my shoes.

The Commission held up Gibson's purse. There would be a hearing. Two things appeared wrong, they told me. Gibson had done a tank job and also he was 37 years old. You couldn't fight in the state after 36 unless you got special permission. That was the next day when I heard. Also Carol came to see me. Carol owned the club, she'd run it for 30 years and kept it going when all the other clubs had their bad years. I'd been with her 18 years.

"Doug," she said, sitting down across from my desk, "another stinker like that and I've got to let you go, I've got to get another boy."

"Listen, it's those heavies, those heavies always stink. We can get one good heavy in the ring but we can't get two, you just don't have that kind of money."

"You get out of the gate."

"Impossible."

"Jenners does it across town."

"Jenners got the Palace. He can scale the prices. This place is 100 years old, Carol. Why, there are only two restrooms in the whole auditorium. You ought to see the men's room. Urine seeps one inch across the floor. 14 guys in line behind each urinal. I don't know what goes on in the ladies' room. They've got to squat. It must be hell. There's no way we can scale 100-75 and 50 and get away with it and you know that as well as I do."

The phone rang.

"Listen, Shithead, you've got a woman in your office. I can hear her breathing."

"I'll call you back, Harry, I'm in conference."

"I can hear her breathing! Are you going to eat her box?"

"No, Harry, that's impossible. I'll call you back. We might give you $500 for a semi. That's tops."

"Shithead, you're so tight, you've never ever given me *anything*! And what's a semi? Who wants half a fuck? I'm going to bring you my goldfish."

"You do and I'll run your ass out of the state!"

I hung up then took the phone off the receiver. Carol looked at me. "That was a woman on the phone, wasn't it?"

"What?"

"I could hear her voice, Doug. I want you to keep your sex life out of the office. And no more stinkers like that last one. The market just dropped below 700. Each month some new country discovers an atom bomb. It's a new world. Nobody is allowed any more mistakes."

With that she walked out.

Next week I've got a kid from Japan. They never make a bad fight; most of them can't hit but they make it up with guts. And I've got this 17 year old Mexican kid, he's run off 6 straight and the girls haven't gotten to him yet. And neither of these guys weighs over 128 pounds. I feel fairly safe. I should have married Carol, though, ten years ago when we were making it.

Sally and I argued almost every time we got drunk, and the arguments were vile and violent, and we drank almost all the time, and the arguments were LOUD and destructive, and we were evicted from place after place. We'd walk down the street and say, "We lived there. And we lived in that place too. Remember when we lived in that place?" Most of the evictions were via a notice under the door; they didn't care to contact us personally. Sometimes though, we were confronted personally but usually a day or two after our argument. Once I had mounted Sally and as we were working away I heard a key in the door. It opened and there was the manager. He pointed a finger down at Sally: "YOU'RE OUT!" he said. Then he paused and looked at me: "AND YOU'RE OUT TOO!" Then he walked out, closed the door, and we continued.

We began in most new places with a bit of dignity. Sally would tell the manager about me: "He is a fireman." Or, "He's a surgeon's assistant." Or, "He's on vacation." That was the one Sally used the most. In one place a young couple seemed to take a liking to us. They promised us all new rugs. And while we were at the bar one day they had put them in. New rugs. All red, bright red. Quite appropriate, I thought. Two days later while we were asleep there was a POUNDING on the door. "YOU PEOPLE GET OUT OF HERE AND GET OUT OF HERE NOW! YOU'RE DRIVING AL THE TENANTS IN THIS BUILDING CRAZY! I'M GOING TO LOSE MY JOB!" I got up in my shorts and opened the door. "Listen, man, we've got almost a month left on the rent. No chance of us clearing out now." "I'LL PAY YOUR BACK RENT! JUST GET OUT! CHRIST, WHAT HAVE YOU DONE TO THE RUGS? LOOK AT THAT LAMP! YOU PEOPLE NEED A BOXING RING, NOT AN APARTMENT!" We moved out.

The place we lasted longest was the HALCYON ARMS on Union Avenue, a few places up from the TEAMSTER'S UNION headquarters. They had a desk in front and you had to get your key and leave your key when you went in and out. The guy at the desk we named Sleepless because he seemed to be at that desk 24 hours. When he slept was the mystery, and it might have helped the situation. He was too sleepy to care.

The time I'm thinking about here as I write this was this certain time that Sally left. Sally was always leaving me but this time, somehow, it seemed more definite. It was confusing to me because I didn't know whether to be sad or happy. One likes to pinpoint the emotions or else all seems wasted.

I sat there with my fifth of Scotch and my beer and looked out the window. Sally was out there somewhere. The note had been very definite: BASTARD I CAN'T STAND YOU ANY MORE BUT I WANT YOU TO KNOW THAT I LOVE YOU AND THAT I'LL NEVER FORGET YOU EVER . . . SALLY

She hadn't done the dishes or made the bed, had taken all the cigarettes. I walked to the closet. Most of her clothes were still there. I sat down and had another drink. Under the bed I could see one of her pink slippers and next to the slipper was a pair of shit-stained panties. I got up and walked around. There were hairpins everywhere, in the ashtrays, on the dresser, on the floor, in the bathroom. Her magazines were on the floor, by the bed, magazines with exotic covers: MAN RAPES GIRL, THEN THROWS HER BODY FROM

400 FOOT CLIFF . . . 12-YEAR-OLD BOY RAPES WOMAN AT THE ZOO . . . LOVE BANDIT DRINKS THE BLOOD OF HIS VICTIMS. Inside were pictures of beheaded women, of people baked in ovens, of cops digging into murderers' graves outside Bakersfield.

In the dresser next to the Kleenex were all the notes and letters I had ever written her, all neatly bound with 3 or 4 sets of rubber bands. And then there were the photos, all the photos. There was one of both of us crouched on the hood of our '58 Plymouth, Sally showing a lot of leg and grinning like a Kansas City gun moll from out of the twenties and me showing the bottoms of my shoes with the circular waving holes in them. And there were photos of dogs, all of them ours, and photos of children, most of them hers.

Then the phone rang. It was Sally in some bar. I could hear the juke box. "I just want you to know, you son of a bitch, that I'm not coming back." Then I heard a man's voice: "Sally, Sally, forget the fuckin' phone and come back and sit down with us!" "You see," she said, "there are other men in the world beside you." "Your opinion only," I said. "I could have loved you forever," she said. "Get fucked," I said and hung up.

I poured another drink and while looking for a scissors in the bathroom to trim the hair around my ears and in my nose I found a brassiere in one of the drawers and held it to the light. The brassiere looked all right from the outside but inside was this stain of sweat and dirt and the stain was darkened, melded in there as if no washing would ever take it out. I drank my drink and then began to trim the hair around my ears. I decided that I was quite a handsome man and I'd lift weights, go on a diet and get a tan. I deserved better than Sally.

The phone rang again. I lifted the receiver, hung up,

lifted the receiver again and let the phone dangle by the cord. I trimmed my ears, nose, eyebrows, drank another hour or two and then went to bed and slept.

I was awakened by a sound I had never quite heard before. It was loud, deep and persistent. It was like a thousand wasps burning to death. It came from the dangling telephone, still off the hook. I picked it up. "Hello."

"Sir, this is the desk clerk. Your phone is off the hook."

"All right. Sorry, I'll hang it up."

"Don't hang up, sir. Your wife is on the elevator."

"Who?"

"She says she's Mrs. Borowsky."

"All right. It's possible."

"Sir, can you get her *off* the elevator? She doesn't understand the controls . . . her language is abusive toward us but she says that you'll help her . . . and sir . . ."

"Yes?"

"We didn't want to call the police."

"Good."

"She's laying down on the floor of the elevator, sir, and, and . . . she has . . . urinated upon herself."

"O.K." I said and hung up.

I walked down the hall in my shorts, drink in hand, cigar in mouth, and pressed the elevator button. Up it came from the bottom floor, one, two, three, four. The doors opened and there was Sally . . . and little delicate trickles and ripples of water lines drifting about the elevator floor and some blotchy pools.

I finished my drink, picked her up and carried her out of the elevator, threw her on the bed and pulled off her wetted panties, skirt and stockings. Then I put a drink on the coffeetable near her, sat on the couch and had a drink for myself. Suddenly she sat straight up and looked around.

"Borowsky"? she asked. "Over here," I waved my hand. "Oh, thank God."

Then she saw the drink and drank it right down. I got up, refilled Sally's glass, put cigarettes, ashtray and matches nearby.

"Who took my panties off?"

"Me."

"Don't you go playing with my panties. I'm mad at you."

"You pissed yourself."

"Who?"

"You."

She sat straight upright. "Borowsky, you queer, you dance like a queer, you dance like a woman."

"I'll break your goddamned nose!"

"You broke my arm, Borowsky, don't you go breaking my nose . . ."

She put her head back on the pillow. "I love you, Borowsky, I really do . . ."

Then she started snoring. I drank another hour or two, then I got into bed with her. I didn't want to touch her at first. She needed a bath, at least. I got one leg up against hers; it didn't seem too bad. I tried the other legs. I remembered all the good days and good nights and I slipped one arm under her neck, then I had the other around her belly and my drunken penis gently up against her crotch. Her hair came back and climbed into my nostrils. I felt her inhale heavily, then exhale. We would sleep like that most of the night and into the next afternoon. Then I would get up and go to the bathroom and vomit and then she would have her turn.

I figured 500-plus air might make this community college outside Detroit worth my soul so I got on *American* and worked the stewardesses for extra drinks. I was to land a day early, and I made it down the ramp waiting for some professor to grab me and one did and I told him, "I'm yours now. How can you tell what you've got until it gets off the plane?"

"We can't. My job's more or less on the line each time but it's worth it." Each year he went out and got one. It had been Ginsberg, Stephen Spender and James Dickey in the last three years and he still had his job. I warned him that I had been thrown out of the women's dorm at the University of Kansas after a reading and we walked toward his car. He drove me to a hotel in Detroit and left me with a mass of phone numbers and instructions. The university was getting the room and board, he assured me. After he left I took a shower and phoned down for drinks.

I had been drinking an hour or so—picking out my poems—when the phone rang. It was my buddy Slim de Bouffe who came in at 5 feet and 265 pounds and played with poems and booze and women. He liked my shit. When he knocked on the door the room knocked back. He wrote poems with a hammer. I told him to come on in.

There wasn't much to the night, mostly drinking, and stories about bad luck with women and good luck with women; about the poetry hustle and the poetry grind and about some of the good people in it and some of the other kind. Slim had a way of dropping little wisdoms out of his mouth as if they didn't count, as if he were asking for a match or giving directions to the nearest whorehouse. You had to listen carefully to Slim but it was worth it. It was worth some hours of listening. He left late that night and I went to bed and slept in that 100-year-old hotel in the middle of Murder City and I slept well.

Awakening was another matter. I was on the fourth floor and the windows looked out on a building with a flagpole on top of it. I gagged, went to the bathroom, had a minor vomit, opened a warm beer and got the switchboard woman.

"Yes sir?"

"I have a complaint."

"Yes sir?"

"Look, I'm going to be here 2 or 3 nights which means that I'm going to wake up with 2 or 3 hangovers."

"You'd better send your complaint to God, sir."

"All right, connect me."

"He's unlisted."

"Don't I know. Look, as I was saying, I'm going to wake up here every morning and you know the first sight that will meet my eyes?"

"No, I don't, sir."

"The American flag."

"The American flag?"

"Absolutely."

"You mean you don't like the American flag, sir?"

"Of course not. It has these red and white stripes, they wave in the wind, and then there are the stars, there are all these stars up in the corner, you know, on top of the blue . . . I wake up sick. I've got to read poetry at the university, they're going to put me on video tape."

"Sir, I *like* the American flag!"

"Fine, I'll take your room and you take mine."

"Have you fought in any wars, sir?"

"Yes, first I fought for Franco in Spain and then . . ."

She hung up on me.

It was hot under the video lights but I worked from a bottle of 100 proof vodka and, when that emptied out, Slim de Bouffe went out into the night and came back with a six-pack. I finished it up under that and the applause seemed fair enough. I fielded some easy questions, got the 500 dollar check and got out. They told me they'd mail the air within ten days. I had to work a bookstore-signing for 50 bucks. Then a night's sleep and back to L.A. where I had figured this new system on the harness races. The sophisticates always sneered when I talked about the races. The sophisticates always thought soul could be found in the obvious places; that's why they were sophisticates instead of artists.

There were 600 people in the bookstore. The owner had advertised in the main Detroit newspaper. We couldn't move. Drinks and food had to be passed hand-to-hand overhead. I drank everything they handed me except wine. I signed books and screamed back insult for insult. I was high up in the sky. I beat their meanness with a more clever meanness. Civilization. They wanted to suck me dry and trash me. I'd come up through the alleys like Jersey Joe and old Jimmy Braddock. They couldn't trap me with love. Adulation, maybe. I read a couple of poems from *Burning* that somebody shoved at me. Then I fought my way out, cursing that whole gang of bloodsuckers. I got to the curbing and a car pulled up. "In here, Bukowski!" I jumped in and we drove off.

"You're just like a rock star, baby," said the kid at the wheel. I looked around: a car full of female groupies.

"Like hell. Either these women get out or I get out. All I want is a ride to the hotel."

The kid at the wheel pulled over to the curbing. "All right, girls, get it out. Now!"

They got out and we got some dock-hand, back-room cussing from those lovelies and then the kid put it to the floor and we went down the street.

"Eddie Mahler," he said.

"I'm Charles Bukowski," I answered.

The kid, Eddie, he was good. The street was very dark as all Detroit streets seemed to be. Eddie had a little game. He'd see a car up ahead and come alongside. Then he'd smash his car into the side of the other car. He'd bounce it good. Then he'd come back and hit it again and again. He'd keep hitting that car until it climbed up over the curbing and stopped. Then Eddie would stop the car and glare at them and I'd sit there and glare at them right along with Eddie. Then we'd drive off and find another car and do the same thing. We got 4 or 5 cars that way.

"You're a vicious son of a bitch, Eddie. I like you."

"You and Rod McKuen are my favorite poets."

"What?"

"Yes, you two guys are the only poets I can stand."

I let that go. Soon we seemed to be driving along in the country. There were trees and space everywhere. Eddie stopped the car. "Get out," he said.

I got out.

"O.K," he said, "I want that 500 dollar check. You're going to sign it over to me, Edward Mahler."

"And you're going to suck your mother's left tit."

The first punch came so fast I couldn't see it. I swung from the heels and missed his head by two feet. He sunk one

126

into my gut and I dropped to my knees and vomited up ten dollars worth of booze. I got back up.

"What did you say that name was?"

"Eddie Mahler."

"Got a pen, Eddie? I lost mine giving out all those autographs."

"Sure."

I walked over to his car and put the check on top of the car roof. It was very wet in the moonlight. I signed the check over to Eddie, handed him the check and the pen and we got back into the car. "The least you can do, punk, is to drive me back to the hotel."

"Don't call me a punk."

"Drive me back to the hotel, punk."

He started the car, and we drove off. "I want you to meet my mother first. She's always admired your stuff."

"All right."

"You don't mind?"

"Compared to what's happened, that's easy."

"Sure."

"Eddie, if this ever gets out, I'm finished. I'm supposed to be the tough guy, the man of the streets. Hell, if this gets out nobody will ever buy my books."

"I don't want to compound anything. I'll keep quiet."

"I'm not speaking of morals or ethics or anything, Eddie, but that money's really mine. And . . . hey, shit, what happened to my wristwatch?"

I looked over and Eddie had on two wristwatches. "Give me my wristwatch, punk."

Eddie slipped my watch off. I put it back on. "One time I'm on the floor drunk, passed-out and I feel somebody lift my wristwatch, then I feel somebody pulling at my finger, he's trying to get my ring off. I look up and he's got out this knife, he's going to peel down my finger to get my ring and it's not worth $3. You ought to have heard me holler. He scattered."

"I'll pay you back $100 a month from this check I took from you," said Eddie.

"No good," I said, "you're driving me back to the hotel. Then we're going to sleep it off and I'm going to duke it out with you again when I'm sober."

"O.K, but first I want you to meet my mother."

Eddie's mother was very nice. A young blonde. I mean young compared to me. Neither Eddie or I mentioned anything about the check. His mother mixed us all some drinks and we drank an hour or two, then left. Before we left Eddie went to the closet and gave me one of his shirts, a nice purple and white striped job. I put it on, mine had somehow gotten bloodied and ripped during the fight. Before we left, Eddie's mother got out these photos of her ex-husband, a rather famous gangster who'd been gunned down by the cops. We all did a bit of mourning and weeping for him, me mostly. Then we had another drink and left.

In the hotel in the morning I awakened first, shit and showered. Eddie was out. My first thought was to sneak downstairs and holler cops. But somehow that was out. I got back into bed and opened a warm beer. No refrigeration in the fucking place. Eddie rolled over. "Hey," he said.

"Yeah?"

Eddie got up, went to his pants and took out his wallet. He walked over and handed me the check. "I knew I could never take this. I knew I'd give it back when I woke up in the morning."

"Eddie, I'll take it."

The kid started getting dressed. "Care for a warm beer?"

"O.K."

I broke one open for him. Eddie finished dressing, then finished the beer. I found a pen and wrote my address down. "Write me, Eddie."

He took the slip of paper, put it in his pocket and walked out the door. That's about all there was to that reading except I met Slim de Bouffe and his girlfriend in this bar later, they were going to get me to the airport and I told them the story as we drank green beer in a place they were mopping up with a very strong disinfectant and we almost vomited together. "You mean you couldn't take him?" asked de Bouffe.

"I couldn't take him," I answered.

Then we all got up and walked over to a sweeter-smelling place.

They were both 7 years old and they found the hole in the fence and crawled through.

"He usually sits out in the yard in this chair. He just sits there looking kind of mad."

"He might kill us, Billy."

"Look, Red, he's in enough trouble, he won't kill us."

"You say he looks mad."

"He's just pissed. He don't go to the market or eat out or anything. He sends people out for his things. We got to look out for his people."

"I'll bet he has guards everywhere."

"Not too many, Red, just two or three. I come here every day. I never been caught yet."

"You like to look at him, Billy?"

"Yeah. Only today I think I want to talk to him."

"Talk to him?"

"Yeah. Now keep down low against those bushes. Now lay down here."

"O.K."

"See him, Red? He's sitting in that big chair with his cane, he's just looking off into space, looking mad."

"I see him."

"Let's crawl closer."

"How about the guards?"

"Oh, they just walk around. They get careless. If we had a gun we could kill him right from here."

Billy pointed his finger, moving his thumb down: "Pow!"

"I'm scared, Billy!"

"Me, too. That's the fun of it. Keep crawling closer."

"It's him, Billy, it's him! I've seen him on TV, I've seen his picture in the papers!"

"Sure it's him, Red. Who do you think he is?"

"He does look mad! It's just like seeing God!"

"It's better, we can talk to him."

"You—still going to talk to him?"

"Yeah, yeah, I've made up my mind. Keep crawling toward him."

"I've pissed my pants, Billy."

"It doesn't matter. Keep moving up."

"I pissed my pants, Billy, I'm so scared I pissed my pants."

"I could hit him with a rock now. Red. He's just looking off into space. Soon we'll be able to reach out and touch him."

They crawled closer. Soon they were out of the brush and they crawled along the lawn, closer and closer. They were 12 feet away, then six. Then they stopped. They just remained quiet, breathing.

Finally Billy said, "Hey!"

The man in the chair was jolted upright, dropping his cane. "*Christ!* . . . what is it?"

"We came to talk to you," said Billy, standing up. Red stood up too, looking down at the spot on the front of his pants.

"Red pissed his pants, we're sorry about that."

The man picked up his cane and pointed it at the boys.

"You goddamned kids get out of here!"

"We want to talk to you."

"There's nothing to talk about. Now get your asses out of here!"

"My father didn't vote for you," said Billy. "He tells people that."

"Well, the way it worked out, somebody must have."

"Why did you do it?" asked Billy.

"Do what?"

"Do what you did."

"You kids live around here?"

"Sure. What do you think?" asked Billy. "You think we flew down from Mars?"

"It wouldn't surprise my ass in the least."

"Why do you use dirty language?"

"Sorry."

"All your men were sentenced to jail. Aren't you sorry for your men?"

"All men are guilty of something."

"Do you mean all men should be in jail?"

"I didn't say that."

"Does your wife still go to bed with you after what you did?"

The man lifted his cane and pointed it at Billy. "You stay out of my sex life!"

"I'll bet she doesn't anymore."

"What do you know about sex?"

"Plenty."

"O.K., what is it?"

"It's something to do to make yourself feel good so you can go on and do all the things that don't make you feel so good."

"That's not Webster but it's not bad."

Then there was silence. The man turned and looked off into space again. Some minutes passed. Then Red said, "I kind of like you, anyhow."

Billy turned to Red: "What the hell's wrong with you? He's no good. He ought to be in jail with the rest of those guys!"

"I guess you're right."

"I guess, Red," said the man, "the least you can do for me is vote Republican when you grow up."

"Herbert Hoover was a Republican and he let the people starve to death!" said Billy.

"How do you know that?" asked the man.

"My uncle told me."

"O.K., that's good enough."

"Both those Kennedys were good guys and look what happened to them."

"I've heard."

"Somebody ought to kill you!"

"So my wife can go to bed with another man?"

"No. Just because you STINK!"

"Boys, I think this interview is over."

Billy and Red stood there looking at him. A solitary bird flew past between them, quickly, looping up and down like a fantasy and then it was gone. The man leaned upward in his chair. Then he screamed out: "HARRY! DOUG! OVER HERE!" quickly but heavily. They were young and well dressed and had revolvers drawn. They were each adorned with the latest hairdo and the latest clothing style.

"WHERE THE HELL'S MY SECURITY? WHAT YOU GUYS BEEN DOING, PLAYING SCRABBLE IN THE ROSE BOWER OR WORSE?"

"How'd these fucking kids get in here?" asked the taller of the security guards.

"Ask them," said the man.

"How'd you kids get in here?"

"A hole in the fence."

"But everything's wired!"

"What's wired?"

"Oh, shit, we got to check the wiring," said the taller of the security men to the shorter, "get your ass on Mr. Bell now and get Del Monico over here, and FAST!"

"Listen," said Billy, "I think we'll be going home now."

"Hold it now!" said the remaining security man, "don't move!"

"Let them go."

"Don't you want me to process them?"

"What the hell you going to find? You'll find that one of the kids has pissed his pants and the other has a father who is a plumber and gets drunk every Saturday night."

"All right, kids," said the security guard, "you can go now."

Billy turned and began to run and then Red ran after him. Red was a better runner than Billy and he passed him and got through the hole in the fence first.

"Anything I can do for you?" the security guard asked the man.

"Yeah. Get the hell out of my sight, Now!"

It was done and the man in the chair leaned back again. You could hear the ocean if you really listened. He really listened. He still held the cane in his right hand. The veins of that hand were not relaxed.

Harry walked into the bar and sat down. "Scotch and water," he told the bar-keep. Harry had some thoughts on bars. They were infested with the second-lowest breed of humanity. The race-track's got the first lowest breed of humanity. Having just gotten in from the track he was completing a meaningless day. At least the jukebox wasn't on and nobody was shooting pool. He remembered the days you used to be able to come into a bar and stare into the mirror until you got drunk. Or you beat the shit out of somebody or got the shit beat out of you. And you used to be able to win at the racetrack and occasionally meet a woman of high quality. But why cry? Everyone lived in the same world as you did. Or so they said. He got the first drink down and ordered another.

When he looked up there was a lady in her mid-40s, large purple blouse, sagging breasts, overtight skirt showing pot belly, two heart-shaped blue earrings on long silver chains, and in the center of her face—a blaze of orange lipstick, glistening wet. The earrings fascinated Harry. The lady managed to move her head just enough to keep the earrings bouncing inanely—the blue hearts leaped and jumped and whirled on either side of her head. "Hi! I'm Janice!"

"Harry."

"You new in town?"

"In the world."

"*Ta*! Ain't that somethin'? Can I ask you somethin'?"

"Shoot."

"Shoot"?

"Speak."

"Are you a slave or a master?"

"I remain humble among the multitudes: I'm a slave."

"What's a slave?"

"A man who can't reach his own asshole with his dick."

"You're bitter."

"No, I just can't reach."

"Do you believe in love?"

"Yes, but only for other people."

Janice got up and brought her drink down, blue heart earrings jumping like jazz discovering Bach. She had on false eyelashes two and one-half inches long. "I wanna buy you a drink."

"O.K."

"You like money?"

"Better than youth, fame or virgins."

Janice ordered the drinks and said, "You come home with me and you've made yourself 50 bucks."

"Fine. I'll do anything but drink buttermilk."

"Oh, good, then we'll make it 75 bucks."

They drank up and he followed her out. It was a pink Mercedes. She angled off from the curbing, breaking traffic in half, horns going, the blue hearts jumped . . . She swirled up a half-moon driveway and pulled in front of a large three-story house. The garage door opened like a large, terrifying and mindless mouth but she jumped out of the car, opened Harry's door and pulled him out.

"Come, my darling, I just can't wait!"

"I wonder," he said, "what the third-lowest breed of humanity does?"

He followed her up the stairway and into the house.

Nice, he thought, a guy like Sugar Ray Robinson could use something like this.

He found himself in a large leather chair overhung with a lamp on one side and a parrot on the other. Janice ran into the other room. Then the parrot looked at him and said, "Now eat your *spinach*, darling."

"Oh," said Harry to the parrot, "why don't you go flog yourself off?"

"After you eat your *spinach*, darling!"

"What?"

"Now eat your *spinach*, darling . . . "

Janice came in with two large drinks, gave him one, then sat on the couch across from him. Harry drained half his drink; his temples damn near gagged and a photograph of *Man of War* coerced before his eyes, then vanished. He drained the other half.

"Keep them coming," he said.

Janice walked into the other room. Harry stared at the parrot. The parrot stared back. Then the parrot looked away, bored.

She handed him the drink. "What I want you to do, you may not like."

"For $75 I believe that any man could stand a minor diminishment."

"Maybe. Drink your second drink first."

Harry did that. Janice got up and walked out. He waited. Janice walked back in.

She threw the material on his lap. "You put that stuff on."

Harry picked it up and looked at it. "Great Grandmother

of Christ, don't you know I'm half-crazy already? This could carry me into the shit-stained land of absentia."

"Seventy-five bucks. Put it on."

"Yes."

"The bedroom," she said, "is one sharp corner to the left."

Harry carried the stuff into the bedroom: a little boy's short pants—black—and a blouse, ruffled, silky and white; underwear with designs of rockinghorses, moons and candy canes upon it; two ankle-length stockings, white.

He worked his way into the stuff and walked out. Janice put another drink into his hand as he sat down. He drank it halfway down—no vision of *Man of War* this time.

No vision at all.

"You're a nice boy," she said.

"Now," said the parrot, "eat your *spinach*, darling!"

"What have I got myself into?" asked Harry.

"Seventy-five bucks."

"Did Job have to suffer like this to stay on the payroll?"

"You keep saying clever things! You *are my bright* little boy!"

"Look, why don't we just fuck and get it over with?"

"If you keep saying things like that, Harold, I'm going to have to wash your mouth out with *soap*!"

Janice got up and walked to the telephone, dialed, waited.

"Harriet? Harriet, my boy is back home! Won't you come over and see my boy? You *will*? I'm so happy! We'll be waiting!"

Janice hung up.

"Another drink," said Harry. Janice went to the kitchen and stoked up another, brought it out, handed it to him. "Now Harold, I got a note from your teacher today and she said that you had been *bad* in school, that you had pulled a little girl's pigtail and stuck it in the inkwell! Why did you *do* that, Harold, bad boy!"

"Because she'd been finger-fucking her sister while the other girls were playing volleyball!"

"Harold! I *told* you about dirty words! One more time and you get the soap!"

"Now," said the parrot, "eat your *spinach*, darling!"

The doorbell rang about 10 minutes later and Janice got up and answered it. "Harriet! And I'm so *glad* you've got Timmy with you!"

They walked in and Harriet was an almost carbon copy of Janice. She had some guy with her. He had on little boy's pants—black—and a blouse, ruffled, silky and white; underwear with reindeer and stars interspersed with rocking-horses, and two ankle-length stockings, white.

"Harold," said Janice, "I want you to meet Timmy."

They shook hands. "How you doing, man?" Harry asked.

"All right, I guess. How you doing?"

"Fair to middling."

"Me too."

Timmy sat down in a chair across the way and Janice went in to mix new drinks. "I want you boys to get along now," said Harriet.

"Now," said the parrot, "eat your *spinach*, darling!"

"This recession is a living hell," said Timmy to Harry.

Janice brought the drinks back in and handed them out, then sat down. "Harold has been a *very* bad boy! Just this morning we had hard-boiled eggs and he said he didn't like the yolk and he didn't like the white. Then he dropped the jam right onto the front of his shirt!"

"You think the Dodgers will repeat this year?" Timmy asked Harry.

"It's a cinch," said Harry, "they're going to learn how to use Ferguson, and Lopes will get off faster at the bat."

"Timmy has been *very* bad too," said Harriet. "He left his tricycle out in the rain and all the spokes got rusted. He needs a *spanking* very badly!"

"Harold needs a spanking very badly too. He pulled a little girl's pigtail and then stuck it in the inkwell!"

"I *told* you . . . she was . . ."

"*Harold.*"

"These boys are acting very *badly*! I think I'd better take mine home!"

"Mine needs some chastising too."

"All right, Janice, I'll phone you tomorrow. We're leaving. Timmy!"

"Christ, at *least* let me finish my drink!"

"No, no, we're *leaving*. Timmy!"

And she took Timmy and led him out the door by one ear, the clear night wind blew in, and then they were gone.

"Now," said Harriet, "*you* go to the bedroom!"

Harry walked into the bedroom. It was dark in there. But he did have his drink with him. He finished his drink and rolled the glass across the rug. He unlaced his shoes and stretched out on the bed. It was one of those neighborhoods where you could hear the crickets rubbing their legs together. He listened to the rubbing of the legs. It made things seem fairly all right.

Then he wondered, should I take this stuff off and wait for her or should I let her undress me?

It was the first bit of uncalculated, mathematical wisdom he had come upon in some days of weeks, but he still hoped she'd bring one last good drink.

Harry bought a newspaper and walked into the travel agency. A woman in a yellow skirt, white blouse and high heels was bent over placing something in the bottom drawer of a filing cabinet. Her skirt hiked up and Harry stared at the back of her legs. The legs were good. When the woman turned around Harry elevated his glance. The woman was in her mid-40s but she still radiated sex. She was almost plump and the skirt fit tightly, so tightly that Harry could see the garter belt that held up the stockings.

"Hello," said Harry, "I need a ticket."

"Please sit down," the woman said. All her clothing pulled at her as if she wanted to get out of it. When she sat down she crossed her legs and Harry found himself staring up her legs. She noticed and smiled slightly.

"Where to," she asked.

"Detroit," said Harry, "regular coach fare."

"Round trip?"

"Yes, round trip."

"When do you want to leave?"

"Oh, sometime Thursday afternoon. It doesn't matter much when I arrive. I read Friday night."

"Read?"

"Oh, pardon me, I'm a poet."

"Oh, a poet . . . how strange. Do they pay you to read?"

"$500 plus air this trip."

"What kind of poetry do you write?"

"Sex."

"Sex?"

"Yes, sex."

The woman checked her schedules.

"I can get you on a flight out of L.A. International at 2:48 p.m. *American*."

"Fine."

"Return trip open?"

"Yes."

"You must lead an interesting life."

"It's all right."

"I'm Mrs. LeMon."

"I'm Harry Benson."

While Mrs. LeMon dialed the telephone Harry looked up her legs again. She had recrossed her legs and the skirt had climbed higher. It was hell to be a leg man and come across the rarity of high heels, long stockings and garter belt. All the modern women had gone to pantyhose, which de-sexified everything, or pants. Well, if women didn't want to be sex symbols that was their right, and if they wanted to be that was their right too. Harry forced his eyes from her legs and read the paper.

"Look," said Harry, "here's a Superior Court judge who has authorized castration for two men who pleaded guilty to child molestation."

Mrs. LeMon hung up. "I've got you on flight 248, *American*, 2:48 p.m. What did you say?"

"These two guys have been molesting little girls and they might get their balls cut off."

"I think that's terrible," said Mrs. LeMon.

"Me too," said Harry. "Some girls are terrible little teases and a man gets hot."

"I'd like to read some of your books."

"You wouldn't like them."

"What are they about?"

141

"Just stories and poems."

"About what?"

"Rape, child molestation, oral sex, garter belt freaks, high-heeled shoe fetishes, whips, leather, all that crap."

"And they *pay* you to read that?"

"Oh, I mix in a little spring and love and death and laughter. It confuses them. Look here, it says that the exiled Russian author Alexander Solzhenitsyn is visiting Canada. He's got it made. They toady to those kinds of freaks. He'll probably lay five or six Eskimo virgins. He can't write worth a damn."

"Do you like virgins?"

"I like mature women, slightly overweight sex symbols."

"I like your sense of humor."

"I'm serious."

"Cash or credit?"

"Cash. How much is it?"

Mrs. LeMon told Harry how much it was and he put the money down in front of her.

"Mrs. LeMon, I know this making out of the tickets takes some time. I think I'll go out and get a beer and a sandwich."

"Why don't you go out and get your beer and drink it upstairs? My apartment's right up that stairway. There's meat in the refrigerator and some Russian rye. You can make a sandwich, drink your beer and rest while I'm making out the tickets."

"O.K. I'll be right back."

Harry found a liquor store two blocks west. He got a six of Bud in the bottle and put a dime in the parking meter in front of his car as he walked past. When he got back to the travel agency Mrs. LeMon was making out the tickets. Her skirt was hiked higher. He didn't look at her face, he looked at her legs and said, "Hi!"

"Hi!" she answered.

Harry went up the stairway. It's like a movie, he thought. Someday I'll write about this. He opened the door. It was a nice apartment. Female. Real female, old-fashioned female. Harry had once dreamt he had fucked his mother; it had been the wettest wet dream he had ever had. Sex was doing what you weren't supposed to do. That's one reason marriage didn't work; it became a job instead of a raid into the unknown. He was really a puritan and the breaking down of the mores made him horny forever; that along with vitamin E and a late start in the game.

He broke out one bottle of Bud and put the rest in the refrigerator. He had to be the best poet in the game today. Everybody agreed that Bukowski was slipping, Ginsberg was a nice old bore and Creeley was drinking a quart of whiskey a day. Duncan was too precious, Lowell was too careful and Ferlinghetti was hampered by an alcoholic wife.

Harry sucked on the beer and walked over to her dresser. He opened the second drawer down and he was right— there were eight or 10 pairs of panties. He went through them and found a pair he liked: black, netted and laced. He unzipped and pulled it out. He took the panties and folded them over his cock and began rubbing them over his cock. Harry watched himself in the mirror, grinning, and he kept rubbing. His cock began to swell and the head puffed up and out of the panties. He watched himself in the mirror, then his mind said, Jesus I got stop or I'm going to lose it. He zipped up, poking it in and put the panties in one of his rear pockets. He finished the beer, went to the refrigerator and opened another one. He looked in there. Why was it that almost all women ate cottage cheese and yogurt and cheese? Soft stinking cheese. And doughnuts and *See's* candies?

He took the beer and walked over to the couch and sat down. He'd thrown the newspaper down there. He picked it up:

55 FELLED BY FOOD

Nuevo Laredo, Mexico (AP)—More than 55 persons who attended a Knights of Columbus luncheon at the Lion's Club convention hall were hospitalized with food poisoning, officials reported.

Bastards, thought Harry, serves them right. Anybody who goes to Mexico deserves to be reamed and creamed.

The door opened. It was Mrs. LeMon. "Hi!" she said.

"Hi!" said Harry, "who's running the store?"

"My son, Gary," said Mrs. LeMon, sitting down.

"Is he competent?"

"Oh my, yes."

"Will he come up here?"

"I told you he's competent. I told him not to come up here no matter what happened."

"Suppose I'm some kind of kook."

"You're not. Your face is too kind."

"Really?"

"Really."

"Pull your dress higher. I love your legs."

Mrs. LeMon pulled her dress higher. Harry bent down and kissed one of her knees. Then he spread her legs and bit her hard four or five inches above the knee.

"Oooh, that hurt, don't do that!"

"Go in and piss."

"What?"

"I told you to go in and piss. Women pissing make me hot."

"But I don't want to pee."

Harry put the bottle down and slapped Mrs. LeMon across the face, hard.

"Oh, don't do that . . ."

"I told you what to do! Now go ahead and do it!"

Mrs. LeMon went to the bathroom. Harry finished his beer and brought out two more, opened them, put them on the coffee table. He heard the toilet flush. Mrs. LeMon came out and sat down.

"Drink up and relax," said Harry. "That Vietnam evacuation was really a mess. The whole goddamned army and their wives and their whores trying to scale the walls of the U.S. Embassy. Old people caught in barbwire and bleeding to death and Marines bayoneting anybody the TV cameras weren't on. All to come to America and replace the Puerto Rican as the most despised racial group in America. Suck my dick!"

"I don't *do* that."

"70,000 collaborators swimming in the ocean and begging for mercy! Suck my dick!"

"I told you . . ."

"Well, then, drink your beer and show me more leg!"

Harry drained the remainder of his bottle without stopping. "I saw some wine in there. Can I drink your wine?"

"Sure."

The wine was three-quarters full. Harry stood in the center of the room and took a good hit.

"Stand up!" he told Mrs. LeMon. "You got me hot. You got that ass and those legs. A woman your age doesn't deserve to have that. You got me hot. STAND UP!" I said.

Harry put down the wine bottle and took off his belt.

He folded it double and then lifted Mrs. LeMon's dress. He lifted it above her waist, exposing the thighs, the panties, the garter belt, the white skin between the stockings and the panties.

Harry began to beat her alongside the legs, starting low around the ankles and working up, gradually increasing the tempo and the force, then he got to the upper thighs and thrashed, saying, "You whore, you goddamned whore . . ."

Mrs. LeMon tried to hold in her screams so her son, Gary, downstairs, wouldn't hear her. Then he spun her and beat upon her ass viciously. She fell to the floor, weeping. Harry disrobed. He walked over, took a good hit of the wine, then walked up to Mrs. LeMon. She appeared to be shivering. Harry grabbed her by the hair and pulled her upward. She screamed as he did so, loudly.

"Goddamn you, shut up! If your son comes up here I'll kill both of you!" He kissed Mrs. LeMon, spreading the lips of her mouth open. Her face was wet and she was convulsing. He worked her panties off and got it in, taking both hands and spreading the cheeks of her ass wide, extremely wide. He saw her ass in the mirror and himself bent over her like leprosy. They worked across the room knocking over the coffee table, banging into a wall. Her cunt was too large for him. Too many babies. He had to get her in front of the mirror and watch. He finally came. He threw her on the bed. She seemed to be convulsing. He saw a high-heeled shoe on her rug. He dressed, watching her. Fully dressed he opened his shirt a few buttons and dropped the high-heeled shoe in. Then he heard her voice: "You're leaving, aren't you?"

"Yes, I'm going to Detroit, *American*, flight 248."

"I love you, Harry."

"What? That wasn't love. That was raw sex shit, dementia. I'm not proud of it."

"I know I'll never see you again. Kiss me goodbye, that's all I ask."

"God, this is grade-B movie."

"Harry . . ."

"All right!"

He got into bed next to her with his shoes on. Her mouth opened. He closed on it. And held. She was crying, rushes of water coming out from under her eyelids. The high-heel shoe was between them in his shirt and the heel was stabbing into his chest. Harry pulled away. He got up and then noticed the nightstand on the other side of the bed. There was half a pack of cigarettes and a pack of matches. The matches said: "Save-on a GREAT place to shop! The quality drug stores . . ." He took out a cigarette and lit it. *Lighted* it, as the intellectual writers said. Then he noticed a book on the nightstand. He picked it up: Jong's *Fear of Flying*. Mrs. LeMon seemed still at last. The wine bottle was on the floor on its side. He picked it up and found one last hit. Then he walked out the door and went down the stairway. Gary was down there. He looked bright but introvert, no challenge. "Is Mom all right?" he asked.

"She's pleased," Harry told the kid. The kid caught it. He liked the kid's kool. One thing about the new generation, they either understood very much instinctively or they became murderers without feeling. There was very little middle ground, and maybe they were right because it was the middle ground, that vast jelly-like totality of billions and billions following all central signals, that had kept the world crawling over and over itself again and again, bored, fatted, starving, inane, feeding on nothing, giving nothing, being nothing.

Harry walked toward the door of the travel agency. He got his hand on the knob when Gary spoke:

"Mr. Benson?"

"Yes?"

"You forgot your tickets."

"Oh?"

Harry walked back. The kid handed him the tickets enclosed in a neat blue leather folder. "Thanks for coming to see our agency. I hope you'll use us again on your next flight."

Harry took the tickets and walked back out the door. He walked back to his car. There were 12 minutes left on the parking meter. He got back in the car, it started; he took a left on 6th street and a right on Vermont. Traffic was bad and Paul Williams was on the radio. He didn't like either one of them. It was, perhaps, a matter of utter obviousness. He took out the high-heeled shoe and stuck it up on the dash. Yes, much better.

He'd kill them in Detroit.

I turned the car into The Bug Builders in Santa Monica and began walking. I'd blown an engine down there some months past, had gotten a rebuilt and was in for the 3,000 mile check-up. I lived in L.A. and knew I had hours to wait. It was 10:15 a.m. I found a restaurant open and walked in. There was only one man in there, at a back table. I took a table at about the center and the waitress brought me a menu. Breakfast. I ordered ham and eggs, scrambled. I was hungover but thought I might hold it down. I had a paper and opened it. "Dodgers lose." That cheered me a tick. When the waitress brought my breakfast she refilled my coffee cup.

Fine girl with an ordinary ass. I began eating and then two people entered—a boy of about 23 and a woman of 50. They took the table directly across from mine. "That Helen keeps coming in when I'm looking at television and she *insists* on talking. And she talks in this *LOUD* voice!" said the boy. "I tell you, next time she does that I'm going to turn my television on so *LOUD* she won't be able to be heard! I'm going to *do* it, so help me!"

When I finished eating I stood up and belched as I left the table.

I walked down to the mall. A cop was giving two kids with bicycles citations. *LEPKE* was playing at the movie but it didn't open until noon. A girl with very good legs and a miniskirt walked by. She saw me looking at her and turned her head and stared at me as she waited for the signal.

What's she thinking? I thought. If one only knew what they were thinking.

She crossed the street and I watched her haunches revolve. Then I noticed that she had a wrinkle in her skirt where she had sat down and I lost interest.

I walked down Santa Monica to Ocean, then crossed the street and walked through the park. I turned onto the pier and walked along it. The people on the pier were unconcerned; they were neither happy nor sad. They rattled about in the Penny Arcade and bounced against each other in the electric cars. The fishermen weren't catching much. I walked down one side, came up the other. Coming up the other I came upon two young girls, each about 16. One was sunbathing on top of a cement bench, head down. The other was underneath the bench with her head sticking out toward the ocean. She had the sexiest lips I had ever seen on a woman, a girl. The appeal of those lips was jolting. One doesn't expect lips like that from under a stone bench at

11:25 a.m. And between those lips, on the side toward me, stuck out a tiny tip of a tongue.

Never had I seen anything more astonishingly sexual and lush. And her eyes were on mine. The effect was so strong that I had to turn away. When I looked again it was as before. I walked on. What does one do? What is the password, or what hope, when a man is 54 and still feels all those designs and patterns and traps and wonderments? Why didn't they hurry up and fix my fucking car?

I crossed and walked down the stairway to the boardwalk that led to Venice. I was still badly hungover. Breakfast hadn't helped much. It was hardly down. It hung about halfway up and halfway down. "Drunkenness and suicide are the bedmates of the writer," somebody had almost said once. It was true; I'd never known a good writer who was not either an alcoholic or a doper or both.

"Charles!"

I walked over. It was a man about 28, dark-haired, big. He had on glasses and needed a shave. "You don't know me," he said. "I've read your books."

"I'm sick," I said, "and walking around while they fix my car."

"My car's at Sears. I'm getting a new battery. Can I buy you a drink?"

"Too sick. I never drink before noon."

"I'm sick, too."

"Come on. Let's sit down. I'm wobbly."

We walked over to a bench facing the ocean. "Venice depresses me," I said, "especially when you get down to that Jewish sandwich shop and these hard cases, these Tim Leary dropouts demand 20 cents."

"Yeah, it's bad. And the liberals down here, the anarchists, the Communists—nothing's happening, Mrs.

Jones—so they turned into transvestites. They're really only half into it but they're into it."

"What do you do, kid?," I asked, "just sit on these benches and rot and wait?"

"I write scripts for television." He named one of the shows he wrote. I didn't know it. All I watched on television was the boxing matches. He went on: "I just wrote two scripts, got $6,000 for each of them. Each took about eight hours. I hardly remember writing them. The money's so easy I can't resist, I can't stop."

"You've got a right. It beats working for McDonald's."

Just then a large tractor affair making much noise and painted yellow came by behind us. My friend held his ears. "Jesus, I can't stand it! What are they doing with that thing? What does it mean?"

"It doesn't mean anything. The city buys those things and then sends them out to belabor a couple of guys sitting on a bench with a hangover. That's their function. It's that simple."

"It's disgusting."

"You shouldn't be out here. You ought to be home in a chair with a vodka-7 in your hand."

"I have come out here to get away from my wife."

"Sorry."

"I came in drunk last night and she says I hit her. I don't remember. It was something about two ashtrays, one was on top of the other. I couldn't stand it."

"A lot of things preceded those two ashtrays."

"Yes."

"I have trouble with women, too."

"Yeah, I've read your shit."

"They read your writing, they know what you are. Then they come in and try to change you. Don't drink, if you love me. Learn the fox-trot. Attend the family picnic. See your local pastor."

"Why do they do that?"

"I don't know why, totally. But I think I have part of it. The woman is the child-bearer and the child-trainer, whether she knows it or not, whether she wants it or not she has this inherent streak. Raising a child to most women means raising it as per the woman's knowledges and prejudices. It's hard work. So she begins by trying to be the man-trainer. If they are able to train the man, they feel that surely they'll be able to train the child. We are the great testing ground for somebody else's future."

"Maybe that's why I hit her."

"No, it was the ashtrays."

"I've got a secretary. She's not much but I fuck her."

"That's what secretaries are for, especially if they are women's libbers."

"Do the women hate you?"

"No, they hate the men who agree with them."

"My secretary helps me write."

"That's good. What do you do, tape it and let her type it?"

"No. I lay down on top of her and I play with her tits. I keep laying down on top of her and playing with her tits and she writes. Soon it's over and we've got something."

"It comes harder for me. I use two sheets of paper and a carbon."

"That whole TV scene is too bizarre, it really is. After lunch the producers will send out a chauffeur in a limousine and they'll come back with some 13-year-old girls."

"Marvelous. Think of a 13-year-old girl. It must be goodness beyond goodness."

"That's not for us, my friend."

"No, you'll just keep writing your scripts and sitting here on this bench for 40 more years. Not much will change."

"Yeah?"

"Yeah. See those bars holding up those swings? Well, they'll be a little thicker, that's all. And rounder. And they'll be of some silver substance that will glow in the sun."

"Yeah. And the women will just wear little dots over their cunts and tits, the littlest of dots."

"Yes, only the cunt will have moved up from between the legs and be placed under the left arm pit."

"Oh no. And guys will walk about on two cocks like legs."

"That's it. Well, I have to go see if my car is fixed."

"I have to go see if my car is fixed, too."

"Your name is?"

"Joe."

"I'll see you again sometime, Joe."

"Yeah, sometime when my car is getting fixed and your car is getting fixed."

I left him there and began the long walk back to 6th street. Everything was all right for some blocks, and then when I was four or five blocks away from the Bug Builders I heard footsteps behind me, female footsteps. I was walking slowly and she was walking just as slowly about a yard behind me and a little to the left toward the street side. It went on for a full block. On the next block she still followed me.

This can't be true, I thought. I'm addled, goofy, inept. It's the hangover, the sea air.

I slowed to let her by. As I slowed, she slowed. I slowed more; she slowed. I gave up and walked my normal pace. She followed along, a yard behind and a little to the left on the street side. Then we came to a signal. We both waited, her just the same distance behind me. When the signal changed I bent over as if to tie a shoelace. She walked past me and across.

On the next block I followed her, just a yard behind. She was bowlegged, just a bit, about 32, but she had a most marvelous behind. Well, not quite. It seemed a bit *square*, somehow. But after a while I got to like that squareness. It revolved with the power of the mare who knew she was there, still dangerous and damned able; not just able to catch the cock but the soul, too. It was under a tan dress and it moved. Her hair was very black and knotted into a tight, stern bun, and you knew if it were let loose it would flow down to her hips. And the hips were much there. My eyes went from the buttocks to the hips to the neck, down to the hips again and then settled upon the buttocks: the power to save a man or kill a man or ignore a man. I followed her for two blocks. Then at the next signal she crossed the street away from me. I stood and watched her. She walked across the parking lot and toward a small semi-grocery and liquor store. Just as she got to the doorway she turned and looked back at me. Her face flushed a deep red. Then she walked into the store. I was on 6th street. Bug Builder's was three-quarters of a block the other way. I walked on down and into the office. I was lucky: my car was ready.

I met the Crottys quite by accident. That is, I was looking for a new place to live and they both came to the door and looked at me through the screen.

"I saw your 'vacancy' sign. And this woman's pregnant. We need a place to live."

The woman's name was Darlene and I had gotten her pregnant after taking her to the racetrack. Mrs. Crotty got the key and took us to an apartment in the upper back. I took the place and Mr. and Mrs. Crotty simply became people I paid the rent to. He was 58, she was 55. The only time I saw them was when they drove their Volks to the market. They had no visitors except a son and a daughter who came by separately and sporadically.

Darlene and I lived together without much velocity or hope. The child was born, we lived together three more months, then the split came. Darlene and the child moved a few blocks away and I moved down to the front court.

It was a good place to drink beer, there by the front window facing the street. The typewriter was there, and outside large green brush covered everything, along with the vines and small trees.

The Crottys, who hadn't liked Darlene, became noticeable. I'd come home and find large paper bags against the door. The bags contained various items: green onions, oranges, apples, tomatoes and sometimes a shirt. Mrs. Crotty would knock in the mid-afternoons. "Don't eat anything, I'm going to bring you a plate." The plate was most often fried chicken, mashed potatoes and gravy, green peas, tomatoes and green onions, plus biscuits. She also made a good boiled beef plate. And every other night Mrs. Crotty would come down about 8:30 p.m. slightly intoxicated, and say, "Come on down and drink with us."

When I came down, Mr. Crotty would be passed out across the table, head in arms; he would be in his undershirt and tan army pants. Full and near-full bottles would be here and there about the table. The breakfastnook was always very clean and the red radio would be on to a popular music station. "Paddy," she'd say, "wake up. We've got a guest."

Up the head would come and he'd look at me. "Hi! How ya doin'? Have a drink."

Mrs. Crotty would set a full quart of Eastside in front of me. We'd drink from early evening until 3 or 4 in the morning. Most of the nights were the same. We'd sing the old songs, songs of the twenties and thirties. We'd talk about the crazy people in the neighborhood or about crazy people we had known. Mr. Crotty was a good storyteller, but he'd soon pass out again.

"Well, Mrs. Crotty, I've got to go."

"Oh, shit, stay. That old fart-sack , just because he passes out it don't mean nothing."

I'd stay or Mrs. Crotty would get angry. Sometimes, although not too often, I'd kiss her, a long hard kiss, spreading her lips back. Finally, after many more cigarettes and a few more bottles of beer, I'd leave.

The conversations, each time I went down there, were about the same. Mrs. Crotty and I would discuss our hemorrhoid operations. We'd talk all about the depression days of the thirties. We'd talk about the days we used to sit around in bars. And like all drunks, we'd get around to God, finally. But the Crottys got very upset when God came around, or the Pope; I wasn't very much interested in either of them and it made them furious, almost to the point of murder. I tried to stay away from that area.

The drinking was every other night and sometimes I got out of stride or I'd be at the typewriter. Mrs. Crotty would come down.

"We're drinking. We'll be looking for you."

"I can't make it."

"Can't make it? Why?"

"I'm at the typewriter."

"Ah, piss on that typewriter! Come on down, we're drinking!"

"I've got to finish this thing."

"Come on to the door. I want to tell you something."

"O.K."

"Listen, you rotten son of a bitch, I told you we're drinking. Now you son of a bitch, come on down!" Mrs. Crotty never swore when she was sober.

"I'm sorry, Mrs. Crotty. I can't."

Then she would unleash her total drunken vocabulary. She was pretty good. She would reappear in 30 minutes and make another pitch. If I didn't respond, I'd get the note under the door next:

"Bastard, you never paid me back that 50 dollars I lent you and if you don't pay it back I'm going to the police."

One night I didn't make it down and somebody bumped into their court with their automobile while trying to park in the apartment house lot across the way. I heard his voice:

"HEY, WHERE IN THE HELL DID YOU LEARN TO DRIVE?"

"WHO ARE YOU?" the guy in the car hollered back.

"I'M PATRICK CROTTY AND I OWN THIS GOD-DAMNED DUMP, THAT'S WHO I AM! WHO THE HELL ARE YOU?"

There was no answer.

Meanwhile the Crottys and my days went on. Then I met a madwoman, her name was Gerda.

"I don't like the Karates," she said.

"It's the Crottys," I said.

Gerda would stand in one of my windows and scream into the street. She screamed as if I were mutilating her.

"What the fuck you doing?" I'd ask.

"I'm enhancing your reputation."

"Let's leave it the way it is."

Gerda was mad. The front door to my place was made of glass. If she came over and I wasn't home, she'd break all the glass panels out of the door. Sometimes she'd do it when I was there.

"She's crazy," Mr. Crotty would say replacing the glass panels, "what do you see in her?"

"I guess it's her body."

There were pieces of glass all over the rug. I always drank barefoot in my place and I gathered all these pieces of glass in both feet. I had to go to a doctor and have them sliced out.

"How did this happen?" my doctor would ask.

"A woman."

After a month or so I left the Crottys. I moved out and went to live in Gerda's house. She charged me rent, too. Then I broke the glass out her front door. Gerda and I had difficult days and nights. One night she ran me out and I went to a motel on Western Avenue and drank a quart of Cutty Sark. In the morning I went over and got my shit, packed it into my car and drove around looking for a place to live. I passed the Crottys. There was a sign on the front lawn: VACANCY. I went back and knocked.

"What happened?"

"She ran my ass off."

"I told you she was crazy."

"I know. I saw your VACANCY sign. What you got open?"

"It's your old place. We fixed it up nice."

"Can I move back in?"

"Sure, but it's 10 bucks more, we fixed it up."

"All right."

I gave them a month's rent and moved back in. It had been fixed up all right. They'd even taken the glass door out and replaced it with a wooden one. Brown bags full of goodies appeared at the door again, plus the free dinners. We had our Eastside drunk, sang songs. Mr Crotty passed out and I kissed Mrs. Crotty.

Then two or three nights later I vanished. I was gone overnight. The next day I came back about evening. Mr. and Mrs. Crotty were standing in the driveway.

"Where have you been?"

"Gerda's."

"I thought so," said Mrs. Crotty.

"I'm moving back to her place."

"But she's insane, don't you know?"

"I know."

"There's no hope for you," said Mr. Crotty. Then they marched up the driveway and vanished into their court. I went inside and packed.

A week later I was packing again to leave Gerda's place. I didn't even drive past the Crottys. I found a place on Oxford Avenue with roaches behind the refrigerator.

I forgot the Crottys for some months, then one evening I was driving in their neighborhood. They had rented my front court, there were lights on in there. I drove on up the driveway, parked and got out. I knocked. Mrs. Crotty answered the door. Mr. Crotty stood behind her.

"I thought I might bring some beer by," I said.

"We're watching TV," said Mr. Crotty.

"Wrong night, eh?"

"Yes."

"O.K. Maybe I can catch you again on the right night."

"O.K."

I got in my car and drove off. I never went back. I moved

from the roach place to a court at Carlton Way and Western. About a year went by. One afternoon I went into the liquor store at The Market Basket. As I was standing waiting to get my beer bagged, I noticed somebody staring at me. He had changed. He had seemed to have melted. But it was Mr. Crotty standing by the water fountain just outside the grocery department. I walked up. "Christ," I said, "not you."

"Yes, we shop around, you know."

"Where's Grace?"

"She's outside. She'll be in in a minute."

I waited. It was a hot summer day in the low 90s. The glass doors opened and there was Mrs. Crotty.

"Hi!" I said.

"Hank!" she said.

He had melted and she had grown; her face was much fatter, she seemed taller and in all the heat she had on a thick black coat, thick heavy collar, long; her face was redder, she was pale. I hardly remember what was said. Some niceties. We were all sober. Then I left. The glass doors opened and I carried my bagged beer to the car, got in, started up and drove off. I don't think I'll ever see them again.

1.

Well, so Mailer and his cohorts got him out, he was a writer, there was a book, I haven't read it—all I know is what I read in the papers while I'm crapping. So, as you know, the writer put the knife to a waiter, "wasting him" as the boys in my time used to say. Which was not good for Mailer either. All right, here we have two writers and a waiter. No we have two writers. Which brings something to this ribbon which is spinning now before me: a man can be a good writer without being good at anything else; in fact, he can be pretty bad at everything else and usually is. Of course, there are people who are pretty bad at everything else and they can't write either. I might get to reading *In the Belly of the Beast* one of these days. I never could get through *The Naked and the Dead*, feeling it was too close a feed-off on Hemingway. But N. Mailer is an excellent journalist, and while not fit to sit on a parole board, he did what he felt he had to do. So did the other writer.

2.

I have a saying, "You will find the lowest of the breed at the racetracks." I am there almost every day working out my various systems, waiting the long 30 minutes between races. I don't know how many of those 30 minutes I have given away over the years sitting there waiting for a race that is generally over in a minute and nine seconds. And at the quarter horse races most of them are finished in 17 seconds plus a tick. A racetrack never has a losing day. For each dollar bet they give back about 85 cents. In Mexico they give back 75 cents. In some of the tracks in Europe they give back 50 cents. It doesn't matter, the people continue to play. Check the faces at any track going into the last race. You will see the story.

When I came out of the Charity Ward of the L.A. County General Hospital in 1955 after drinking ten years without missing a night or day (except while in jail) they told me that if I ever took another drink I would be dead. I went back to my shack job and I asked her, "What the hell am I going to do now?"

"We'll play the horses," she said.

"Horses?"

"Yeah, they run and you bet on them."

She had found some money on the boulevard so we went out. I had 3 winners, one of them paid over 50 bucks. It seemed very easy.

We went out a second time and I won again.

That night I decided that if I mixed some wine with milk it might not hurt me. I tried a glass, half wine, half milk. I didn't die. The next glass I tried a little less milk and a little more wine. By the time the night was over I had been drinking straight wine. In the morning I got up without hemorrhaging. After that I drank *and* played the horses. 27 years later I am still doing both. Time is made to be wasted . . .

I was out there again today. There are some creatures out there, shirttails hanging out, shoes run down, eyes dulled. Many are there day after day. How they manage to keep going out there is the mystery. They are losers. But somehow they manage to find entrance fee, somehow they manage to place some feeble bets. But today I saw the worst. I had seen him the day before also. He looked worse than any skid row bum, he had a scabby beard, part of the leather had lifted from his shoes showing parts of his feet—he was barefoot. He wore a greasy brown overcoat but he had a bit of money. I saw him placing some bets. He didn't sit in the stands but on some steps outside the stands and he played a harmonica very badly. I looked at him: he had on some glasses but one of the eyeglasses had fallen out and the one that remained was a dark black. As I walked slowly by he started talking to me. He spoke very rapidly: "Hey, ge out ree hoo nar bah!" Sentences followed that were of similar order. I couldn't imagine this fellow placing a bet or driving an automobile. But he had a right to. Who said he couldn't?

And who said he had to *look* a certain way? Or talk a certain way? Society dictated our modes and ways. Maybe he was helpless. I remembered starving in New York City, trying to be a writer. One night I had gone out and bought a bag of popcorn, it was my first food in several days. The popcorn was hot and greasy and salty, each kernel was a miracle. I walked along in a beautiful trance, feeling the kernels enter my body, feeling them in my mouth. My trance was not entirely complete. Two large men walked toward me. They were talking to each other. As they got closer to me, one of them looked up and just as they passed me he said loudly to his buddy: "Jesus Christ, did you see *that*." I was the freak to them, the idiot, the one who didn't fit the mould. I walked along then, the kernels not tasting quite so well.

As I passed the man at the racetrack sitting on his steps I knew that any of us could get lost away from the crowd, some of us even wanted to. I walked down and found a seat. The horses broke from the gate. It was 6 furlongs. I had the one horse in a maiden race. Orange silks. The one horse is usually bad at 6 furlongs but I had a reason for the bet. My horse broke poorly, rushed up, fell back, I lost sight of him, then as they took the curve for home I saw my orange silks again, he was coming from the outside. He seemed to hang in mid-stretch, then he came on again to win drawing out. They put up the price: $14.60. I had it ten win. $73. I got up to go cash my ticket. When I did I no longer saw the man sitting on his steps. I didn't see him for the rest of the day. I'll be looking for him tomorrow. There's a good card going. Three maiden races. I love those maiden races.

3.

What about Fame? they ask me. Will Fame destroy you? Well, now, if I *am* famous and if it destroys me (meaning my talent) then sixty one years of my life will have gone by without my having sensed any of the traps. I think it's easier for a writer to be destroyed by Fame when he is in his twenties. The ladies, the lights, the admiration will do him in. The young have no background to ward Fame off with. Besides, many of the famous are famous not because their work is excellent and original but because the masses identify with the output. And they don't identify with it because it's real but because it is false as most of them are false in their ideals, their actions, their lives. I am thinking now of the richest comedian in the land (they call him a comedian, although he has never made me laugh). This fellow has been dropping one line jokes on the people for decades, beginning long ago on the radio. His jokes are inoffensive and trivial, he has what I think of as an All-American Mickey Mouse Soul. He has burned-out thousands of writers with his flippant little one-liners, and he goes on and on gathering in millions of dollars. His material is thin, inane, useless; he is rich and famous; he is a carbon copy of the masses.

There are writers like this fellow. Their books line the stands of the bookstores in the shopping malls. THE HEARTBEAT'S WAIL. THUNDERBLOSSOM. BLOOD SWORD. These writers are more rich than famous.

Then, there are the *literary* writers of poem, of story, of novel. Their idea is that if something is written tediously enough, if it is involuted enough, if it is hardly understood, then, that's art. Because, you see, this is the way it has been for centuries, they are only carrying on the tradition. These writers are more famous than rich. They are famous because they promote, publish and teach each other, mostly at the universities. They are not rich because they are the only ones who buy each other's books. They complain constantly of the success of such writers as those who put out books entitled THE HEARTBEAT'S WAIL; THUNDERB-LOSSOM and so forth. But they write just as badly, only in another way.

So, you see, if you have FAME you can never be sure that you deserve it. You may have your FAME for all the wrong reasons. This might be my case. So, you see, if I have FAME for all the wrong reasons I am already destroyed, and if I have it for the right reasons, I can never be sure of that, so there's only one thing to do: go on typing, as I have been doing here.

4.

In my old starvation days, prowling the libraries, I did a great deal of reading, mostly in the libraries. The old L.A. Public Library was my favorite. After sitting in Pershing Square and listening to the boys argue about whether there was a God or not I would walk over to the library. After eating up several rooms of books (not really) I found myself in the Philosophy Room. Those boys had some style. They talked about what *mattered*. Or seemed to. Or should. One of the things they talked about was the need for Solitude. That made sense to me. That need. I mean, when I was sitting at a table reading a book and somebody came to my table and sat down it disturbed me. Why sit near me? And when I looked about and saw other *empty* tables, I felt really repulsed. I know that I am supposed to love my fellow man but I don't. I don't hate him; I often dislike him; I just don't want him about. I feel better alone.

I loved Solitude. Still do. I grow when I am alone. People diminish me. Especially men, they seem quite unoriginal. Women, at times, are useful. Also they are funny and tragic. But too many continued hours and days with them leads to madness.

There must be others like me. I always seem to be living with a woman and one acts differently then out of courtesy. But in my in between times of living alone, I had my little delicacies. Like, I'd simply take the phone off the hook, disconnect the doorbell, pull down all the shades and go to bed for 3 or 4 days and nights, just arising now and then to do my toilet, drink water, nibble on a bit of food. These times were precious to me, holy. I was like a battery getting a recharge—off of myself and the absence of Humanity. I have never been lonely. I have been confused, depressed, insane, suicidal, but never lonely in the sense that some person or persons might solve something for me. I never had a television set until I was 52 years old. And I only saw one movie in 20 years—*The Lost Weekend*. I went to check it out for authenticity.

Being alone has always been very necessary to me. At one time I was on one of my hot winning streaks at the racetracks. The money just came to me. A certain basic simple system was working for me. The horses moved south and I walked off my job and followed them down to Del Mar.

It was a good life. I'd win each day at the track. I had a routine. After the track I'd stop off at the liquor store for my fifth of whiskey and my six-pack of beer and the cigars. Then I'd get back into the car and cruise the coast for a new motel room. I liked a different one each night. I'd find a motel, park my stuff, shower, change clothes and then get my ass back into the car and cruise the coast again—this time for an eating place. And what I would look for was an eating place without many people in it. (The worst, I know.) But I didn't like crowds. So, I always found one. Went in and ordered.

So, this particular night, I found a place, went in, sat at the counter, ordered: porterhouse steak with French fries, beer. Everything was fine. The waitress didn't bother me. I sucked at my beer, ordered another. Then the meal came. Goddamn, it looked good. I began. I had a few fine bites, then the door opened and this fellow came in. There were 14 empty stools at the counter. This fellow sat down next to me.

"Hi, Doris, how's it going?"

"O.K, Eddie. How ya doing?"

"Fine."

"What'll ya have, Eddie?"

"Oh, just a cup of coffee, I guess . . ."

Doris brought Eddie his coffee.

"I think the fuel pump on my car is going out . . ."

"Always some damn thing, huh Eddie?"

"Yeah, now my wife needs new plates, Doris."

"You mean houseware?"

"I mean mouthware!"

"Oh, Eddie, ha, ha, ha!"

"Well," Eddie said, "when it rains it pours!"

I picked up my plate and my beer, my fork, my knife, my spoon, my napkin, my ass and moved it all the way over to a far booth. I sat down and began again. As I did I watched Eddie and Doris. They were whispering. Then Doris looked at me:

"Is everything all right, sir?"

"Now," I told her, "it is . . ."

Nothing diminishes me like the crowd.

Say like on New Year's night at midnight, everybody screaming, joyous, celebrating; I feel completely denuded, foolish, unhappy. If I am in a room full of them. If I am alone it's better. New Year's Eve is like any other eve to me: I drink.

Or standing with a group, being sworn in to a government job, I feel like I am eating shit stew, facing the flag, pledging allegiance. I always get out of that: I move my lips but in the sound of all the voices I don't have to say any words and nobody knows.

There are certain privacies that are joyous and necessary. I maintain that I have certain inherent rights to oneness and that I am my own keeper. I am not cranky about this bit, just a touch fucking rigid: it creates a comedy of my own that I can laugh at, though soundlessly.

Some refuse to believe that I have these certain beliefs. There was this lady I had lived with for a year or so, a live one, a bit offed by shock therapy but better than most, she said in her cups, one night:

"Ah shit . . . I've read your stuff, I've heard you talk . . . you're such a LONER! You're such a fuckin' RECLUSE! How come then you WRITE your stuff and then you send it OUT?"

"It helps pay for all that swill you jam down your throat."

"You mean drink?"

"Yes."

"That's no answer! You're copping out!"

She was right, of course.

I remember reading in the papers about this guy they found in the park. He'd been living in a cave there and coming out at night and living off the picnic scraps. They caught him. And took him off. And when I read that I thought, there but for the grace of the typewriter goes me. The keys are my solitude, my luck, my picnic scraps. Hate me but buy my books. And read the old philosophers on Solitude. And don't write me, phone me, or write like me. And if you ever see me anywhere it isn't me. Forget it.

1

People who call other people assholes generally are.

2

When you've considered everything, you've considered too much.

3

Human relationships do not work.

4

Brilliant men are created out of desperate circumstances; fools are also.

5

When you marry the woman you also marry her entire family.

6

Most men who sleep late in the morning are a superior breed.

7

Women are braver in situations they have to face alone; men tend to get braver in and before crowds.

8

I have never met a nonimmaculate cat.

9

The poets do the least to become known.

10

Fame is too often the result of bad public taste; Immortality too often a matter of poor critical judgment.

11

I'm often delighted when something terrible happens to me. It's not so much a matter of masochism, it's more a feeling of a balance come due; it has to happen, and since it does happen, one greets it with an oblique delight—feeling that after that better things are sure to follow???

12

Keep your sunny-side up. Nobody wants to hear about the night your mother kicked your ass in the deli takeout parlor . . .

13

All the women in my life have become the Reoccuring Woman: their complaints have been just as similar and just as realistic. So I judge them, in comparison, only upon the artistry of their head-jobs and their kitchen work, faithfulness and so forth. And when I line them up in this fashion I can't come up with a winner. Just a loser: me.

14

Whenever one of my women goes to another man in preference to me, I am thoroughly astonished, especially when I meet him in person. But all things are illusionary, including those dull, drab sons of bitches, so it's all right, I suppose.

15

Dostoevski was precisely passionate, but when he ended up with Christ in his lap I wrote him off as going the long way around to find what most idiots accepted in the beginning. Not that I didn't find his journey vibrant. For this, I almost forgave him his final Error. Tolstoy, who ended up the same way, was simply dull throughout. Which I can't forgive.

16

Religion is not the Opium of the People. It's a peanut-butter sandwich. On white bread.

17

A whore is a woman who takes more than she gives. A man who takes more than he gives is called a businessman.

18

When the agony of all the people is heard, nothing will be done.

19

I am only a realist in certain areas. For instance, it discourages me that people have upper and lower intestines. As I watch people, I am conscious of these (and other) parts. I'm hexed. For instance, when a man says to me, "She's really a beautiful woman," I feel like answering, "I won't know until I examine the healthiness of her excreta."

20

The best people are the ones you never meet.

21

I much prefer it when a woman discards me. Then I am sure that the error is hers.

22

I have met both the rich and the poor and have found them to be equally unnatural in their positions.

23

There is a certain actress who must be nearing 70, at least, for I saw her in movies when I was a boy and I'm now 62. But she is photographed again and again as looking 32. It has gone on for decades. Marvelous, I think, young forever! And she is often photographed with her sisters, and they've all held on well. They are all photographed smiling together, heads always held upward to hide the neck lines. Marvelous, I think, we all need the dream.

24

One of the most depressing places to be upon the earth is to be sitting in some Los Angeles café at 9:35 A.M. and having the waitress hand you the menu of various egg delicacies as her ankles are thin and her buttocks resigned, she has been used and abandoned by her men and she just wants the rent and a way to go, and then you look up and in a mellifluous voice full of victory and hope and understanding you order item #3, the cut-rate special.

25

A criminal might be defined as one outnumbered by those who generally don't do what he does except in secret or different ways.

26

Check your ass for the shining candle.

27

Of all the women who have claimed they have hated me I have believed all of them.

28

It's exactly as good as it's ever going to get.

29

Will Rogers once said, "I never met a man I didn't like." I never liked Will Rogers. But I liked his statement. I liked some men, temporarily. But somehow I didn't like him. But he was probably luckier than I was and most probably a better man to be around. If you liked pussycats.

30

One night Babe Ruth, who was one hell of a drinker, held Rabbit Maranville, the shortstop, out of the window of their 12th-floor hotel room by his heels.

"Go on, you fucker, drop me!" the Rabbit screamed in this story I read.

I like that story. It would have been a much better one if he had dropped him.

31

One of the great things is when a Suicide meets a Suicide (it helps more when one is a man and the other a woman) over drinks and they talk about all the times they've botched their tries and they begin to laugh about that, and it's really very funny because you really meant to do it. Now the radio is on, there's a pack of cigarettes on the coffee table and the rug is upon the floor, and life is almost delightful, for a moment . . .

32

That's enough. See you in Dresden.

I was past midnight. The drinks had come, I never knew quite from where, and some cigarettes too. And the juke just blazed away. Hours of stale cigarette smoke had turned the air blue gray, and the flies and roaches were dulled and sickened and drunk, and the patrons too. It was a place no sensible being would ever want to be in, but not being a sensible being, there I was.

The urinal was impossible, walking in there you were hit by a deadly waft of a century of piss and puke. And nobody ever used the toilet, it was dark and caked and dry and there wasn't any water in the tank. And the lid had long been gone, the tank lid, the toilet lid, and the whiskey and beer spiders had taken over, threading their webs in there, waiting for something.

I refocused on myself and found myself sitting next to this guy I had never seen before. He was in his mid-30s, wore this leather jacket. Maybe he had been buying me drinks. I didn't know. Nobody else sat near us.

He had a pack of cigarettes near his drink. Pall Malls. I reached for his pack, got it, pulled a smoke out and lit up.

"Did I tell you you could have a cigarette?" he asked me.

"No."

"Don't go touching my cigarettes again!"

He pulled the Pall Malls back in front of him.

Everything was so weary. There was always some-body flexing up against you. They couldn't bear up with the slightest joke, the tiniest confrontation. Everything was a challenge to them. They awakened angry every morning and they stayed that way. They didn't want to lose and they didn't know how to win. Constipated lives full of shit.

I reached over, pulled the Pall Malls back, took a ciga-rette out, broke it in half, threw it back into the ashtray.

He just sat there.

He sat there a long time.

He looked straight forward.

Then he spoke.

"Listen, I just got out of jail for aggravated assault! I don't want to go back there again!"

"Don't fuck with me then." I told him.

We both sat there. It was a hot stupid night. We breathed in the gray blue smoke as the rich were out on their sail-ing ships or drugged to sleep. The trouble with life was that there were only tiny periods of action between all the vast spaces and the people just waited as Death sat on his red hot laughing ass.

"Just don't fuck with me!" he repeated.

"Get yourself a hobbyhorse with a wooden asshole and you'll feel better," I said.

I could feel the anger ripping through him. I wasn't lucky enough to have anger. With anger you could react, wrong or right. I just had a pale and tired disgust. He was drinking whiskey. I was at the bottom of a stale bottle of beer.

"Buy me a drink," I said, "a whiskey."

He motioned Tommy down.

"Two whiskeys."

They arrived and I drained mine down. He drained his.

"Two more whiskeys," he said to Tommy.

"It's all right," I told the guy, "I don't want to overbum."

"Drink up," he said. "I'm getting ready to kick your ass."

The whiskeys were before us.

"You mean if I drink this, you're going to kick my ass?"

"Right."

"You know I can't turn down a drink?"

"I know."

"It's not fair," I said. then reached down and got the whiskey, drained it.

He drained his.

"Let's go," he said.

"Wait," I said.

"What is it?"

"One more," I said, "to dull the pain."

"Two whiskeys," he said to Tommy.

The whiskeys arrived. They sat there golden and powerful among the dead flies and the half-dead patrons. My father had always warned me that I would come to this. He had wanted me to be an engineer. Jesus Christ, that would have been worse than this.

I drained my whiskey. The guy got his. Then I stood up and walked toward the front bar door, opened it and walked out. It was dark out there. He was lit up a moment in the doorway, my mind noted a neon sign and I didn't even see it coming.

I was flat on my ass. Sprawled like a fucking land crab. No pain. Just a slight tinkle of wonder. The guy was good. I was too. At absorbing punches, punches and drinks. I could take all they could offer. Sometimes I just wore them down; other times, I didn't.

I got up, swung and missed, but as he sidestepped he

slipped into some fresh puke somebody had recently deposited and I hit him in the throat, heard him give a little gulp, his eyes rolled a bit in surprise—he was used to winning—then I dug a left hook toward his gut, he blocked it with his elbow, countered with a hard right to my chin and I was down on my ass again, feeling strange, as if I were in too deep with no place to go. He kicked at my head. I saw it coming, grabbed his shoe, was surprised to have it, lifted it up as I stood up—and he was on his ass.

I stood back then, thinking maybe we could call it like that. Let it be, you know.

I knew I had been lucky. He knew it too.

He got up and came on in. I shot a jab. It was useless, I didn't have my shoulder behind it. I took his next shot fairly well, was almost proud, then he blasted me with his next and I was down on my ass again as the prowl car pulled up. I saw it. I was happy to see it. I sat there smiling at the prowl car.

Then I felt him lifting me up. I heard him saying, "I'm just taking him home, officers, he's going to be all right."

They sat and watched as he walked me toward his car, unlocked it. Then he put me in the front seat. Then he got around the other side and got in, started the car. The cops watched us drive off.

He kept driving through the city streets, then we were in a dark area, open country, much space, many trees. He just drove along.

Maybe he's taking me out here to try to finish me off, I thought.

But that wasn't bothering me.

"Hey," I said, "I need a goddamned drink."

"There's a pint in the glove compartment. What's your name?"

"Hank," I said, reaching in and getting the bottle.

"I'm Robert," he said.

I peeled the pint, opened it, took a hit. I passed the bottle to Robert, he took a hit, passed it back.

"What do you do?" he asked.

"Nothing."

We drove along and then Robert said, "Watch this . . ."

There was a small car in front of us. Robert pulled up alongside and stared at the two guys in the other car. They were a couple of kids, maybe 19. Robert kept driving along and staring at the guys. They looked scared. They pulled ahead and Robert went after them. He caught up with them and then banged the side of his car into them. They almost went off the road. They both started screaming.

"Hey, what the fuck are you trying to do?"

"Are you crazy?"

Robert just drove alongside of them and stared. Then he banged his car into theirs again.

"Hey! Jesus Christ, you asshole!"

Robert banged them again, and this time the driver lost control, he spun off the road, piled into some brush. Robert drove off the road blocking their exit.

"Which one do you want?" he asked me.

"I'll take the guy who gets out second."

We climbed out and waited. The car door opened and a kid in a gray sweatshirt got out. A nice blond boy.

"You fucking guys crazy?" he asked.

Robert walked up and cracked him with a right. The kid dropped to his knees and held his head.

"Jesus, what did you do that for?" he asked.

Robert grabbed him by the hair and banged his head against the side of the car.

My guy got out of the other side of the car. I walked to-

178

ward him. Before I could get to him he reached into his back pocket, got his wallet and threw it toward me.

"Please take it," he said, "just don't hurt me."

I picked up the wallet, took the bills out, stuck them in my pocket, threw the wallet back.

"You should never turn down a fight," I told the kid. "It weakens the will."

I turned and looked over at Robert. His guy was out cold and he was stripping him of his wristwatch and a ring.

"Come on, Robert, let's get out of here."

Then the guy had me from behind, he had me in a good choke hold, I couldn't breathe, shots of bright red flashed; I kicked backwards, landed on one of his shins. His grip slipped slightly and I was able to turn sideways but he got the grip on me again, but I reached for his balls, yanked, and he let go. He doubled over, holding his parts. I walked around and kicked him in the ass. He flopped over on the ground, moaning. I stood there looking at him. Just a kid who wanted to fuck the chicks. Just a kid who wanted to go to college.

Robert walked up beside me. He kicked the kid in the head, hard. The kid straightened fast, like he had been electrocuted, then he went limp.

"You don't have to do that, Robert. Show some mercy."

"Mercy is for suckers."

"You didn't have to do that."

"Yeah, I did. Now forget it."

"I didn't like that."

"What you don't like doesn't matter."

We walked back toward the car, got in. Robert kicked it over and we were back on the road. I took a hit of the scotch, passed it toward Robert. He waved it off: "Naw, I don't drink with weaklings."

"Good. All the more for me."

We just drove along through the night and I sucked at the scotch.

"Just like a baby with his bottle. You alkies are weak," he said.

I didn't answer.

"You can't cut it without the booze, can you?" Robert asked.

"No."

I took another hit as we drove along. I wasn't interested in being weak or strong. I just wanted to get by the hours. I wasn't even interested in impressing myself.

"My father was a drunk," Robert said.

"Did it kill him?" I asked.

"The cops killed him."

"Oh."

This guy evidently came from a long criminal line. I could feel it sitting inside of him, locked there. I sensed something else in him, something that wanted to be kind and easy but the other part was too overpowering. He was just naturally and automatically dangerous. I liked some of that but not all of it. His fury had no humor. It was like a job.

"I'll take that drink," he said.

I passed the bottle over. He took a hit, handed it back.

"Mom just got out. She did five years. Homicide."

"Great. Sounds like a great woman. "She is. You done time?"

"Nothing," I said, "just the drunktanks."

"Stick with me. I'll put you through college."

"Yeah."

We drove along. It was a nice warm night. I felt relaxed. It was nice to get out of that bar for a moment. Those people sitting on those stools were just lonely. It was a lonely world. With everybody pretending it wasn't, pretending that they were handling it. They couldn't even wipe their bungholes. Nothing was drabber than the masses and that's all there was.

"If you want," said Robert, "we can work together every night. You've got a certain cool that most guys don't have."

"I'm not cool," I said, "I'm just tired."

"That don't matter. We can work together."

"I'll think about it."

What was worrying me was that the pint was almost empty. And I knew that Robert's criminal insanity would not be so enthralling without drink. Nothing was without it. Drink elevated me. Without it I was common. I didn't want to be common. It was too hard.

I sucked at the bottle.

"Drink is a form of escape," I told Robert. "I like to escape."

He just kept driving. I liked the sound of the motor and the darkness going by. It was like sailing through Time untouched. Movement was unchallenged action.

"Hey," he said, "I think we got one!"

There was a car ahead. I could sense him elevating into his life-meaning. He was like a tiger closing in on the wildebeest.

It was a small model car, a guy and his girl driving along, a young couple. Robert pulled up next to them and stared. They just looked straight ahead pretending we weren't there. But we were there.

"Robert," I said, "let's let them go. They just want to live."

"That's *their* problem."

The guy in the other car reduced speed, thinking maybe we would go on. It was his mistake. Robert braked and slowed next to them. Then he just leaned his car against theirs and pushed them off the road.

We got out of our car. And the kid got out of his. Ow, he was big. A little drunk, hair down in his eyes. But he was large, big, he was going to protect his girl. Probably a high-school football star, somebody used to winning.

He stood there in the moonlight and puffed out his chest. He was magnificent and he knew it.

"Okay," he said, "I'll take either one of you guys. Who wants it first?"

"Listen, sir," I said, "we were just kind of clowning around. Let's call it off."

Robert looked at me.

"What are you, some kind of homo?"

"I don't think so."

"Okay, I'll handle this hot dog."

Robert moved toward the big kid. His girl got out of the car. She was magnificent too. Long hair, great body. They were the magnificent pair. The kid would someday be a corporate lawyer. She would be a fashion model. They were winners geared to get it all. I felt as if we were trespassing some holy land of the future.

"Kick his ass, Lance!" screamed the girl.

"No problem, Darlene."

The big kid and Robert moved toward each other. Then they circled. It was very quiet. You could hear their feet moving in the dirt. The moon seemed to be watching. Everything inhaled. The weeds inhaled, the trees inhaled, the clouds; then there was a movement, fiercely a fist landed upon a head and Robert dropped.

He got right up.

What am I going to do? I thought, if this guy kicks Robert's ass?

All I wanted to do was to be back in my dirty room, in that bed, covers pulled up, staring at the ceiling, waiting. I did that a lot.

There was another sound. And the big kid was down on the ground. You couldn't even see those shots coming. It wasn't a fight of men, it was a fight of rattlesnakes.

The big kid got up and Robert landed again, not as solid this time but enough to stagger the kid. And as Robert moved forward the girl hit him with something from behind. It stopped him a moment and then he looked at me:

"Take care of the broad while I finish this guy!"

I ran over to the girl and grabbed both of her hands. Christ, she was beautiful! Her eyes blazed in anger and fright, her body whirled, convoluted. I actually got a hard-on just holding her like that. Even in the confusion she seemed to notice that.

She spit in my face. "You ugly beggar!"

Then she brought her knee up and tried to de-ball me. She just missed and I slapped her hard, saw her stagger in the moonlight, her long blond hair jumping deliciously into space. I grabbed her and kissed her, she bit my lip, I screamed, landed one in her gut and she dropped, her skirt falling back, showing long sheathed legs glistening magically.

Then Robert was standing next to me.

"I finished him off," he said. He looked down at the girl. "Let's fuck her."

"No."

I reached down and helped her up. She was a bit crazed. She was very close to me. She looked at me.

"Don't kill him, please don't kill him. I love him!"

"It's going to be all right," I told her. "Please don't worry."

"Hey! What's with *you?*" asked Robert. "I'm going to fuck this bitch!"

"No," I said, "it's not right."

"Do you think anything we're doing is right? Why do you keep drawing lines?"

He gave me a hard push and then grabbed the girl, pushing her toward some brush.

"No, no, no! *Please!*" she said.

"Shut up," said Robert.

Then she must have attacked him, done something against him. He retaliated. She screamed and he dragged her to the brush. I walked back to the car, got the pint and had the last hit. Then I walked over and looked at the guy. I bent over him. He looked asleep. I could see him breathing. He wasn't dead. Fine. He could still be a corporate lawyer. Then I walked over to their car, opened the door, got in. There was a bag on the floor. I looked in there. It was a bottle of expensive wine, only a bit of it gone. My life was renewed. I went back to Robert's car, leaned against it and sucked at the wine.

After a while Robert came along. He stood there looking at me.

"It was great," he said, "she loved it. I fucked her, then I made her suck me off, then I sodomized her. She loved it."

"I'll bet."

"Yeah, she did."

"Let's get out of here—"

"She's waiting for you, Hank. She wants more."

"Cut the crap. You haven't killed her, have you?"

"No, she's just laying out there waiting for more, her legs spread."

"Let's go."

The big kid was still stretched out. We got into Robert's car and started back toward town. Everything was still quiet and dark, except for the gentle hum of the motor. It might have been as if nothing had happened. The trees acted as if everything were the same, and the asphalt road acted as if nothing had ever happened—only the moon seemed to know—and there was a covering over Robert now, like a slime, it climbed all over him, into his eyes, his ears, his mouth; it was under his armpits, it was between his toes, it seeped and crawled him and it had nothing to do with morals, with right or wrong; it was something else, something very ugly and unexplainable covered him.

"See you found a bottle," he said.

"Yeah. I got lucky."

"Even if you didn't have the guts to fuck that bitch you shoulda jacked-off over her body."

"Yeah, I guess I missed my chance."

We were getting back into town, into the poor section. Robert reached somewhere and then tossed a stack of bills into my lap.

"Your half. That kid was loaded."

"Thanks, you're very honest."

"Got to be. We got a good thing going."

I gave him my address. Like a good thug, he knew the city, he got me right there. We pulled in front of the roominghouse. The whole neighborhood had been asleep for at least five hours.

"Listen," he said, "the night's not over. I'd like you to meet my mom."

"I'm sure she's great, Robert, but I just want to go in and get some rest."

I got on out. Then Robert was off in his car.

I got the key out, opened the front door, then walked up the stairway and at the first turn I saw the framed painting of Jesus. He looked pained, like a young guy whose girl had just left him to run off with the dope dealer.

I got into my room, pissed in the sink, got out of my clothes except for the undershirt, got into the unmade bed with all that money and my wine bottle. I had never seen that much money. I bunched the pillow up and sat there in the dark sucking on the wine bottle.

Things went by, things went by fast, things went by so fast that they never took form.

A mouse came out, it clambered up the hot plate, then ran up the handle of my coffeepot, hung there halfway on the handle and looked at me. I could see it in the lightening dark, the lightning dark. It looked at me and I looked at the mouse and it didn't like me there in its room. Then, in a tick, it was gone.

I was alone again, I always felt better being alone. When you're alone, the only problem is yourself. It's nicer that way. You stay out of trouble. I was really a nice guy. I knew that.

I finished off the wine bottle, threw it to the floor, unbunched the pillow, rolled on my belly and, ass-up to the demented ceiling, I slept.

Let's begin by saying this is a work of fiction and then let's go on from there. I first met Steve Cosmos in Paris, at least that's the name he was going under then and the name I remember best. Cristina and I were in Paris because the editors had dragged my ass over there to do interviews for the press. Also, I was writing a screenplay for Jean Sasoon, the French director, and we were staying at his Paris apartment along with his wife, the actress of some fame, who simply went under the name of Barbette. All the whole thing meant was much eating and drinking, drinking and eating, and drinking and drinking. I didn't understand it but I didn't care.

Anyhow, Jean Sasoon loved to talk about Steve Cosmos. Sasoon loved freaks and Cosmos was a freak, and I was a freak, that's why I was around.

So, this night who walks in but Cosmos himself, one of the ten most wanted men on the Continent. Mostly he did things to banks and gambling casinos, but he had many little sidelines.

We shook hands.

"Aha!" he said. "I saw you on TV and you got drunk and gave those shits what they had coming."

"I understand you take from the shits what you got coming," I said.

Cosmos laughed. "Oh, yes, it's an almost continuous thing."

"Pleased to meet you," said Cristina.

Cosmos looked. "Ah, what a *charming* girl! Are you with Chinaski?"

"No, he's with me."

Sasoon had gone to the kitchen where he was preparing something.

"*Ah!*" said Sasoon, a quite culinary "Ah," as if he had devised some magic and delicate blending of cookery. Cosmos, being French, ran into the kitchen to view and taste the moment, perhaps add something to it?

Cristina and I glanced at each other. We had met the great man. I refilled our wineglasses.

Cosmos had a gentle style and grace, you could see that right off. Strange white-blond hair, very straight back, a pink boy's face, a face full of pranks and laughter. His eyes were very large and round.

Then Barbette came in from somewhere. She saw Cosmos and started right in on him vocally. She kept on and on. A concerned tirade. Cosmos gave small answers, acted astonished, smiled, laughed. My French is worse than my German and I have almost no German, but what it was, she was telling him:

"You were seen in a bank today. I have a source. What were you doing in the bank?"

"Walking around."

"Don't you know your posters are out everywhere? They are looking for you!"

"But I was there and they couldn't see me."

"Why don't you hide low? Why do you stick your butt in their faces? You're a fool! What are you trying to do? Do you think you're God? For a man who has been around as much as you, you have the brain of a grasshopper, of a snail! Do you think I would enjoy you in jail?"

"No, neither of us."

"Then why are you such a fool? Why—"

Barbette went on and on.

Cosmos bent his head to the right, stuck his left thumb into his left ear and let his tongue loll out. The message was clear: All existence was stupid and it really didn't matter what any of us did.

Barbette got it, laughed. The lecture was over. Everybody was back to speaking English.

Sasoon turned from his steaming and delicious pots.

"The guy, the other night, he lost all his money at roulette because he played honest and he came out onto the grounds drunk and fell full-length into the lake in his tuxedo, came up dripping mud and slime!"

"Ah!" said Cosmos, "what an ending, yet I'm still here."

After eating we really got into the wine, fine French wine, it really rolled on down and in, you can drink it forever. Corks were pulled and pulled, cigars lit.

Cosmos kept repeating, quite seriously, through a smile:

"I have no interest in the police. They only have an interest in me."

I heard from Cristina later that I was the fool: putting my arms about the shoulders of Cosmos and Sasoon, saying over and over and *over*:

"You guys are my buddies! I really *like* you guys! You guys are my buddies! We all got *class!*"

What Cristina meant about the fool part was the repetition: they had to keep hearing it. But it's difficult in this life to ever meet exceptional men, and along with the good French wine this put me out of balance.

I *do* remember other portions. Cosmos had a trick to pull elsewhere. We all managed to get into Sasoon's car and we drove small dark streets under Cosmos' direction. Finally, along a tall row of hedges Cosmos said, "Stop here."

He stepped out.

"Now leave."

As we drove off, some of us looked back. Cosmos had pulled the neck of his trenchcoat upwards, and as he walked off he looked over his shoulder as if there was something there following him. He was right: it always was.

It was about a year later when we saw Cosmos again. I had finished the screenplay and Sasoon came to America to try to hustle up a backer. A producer. He rented a house on the beachfront down at Venice. Don't get lost. I'm speaking about Sasoon: he rents the house. *Rented* the house. (I hate fucking with tenses, it makes me tense.)

All right. Sasoon had Cosmos with him. They had purchased two expensive motorcycles and two old, long, cheap, gas-eating cars which they considered "class," or as they put it: "great buys." Here in L.A., we might refer to them as "Mexican Specials," which is not racist, only accurate. I've driven any number of Mexican Specials but never by choice, and I don't believe the American-Mexicans do either.

The house was next to a house next to an oil well. The house had 12 separate rooms, each with its own bed, and next to each room was another room with a shower and toilet. This was good for Sasoon, a ladies' man, and he often stocked up with four or five women in each room but he never did fill all 12, although one night he got up to 11. His excellence with the ladies backfired when he was looking for producers because he usually ended up in bed with the producers' wives and this pissed them to no good end.

I met many famous people in that house: producers, actors, directors. The problem with the famous when you meet them is that they don't seem to be very much. They just stand around and sit around with their shoes on and usually don't do or say much. In fact, they appear to be dull. (I usually take my shoes off.)

I wasn't much luckier with the producers than Sasoon was. He had pointed one out to me who was interested in producing my screenplay. I was with Cristina one night and I was leaning against the bar at Musso's and this producer, let's call him Medicino, well, Medicino saw me at the bar and left his table and walked up and said, "Hello, Chinaski."

"Oh, Mr. Medicino."

He got into it. He was going to produce a movie. It was about a writer from the '60s, now dead. I couldn't read this writer. No knock against this writer: I can't read any of the writers. This is all right, it's the way it is with me. Then the bad part came: he told me what he was going to title the movie.

"Wait," I said, "you're not joking: you're really going to call this thing *The Heart's Boomerang*?"

"Yes, I like that title."

"Listen, you use that title and I've got to equate you with some guy in a circle-jerk singing 'God Bless America.'"

I was stunned: Mr. Medicino whirled and walked back to his table without a word. No fuckin' sense o' humor.

"Well," said Cristina, "there goes your screenplay."

"Let's ask the orchestra to stand," I said, and nodded the barkeep over for refills.

Cosmos, down at Venice, was more cheerful. We shook hands and grinned upon meeting again.

"I hear you go to the racetrack," he said.

"Every day. Sometimes at night, too. On a good day I'll listen to some Mahler and play eighteen races."

"You going tomorrow?"

"If I'm alive, of course" . . .

The next day he was there.

"You play the daily double?" he asked.

"No."

"The pick-six?"

"No."

"Exactas?"

"No."

"What do you bet?"

"Straight win."

"No place, no show?"

"Straight win only."

"You can't win any money that way," Cosmos said.

I didn't answer.

Cosmos didn't win the double. He showed me his losing tickets after the race, almost proudly. He had studied the racing form intently but there was no pattern to his betting: 6-2, 4-7, 7-3, 8-9, 10-4, 8-3. Each was a $10 ticket. He was $60 out.

"You see what happened?" he asked.

"What?"

"The eight horse broke down in the first race and the nine broke down in the second, I had a broken-leg daily double."

"The eight and the nine probably would have lost even if they hadn't broken down."

"I had a broken-leg daily double," he repeated as if he hadn't heard me.

After each race it was the same. He showed me a handful of losing tickets but he always had some excuse. Well, at least he had money to shit away from somewhere.

In the eighth race I had two-win on a long shot. It was a little long-shot play I had devised after studying volumes of race results from tracks in Canada, Mexico and the United States.

"I have no respect for you for betting a horse like that," Cosmos said.

"What the hell, it paid seventy-six dollars."

"It was a stupid bet," he said.

That night Sasoon phoned me.

"Steve said he had a broken-leg daily double."

"He had that," I said.

"Cosmos wants to talk to you."

"Put him on."

"Ank," he said, "I feel the pain . . . Life is for nothing."

"Yeah, that's right."

"When I win, I feel nothing, when I lose, I feel the pain. What good is winning? Winning is no good."

He was right, of course, and he was wrong, too.

Cosmos was at the track everyday. He was the worst horseplayer I ever saw. Instinctively he landed upon the shortest-priced stiff, race after race. One day I pulled in close to $600. Steve asked for a $200 loan. I laid it on him.

I didn't see him the next day or the next. That Friday I couldn't make the races, had to have a wisdom-tooth extracted. The dentist gave me a bottle of painkilling pills.

"Only take these if you are in agony," he said.

The agony didn't arrive. I took a handful of the pills, drank a six-pack of beer and drove out to the night harness races.

I was standing in line and I looked over in the next line and there was a fellow who resembled Steve Cosmos, only he had a ragged-looking beard, really scraggly, and he was dressed in floppy, greasy clothing. Cosmos always dressed neatly and cleanly. I looked at the eyes of the fellow. The eyes looked faded. Not the right eyes. This guy was just a second-rate Cosmos. I looked away and forgot about it.

A couple of races later I was checking my program and the line of asses of the hookers along the bar when I felt a hand upon my wallet and I whirled and there was the second-rate Cosmos only it was the real one under all that, and he said, "Ank, I saw you looking at me . . ."

He pulled out two hundred-dollar bills and handed them to me.

"Now that I've reestablished my credit, you ought to be good for $400 next time."

"How'd you get lucky?" I asked.

"The woman I'm in love with—"

"Who's that?"

"The lady with the spinning head."

He meant the roulette wheel. (See: Las Vegas).

Things got bad down on Venice Beach. The screenplay kept crawling back kicked in the ass. The standard comment was, "Nobody is interested in the life of a barfly." They were right, of course. Even the barfly hardly cared. People wanted a loser who became a winner. Or a winner who became a loser. But a loser who stayed a loser? That was too much like themselves. They weren't interested in themselves.

The fine motorcycles went first. Then Sasoon started renting out the rooms. But Sasoon was into leather and all that and he was often absentminded and sometimes he left one of the girls all bound up and gagged upon the fireplace (his sacrificial Altar of Doom) and with an icepick or pliers or a tong lying nearby, and this shocked some of the roomers who wandered about the place and they moved out. Worse, the hardy ones who remained stopped paying their rent. Next, the Mexican Specials went, and next, I heard Sasoon and Cosmos were gone, they were back in Paris. I got the postcard from Sasoon:

". . . going to try the screenplay on the French . . . Barbette has landed a leading role in major stage production . . . will send more news soon . . ."

And a line from Cosmos:

"Life is for nothing."

Three or four weeks later I got a letter from Sasoon who was in Paris:

"Hank,

They got Steve. He's in this ancient prison in Paris, one of the oldest around, a former torture chamber, full of rats. He's very depressed, very. He's gambled away much of his wine rations for the future. You should write him. What he did to get in there was so stupid he won't even tell me about it.

I'm still going around with your screenplay. There has been some interest but nothing definite. But this screenplay is going to make it someday, one way or another, I'll see to that.

Barbette sends her love to you and to Cristina, too.

Jean Sasoon"

Then I heard from Cosmos:

"Well, Ank, the police got me and it was so dumb the way I got caught that I'm ashamed to tell, and won't. My life is over. I will never get out of here. I think of you out there going to the track everyday and I only wish I were standing next to you tearing up my tickets. I will never see you again. Life is ridiculous, it's all a waste. There are a few fine fellows in here but there's nothing we can do, or very little. Well, this is it for me. I never believed it would end like this. There are so many charges against me. I can't believe I did all those things. My lawyer said for me to expect at least ten years, and if I do get ten, I'm lucky. You call that luck? My life is over. Even a butterfly is better off than I . . .

Write if possible.

Steve"

I wrote Cosmos right away. I wrote a long letter, and feeling that it might be read before it got to him, I wrote about how a man of his quality and character should never be in jail. I wrote that he should be honored, that what the world called justice was really a pathetic thing.

I went on and on in the letter, exclaiming what a noble man Cosmos was. I put it on so good that I almost wept.

It took me a bottle and a half of wine to write the letter, and when I reread it and sealed it up I felt that after reading all that they would let him out immediately . . .

Cosmos responded quickly:

"Say, Ank, that was a great letter and I read it over many times. You are right: I don't belong in prison. However, it appears that only you and I believe this. I will never get out of here. This is it. Finis. I might as well be buried alive. My life was good until now. Now I must pay. Well, all the women are yours, and all the horses, and all that good stuff you drink. Think of me sometimes living in this hole with the rats. Even the walls stink. This is my home now, forever, until . . . and then even when I'm dead they'll throw me into some special prison for the dead, with dead rats and dead stinking walls . . . Even death will be for nothing.

Steve"

I was having some trouble with the IRS, which I cleared up, then a chunk of something ripped open my gas tank as I got into a speed duel with some fool on the freeway, and then the freeway jammed and I had to go over the side, and it took three or four days to get that straightened out. Then I wrote Cosmos again, trying to lend cheer. I even enclosed some francs I had left over from the trip over there. And then other standard little pitiable troubles followed, as they will, and I rather woke up one day to the fact that there had been no response to my last letter to Cosmos. Maybe I had said the wrong thing. Or having done a spot of time myself, I realized that some inmates thought those on the outside were out of touch with reality.

It wasn't so. My letter came back with an official stamp upon it in a dark smeared green. Again, forgive my French, but the stamp said something rather like:

MOVED. ADDRESS UNKNOWN.

Great Christ, I thought, Cosmos has dug a hole through the side of one of those stinking walls. What a clever fellow. I was proud of him.

Then I got the facts from Sasoon:

". . . I don't know *how*, but somehow Steve made bail . . . it was quite some sum . . . Then he jumped bail . . . I don't know where he is. But, after this, if they ever catch him in France again he's got life for sure."

I rewrote the screenplay, this time calling it the "jazz-soup version." I mailed a copy to Sasoon. Now he could knock on the same doors all over again. Then I started getting obscene phone calls from teeny-boppers and had to get a new unlisted number. Unlisted numbers last as long as the average marriage: one and one-half years.

I got back into the poem. Tried some oil paintings but just ended up painting various versions of the human face, which is limited subject matter indeed. The horses ran all right but the horseplayers were a dreary group to take. They never admitted failure and kept right on failing. What was really bothering them was loneliness, and absence of brain cells. Sometimes out there I felt as if I were in a giant mental ward, I mean for the insane, you know, with all the doors open and nobody able to walk out. Including . . .

Anyhow, one day the phone rang and it was Sasoon.

"Allo, Hank, it's Sasoon."

"Where you at, Jean?"

"Venice."

"You mean the beach?"

"Well, not exactly. We're in the ghetto, we live in the black ghetto, nice place, big yard—"

"What are you doing there?"

"Well, we want to shoot a documentary of you, all right?"

"All right," I said, feeling sorry for Jean because he had been unable to unload the screenplay.

"Guess who's with me?"

"Barbette?"

"No, she's working, they're shooting something in Algier."

"Who, then?"

There was another voice on the phone:

"I have no interest in the police, they only have an interest in me."

"Cosmos—"

"Thanks for your letters, my friend. I will always value them."

"When you guys coming to see me?"

"Oh, no, you come see *us! In the black ghetto!*"

"Must I?"

"You must."

I got the instructions . . .

Although it was high noon I parked my car in a supermarket parking lot outside the ghetto and phoned in.

Sasoon tooled up in another Mexican Special. After exchanges I got in and we moved toward the ghetto.

"How do you like it?" Sasoon mentioned the car. "It's fifteen years old and only got 20,000 miles on it. This housewife used to just drive it around for shopping, then her husband died and she had to sell it. I really got lucky! You like it?"

"Great, Jean, great."

The exhaust left a gray-blue haze half a block behind us and the tired crankshaft pushed at the weary piston arms that were just aching to slice off and rocket through the hood.

"I got a deal," said Jean Sasoon, sitting very straight and

peering proudly over the long frontal hunk of that moving piece of shit. I inhaled a complete large can of Bud in three swallows so as not to have to answer to that.

We entered the ghetto. The streets were littered with bits of clothing and crap. Stockings. And shoes. But always *one* shoe. And never its mate. Which gave one the strange feeling that somebody had been amputated.

"Ah, look," said Jean, "see that high rise?"

I saw it.

"The people got in there and then refused to pay rent. It took two years and the state troops to finally get them out of there. And before they did, those people ripped out all the toilets, all the wiring, all the pipes, everything, they kicked holes in the walls, set rooms on fire . . . Now it's all boarded up. And people still live there. We got people living under our house, we can hear them talking at night . . . They even have radios down there. Sometimes they have fights, we can hear them cursing . . ."

"Very interesting," I said.

"This is our place," said Jean, and he began to pull into the driveway into a parking area behind his building. Two young boys, black, about eight or nine years old, sat upon their bicycles and refused to budge. Jean slowly inched his car between them. With an artistic dexterity he pushed the large car between them. Suddenly one of the black boys turned his head and said:

"*Hey, man, watch it!*"

Well, I thought, this is really living, and when the large troops come along our balls will be fried, sliced, diced and skewered. We parked, climbed out, went in.

There was Cosmos, sitting on the couch, large cheap jug of wine before him, he was trying to light a beer-soaked cigar. He looked up and saw me: "Ank, son of a bitch, what're you doing in black hell?" He was very drunk.

Sasoon showed me the place. It had two kitchens. And not much else. Except for a tremendous backyard full of weeds. We came back out and sat with Cosmos.

"Look, Ank," he said, "my life is finished. I end here."

"He's going to write me his life story," said Sasoon, "and I'm going to make a film out of it."

"Jean try to make me a writer. I'm no writer. Jean fuck me up good—"

"How's that, Steve?"

"Well, I am ten thousand ahead and then Jean says, 'Let's take a break.' And I say, 'How?' and he says, 'We'll go see Tom Jones.' So we go see Tom Jones. And he's got this big silver cross on and his shirt is open and the silver cross is mixed in with his stinking chest hair and he's dressed in tight-fitting leather and wearing a dildo and he sings his love songs and the women scream. We watch the whole Tom Jones show and then go back to the wheel and I can't go shit. Tom Jones has broken my rhythm. It's Jean's fault: that fuckin' Tom Jones!"

Cosmos lifts the entire jug of cheap wine and takes a tremendous hit.

Sasoon shows me his burglar alarm. It's a large cardboard box with little holes punched in the side. And in pencil, written in longhand: BURGLAR ALARM and also: TARANTULA! DO NOT OPEN!

Just think of that. And I had spend so much money on Westec Security.

We sat and drank awhile. Cosmos just went on and on about Tom Jones.

"What for, I need Tom Jones?"

"He cost me ten thousand!"

"Who is this Tom Jones? He looks like a fuckin' fool!"

Sasoon mentioned some of his ideas for the documentary and then I got out of there . . .

I saw Cosmos at the track the next day. He too had a Mexican Special.

"Jean has me on an allowance. This is my two-weeks allowance. I've got to win. He makes me write. He stands over me in this black shirt while I write. I'm like a slave. I must win!"

Then he put his head into the racing form. I told him I was going to get a coffee. I didn't want to spoil his concentration. I knew that he was going to buy a mass of daily-double tickets.

I met my friend the shrink who ran a nightclub and pushed drugs. He needed three jobs to support his horse habit.

"You need anything?" he asked. "I've got good stuff. Whatever you want, name it."

"Nothing right now, thanks."

I got down 20 win on a four-to-one short and the race was off. I came in a distant second and went over to where Cosmos was sitting. He showed me all his losing daily-double tickets. It was like seeing an old movie all over again.

Cosmos lost all day long.

"Well, there went my allowance," he said. "Maybe I can get a two-weeks advance."

It was very sad. I got him a drink at the bar.

He lifted his drink.

"Life is for nothing," he said.

I phoned Cosmos that night. Sasoon was off somewhere. There was an answering machine. Cosmos' voice was on it:

"I AM NOT IN AND I WILL NEVER BE IN. YOU CAN LEAVE A MESSAGE BUT IT WON'T DO ANY GOOD. WHOEVER YOU ARE, I DON'T WANT TO SEE YOU OR HEAR WHAT YOU HAVE TO SAY. IF YOU WANT TO TALK TO SOMEBODY, TALK TO THIS MACHINE. I DON'T WANT TO TALK."

I waited for the beep.

"All right, machine, go suck yourself off—"

A voice broke in, "Oh, it's you, Ank—"

"You all right, Steve?"

"I drink the wine and feel the pain . . . When I come home there are two black guys in this house. They have a knife. 'Give us the money,' they say. 'What money?' I ask. "There's no money. I need *your* money!' I have this long stick, I hit them over the head with this stick. They run out of the house and I chase them with the stick! Jean is out somewhere fucking. He thinks that burglar alarm works. It's no good."

"You sure you're all right?"

"Yes, I drink the wine and feel the pain . . ."

I didn't see Steve at the track for a week or so. Good, I thought, he's busy writing his life's story.

Then I got a call from Jean.

"You should see this place now! Steve has planted a vegetable garden, built a barbecue and put a fireplace in the house!"

"A fireplace?"

"Yeah, we went out one night and stole some bricks."

"I'm sorry you can't get rid of my screenplay, Jean."

"Don't worry. We will. Why don't you come out? Steve is barbecuing some chicken—"

"Stolen?"

"Oh, no, we got a good buy. Come on out . . ."

It was a Sunday. A terrible day at the track, anyhow. Cristina and I drove out. When we got there everybody was on the red wine and Steve was quite drunk. There were eight or 10 people there. I didn't know who they were. There were no introductions. But they were all into film and they were all Europeans. Which, of course, beats people being into film and being Americans.

Steve had burnt the chicken. It was black and hard on the outside and the insides were raw. And the salad was demented. Stacks of paper plates were everywhere but nobody had eaten, although some had tried. Cosmos just sat and smiled. He had on a chef's hat but there was a smear of dirt halfway up. The eight or 10 people were broken up into groups and didn't seem to like each other.

"Look what Steve did!" Jean waved his arm.

And it was quite a sight. It was obvious that things had been planted. There were paths and designs. It was marvelously done. Poor Steve had busted his ass. And there were chickens and ducks running about the yard.

"We will have our own heggs," said Cosmos. Then he gulped off his paper cup of wine.

"Come and see the fireplace," said Jean.

Cristina and I went in with Jean and there it was. Quite professionally done. Cosmos could do all these things. Spoke many languages. And the garden too had been very professional, very artistic. Steve had taken husbandry or whatever the hell you call it at the university.

We went back in the yard and began on the red wine. Over the fence little black faces watched. Steve threw them pieces of black chicken. Cosmos and Sasoon had settled into the ghetto . . .

The next time I saw Cosmos I was at the night harness

races. He had a big handful of money, fifties and hundreds, and he was with a couple of women and a guy. The guy seemed very intelligent, well balanced. Jean was to tell me later that he was from the French Mafia. They gave Steve money whenever he asked for it. One time Steve had done time rather than reveal something he knew about them, which would have gotten him off.

Steve rushed off to bet and the Mafia guy said to me, "He's crazy."

"I never thought about it that way," I told him.

Steve did hit one exacta that night so he only dropped a couple hundred. I saw the Mafia guy hand him some money for the last race.

I made $68 and drove back on in.

The documentary didn't interest me too much. Jean had picked up a soundman and a cameraman and I got drunk and answered his questions. It was strange when I saw the playbacks, though—I said many odd things, I had no idea that all these things were crawling in my brain. Well, all right.

But Jean said it would take some weeks. But when you're drinking, it's not really work. That's the way I write. But this is supposedly about my friend the gambler, so let me say he had to go to Vegas with a buddy and they were going to rip off the wheel up there. One of Steve's main problems was that he won it crooked and then he'd lose it back honest.

So Cosmos was gone, and then Sasoon had to make a run to Paris and so the house in the ghetto was empty, and an arrangement had been made with a neighbor to feed the chickens and the ducks.

It was strange to me that I had gotten so involved with

these two Frenchmen, and me being of German extraction, even having been born there. But they didn't feel like the enemy to me. I could never have dealt with Americans the same way, I just didn't like them. The only good American guys are in the madhouses and jails, and the women are very hostile and obvious. Well, so, anyhow. . . .

I was at the track and I looked up and there's Cosmos.

"Ank," he said, "I got back, went to the place, and it's locked tight. I don't have a key, I don't know what I did with my key. I got to wait for Jean to get back. What'll I do?"

"There's my place. I have an extra bedroom."

"I'll pay you," he said, "look . . ."

He showed me his wallet. It was so full of hundreds that he could hardly fold it to get it into his pocket.

"No money," I said.

"All right," he said, "we'll do it this way. Whoever wins at the track each day buys the meals and drinks."

"Suppose we both lose?" I asked.

"Are we that bad?"

"Some of us are."

So I drove out to the track each day with a companion. He was still the worst horseplayer I had ever met. He managed to fall upon the worst short-priced horse race after race. And his horses didn't even run. They just wearily trailed the field each race at prices like 5/2, 6/5, 3 to one, 7 to 2. How he could keep doing this so consistently I had no idea. But he did.

I took him to various places for dinner.

Once he complained, "This place is not as nice as some of those other places we've been."

"Maybe not," I answered, "but just this once, force the food and drink down somehow . . ."

Cosmos liked a couple of drinks before and a couple after dinner.

Afterwards we'd go back to my place and I'd open the wine and we'd sit there and then he'd want to watch the TV. So we drank and watched TV. Since he was the guest I let him select the programs. He liked the situation comedies with laugh tracks, the family, middle-class bits. Total nightmares of stupidity. You could guess each new line before it arrived. Steve laughed often: "Oh, this is very funny!"

I put it down as a difference in cultures.

Meanwhile, Cosmos could easily fold his wallet. The hundreds had gotten down to where he could glance at them in a moment.

"You ought to stick to roulette," I told him.

"It doesn't matter," Cosmos had said, "money is for nothing."

"Yeah," I had said, laying out my American Express card to the waiter.

Yes, I know I'm taking too long to tell this, but I want you to get the full flavor, whether it matters or not. It really means something but what it means I'm not sure. What are you doing now, anyhow? Just resting or hiding. Rest and hide within this crap . . .

Sasoon came back and rescued me, I got the call about noon, it was a Monday and nothing was running.

"They stole all the ducks and chickens, they broke in here and got all the food and the wine and all our clothes. They took everything but the typewriter. I don't think they knew what it was."

"Jeez, that's rough . . . Steve's been staying with me. He lost the key to your place."

"Hell, *they* didn't need a key! Has Steve been working on his life story?"

"Mostly, I guess, he's been living it."

"Could you put him on the phone?"

They spoke in rapid French. Cosmos waved his free arm. His pink face became red. They yelled at each other for five or six minutes. Then Steve hung up.

"He's like a father! He wants me to write! I'm no writer! He's going to stand behind me! Can you write with somebody standing behind you?"

"Not unless it's death."

"It's terrible with him! Each day he asks me, 'How many pages did you write?'"

"Writing's like fucking," I told him, "you have to want to do it and then sometimes you fail."

"I don't even want to fuck. Afterwards you have a woman around. What do you do with her? I jack-off! I jack-off to the walls!"

"Well, anyhow, Steve, father wants you back."

"You got any more beer?"

"Sure."

Cosmos drank four bottles of beer, got into his Mexican Special, backed out the drive and was gone. A lucky day for me: two writers in one house were one too many.

Now I could get something done. I took out a coin. Heads I jacked-off, tails I wrote.

I flipped the coin. I landed tails.

I walked in toward the typewriter.

Well, you couldn't have *all* your luck in one day.

Somehow Jean got Steve to writing. I didn't see him at the track anymore. Jean came over with the cameras and the sound equipment one day and we wrapped up the documentary. We drank beer and wine and sat outside and I said things. Responded mainly to questions. My 12 years in the post office, jive-assing with the blacks had taught me how to bullshit my way through. The neighborhood children tossed rocks at us. Some of their parents had informed them that I was an evil man. I drank and wrote dirty stories and lived with women half my age. Why should that bother them?

Afterwards, as the rocks got larger, we went inside. Sasoon showed me some of the pages Cosmos had written. They were quite good. Not the writing but the content. Lively and full of madness. And it was written in English. I had no idea why and didn't ask.

"You've got some good crap here," I told Cosmos.

He really liked that. He showed it.

"Thank you, my friend."

"Good writers watch other people live," I told him. "Great writers live and watch other people live."

"What do bad writers do?"

"Make money."

We drank a bit more and then everybody left. Well, not everybody. I was still there. I was a good writer, a great writer and a bad writer. And pretty fair with the horses.

Let's get rolling: some months went by. Sometimes I saw Cosmos at the track. Sometimes not. He was going through a series of girlfriends. I met some of them. Seemed nice. They all had good jobs, it seemed. But he borrowed money from them, lost it at the track, couldn't pay it back. The girls dropped away. Cosmos put an ad in the paper stating that he wanted to marry a woman with at least five children. He got many reponses and interviewed a great many women. He couldn't find the right one.

"They were all too fat," he told me.

"Why do you want a woman with so many children?"

"It's when you lose after gambling. You've got something to come home to."

"When I lose, all I want to see is a bottle, I don't want anybody around," I told him.

"No, it's nice to have somebody to come home to who doesn't treat you like a loser."

"They will after canned beans and peanut-butter sandwiches."

Cosmos finished his life story. They brought it over to me. I read it. It was very interesting. But a total maze. It needed *work*. They asked me if I might. I told them I couldn't. I was in my own maze.

It was all right. They got some guy. A scriptwriter, temporarily down. Leland LaCrosse. LaCrosse came over and we got totally drunk. LaCrosse claimed Copalla had fucked him over. Copalla owed him money. He was going to sue Copalla. LaCrosse was a very depressed person. He talked about Schopenhauer, he loved Schopenhauer. LaCrosse talked about suicide. He discussed suicide at some length. He talked sense, he was intelligent, but he was bogged down in self-pity. Depressed men seldom crashed through. Sometimes disgusted men did because when you're disgusted it elevates the frame of battle to some logical confrontation. Anyhow, LaCrosse agreed to straighten out the Cosmos script. I liked that: reworking Steve's script would have depressed me.

LaCrosse phoned me one night.

"I'm going to kill myself," he said. "I'm going to cut my wrists."

"That's very painful," I said. "As the blood runs out there will be spasms and contractions. To avoid this get into a tub of very warm water first and after you slice your wrists, hold them under water and stay that way with your body immersed. You'll find it almost painless."

LaCrosse hung up on me.

Evidently he didn't do it. The script got reworked.

Sasoon phoned.

"I'm going to Paris. I'm going to set this thing up. We're going to shoot on a very limited budget. As soon as I'm ready I'm going to send Steve an airline ticket. Meanwhile, he's on his allowance. Keep an eye on him."

"Sure, Jean . . ."

Things got lined up and Sasoon sent Cosmos the money for an airline ticket. Cosmos took the money and went down and purchased the ticket. He was to get a bit part in his own movie. It was to be shot in a famous casino where Steve was not yet in trouble. And best, it wasn't in France. Just near France.

Steve phoned. "You know," he said, "you always said I could stay for a week or two—"

"Yes," I said, thinking, *but you already have.*

"I've got to close this place down and then wait to fly over. I don't want to go now. Jean will put me to work doing some asshole thing. I don't want to go until they're ready to shoot. So—"

"All right," I sighed, "it's all right, Steve."

So again I had a companion with me at the track everyday.

"I have my allowance," he told me.

"Good," I said.

"Whoever wins," he said, "buys the dinner."

"Right."

First time out, he finally won. I got a dinner.

The next time, it wasn't so. Or the time after that. Or the time after that. Or the time . . .

"I don't care if I win or lose," he told me, "I just want to gamble."

"Yeah," I said.

"I can only talk to a gambler," he told me. "Nobody else knows anything."

"Yeah," I said.

Seven or eight days went by.

"If Jean calls tell him I'm not here. Tell him you think I took the plane."

"Aren't you going to?"

"The other day when I told you I was going to visit La-Crosse, I didn't. I went to the airport and cashed in the plane ticket."

"I wondered where you got the new money."

"Tomorrow I will hit it big," he said.

Then he told me that some day he was going to live in a castle with a woman with many children. He would grow his own food. He would have hunting dogs and stock fine wines.

"Do you have any of the plane-ticket money left?"

"Very little. But I feel I'm due for a big hit tomorrow.

Tomorrow and tomorrow and tomorrow. Each tomorrow was the same. Finally, he tapped out. He was standing next to me and he said, "My horse got left at the gate. That's it. I'm broke."

We walked over to the bar and I bought him a drink. You hated to lend a sum of money to a bad gambler; horses just weren't his horsemeat. It was the last race and I handed him a 20 and suggested he consider Night Fire, who was reading five to one. After I spoke, I knew I had said the wrong thing: I had talked him off of a possible winner. He went for a $20 exacta, Slim Bim to Night Fire. Of course they came in in reverse.

As we drove toward his favorite eating place, I thought, son of a bitch, this fellow may be living with me for the rest of my life. He's a fine sort. Inventive. Original in his way. Quite aware of death. Well-lived. He got a little loud and stupid when drunk but we all did. But to live a lifetime? With this buddy? I was used to solitude. Even when I had been a bum I had avoided the missions, preferred the park bench, the alley, anywhere but being with the mob. Being alone was all I had going for me when things got very ugly, it was the only thing which healed me.

Frankly, I was terrified.

"Life is for nothing," he said as we drove along . . .

We had our two opening rounds of drinks at the table and Steve loosened his charm upon the waitress. I was downcast and ordered as if I were the loser. Then I ordered another round of drinks.

Steve looked at me.

"Gamblers understand," he said.

"What do they understand?"

"Everything . . ."

That night at the place, I poured the wine heavily. Steve took out an expensive cigar and lit up.

"I'm all right," he said, "as long as I don't run out of these I'm all right. As long as I have my cigar I will make it."

"How they holding out?"

"Ho! I have *many* yet!"

Steve Cosmos was a class act.

The next day, after breakfast, he asked, "You going to the track today?"

"Yes," I said. "Listen, Steve, how'd you like to *earn* some money?"

"*Earn?*"

I took him out to the parkway in front of the house.

"Look at those weeds."

"I see them, ugly things."

"Yes, you're a landscape artist. Do you have some method of getting them of there?"

"Well—"

"Fifteen dollars an hour—"

"Eighteen—"

"You're on . . ."

I really felt terrible as I pulled out the drive that morning about Steve. I felt like a hunk of shit. I felt like a man acting in bad style. I probably was.

I waved to him and drove off to the track.

As I looked in the rearview mirror he was leaning upon the hoe, contemplating . . .

I had gotten a cable from Sasoon:

"Where's Steve? Phoned the place, no answer. Phoned your place, you do not answer. Ready to begin shooting film. Sent money for air ticket to Steve. Urgent he get here. Reply.

                                        Jean"

It looked like a good card out there. Small fields. I liked small fields. But it wasn't any good: I lost.

When I got back in, Cosmos was well into a beer-drunk. I had a closet full of Budweiser.

He looked up from his cigar.

"I got the weeds. Come, I show you."

We walked out front. He had done quite well.

"There will be no weeds for a year now. You will see."

But he had left one little square of weeds, neatly blocked off, a square of about two feet by four.

"This still needs to be done."

Steve knew as I did, that if we didn't get those out of there all the other work was wasted.

I gave him $140.

Then we went out to dinner.

Need I tell you? We lost it out there the next day. We stopped for a new case of wine on the way in and popped it open upon arrival at the place. We shared a bottle, went out to eat. We tried a new place. The waiter went off for our drinks. The place had piped-in music. When the waiter came back with our libations, Cosmos spoke to him.

"I insist you either get better music in here or shut it off!"

Steve had upbringing. I had come from a lower-middle-class family.

"Steve, do you want to get that plot of weeds tomorrow?"

"If you insist."

"It's up to you."

"It might take some time. The roots are deeply imbedded."

"I'm sure they are."

"Eighteen an hour?"

"Raise you two," I said.

"I'll call . . ."

As the days went on Steve switched to the inner garden. I played the horses in the day and he played them at night. We had some drinks when he came in. Our new pattern was established. When he finished the garden I'd have him paint the house.

I cabled Sasoon to go ahead and shoot the parts without Cosmos.

Then one night Cosmos didn't return from the harness races. I drank a couple of bottles of wine, wrote four bad poems and two good ones. It was just like old times. I figured Steve was laying up with some new girl. I was glad for him.

About 10 A.M. I came down the stairway for something for my hangover and noticed that the guest bedroom door was open. Cosmos had neatly made the bed and upon it was a note:

"*Ank,*

I hit a big exacta last night. Know a guy who wants to buy my car. Am flying over to movie location. I have money for the ticket. I will now be a great movie star. Thanks for letting me stay at your place and for all the good wine.

Steve."

The note made me feel ashamed. I had been so cheap. Steve had pulled it out. I was not very much. I had some way to go. Growing was difficult, I did it so slowly and the years were running out.

How do you say it? Some weeks went by. Then there was a letter from Sasoon:

"*Dear Hank:*

Steve arrived. His part in the movie is to be the director of the casino. We shoot in the daytime. Then at night when the casino opens Steve still thinks he's the director at the casino. He cheats openly at the tables and demands his money. Since we use the casino employees in the movie during the day there is some confusion. Also, since he is not a writer and *an actor he has met some of the people and borrowed money from them. You know what that means. He gave one man a very large check in exchange for funds. The check bounced, came back. The man showed it to Steve and Steve insisted that there must be some mistake, he's going to check with his bank, it's impossible that the check is no good . . .*

Everything else is a mess, too. We are running out of funds. At first we hired the regular people who played the casino at night to act in our movie during the day. Now we must pick up the bums from the street and dress them in proper clothing, which we rent, but it's cheaper that way—and they look just the same as the regular people.

Also, the wife of the biggest producer backing this movie has fallen in love with Steve. She threatens to leave the producer for Steve, and since the producer doesn't want to lose her, they all rather live together, eat together, all that. She is a beautiful and intelligent woman. They go to the gaming tables together and Steve is totally insane, grabbing chips, spilling drinks over himself, shouting passages from Schopenhauer, vomiting upon ladies' dresses, exclaiming that Death is Everywhere, that it is crawling through his intestines like shit, that everything is shit. He is now the brilliant writer-actor. He has been interviewed for several journals but insists that they don't take his photograph, says a camera would destroy his soul, most likely means his ass . . .

Will let you know as more unfolds.

> *Best,*
> *Jean"*

All right, skip two months. Like that. Did you do it? Fine.

There's another letter from Sasoon. He's in Paris.

"Dear Hank:

We finished the movie. Much trouble with shooting Steve. I'd tell him to talk there, say this, then he'd do something else. It kept on and on. It was terrible. But we finished. And since Barbette played the female lead we were all right there. Now editing the film. Steve stayed to be with the producer's wife.

Good luck with your documentary. A major TV station bought it. They are going to show it on prime time. Every night. But they want it broken up into segments of six minutes or less. Much work to be done there but we have fourteen hours of you and ought to get some good segments out of it.

With Steve things are not going as well with the producer's wife as before. She stays with the producer at night in the villa and meets Steve secretly during the day. Steve has borrowed too much money from her which he can't repay. And he has been barred from the casino. I send him bits of money when I can.

He writes me, 'Since I have become a writer and an actor I am more broke than I have ever been. I have holes in the bottoms of my shoes and I sleep with the bums at night on the park benches. I know each of them by name. When it rains we try to hang out in the train station but the police run us off. I am at the absolute bottom, completely dissolute and destitute, and as full of despair, I guess, as a man can get. I am too spiritually weak and inept to even kill myself. If I killed myself where would they put me? Just on another park bench in hell . . . There is no escape from anything. I don't even have the ability to go mad.'"

Poor Steve. I had never gotten the story quite straight because I had heard it from both Steve and Jean, and both times during heavy drinking, but it translates something like this:

As a young man Steve Cosmos had entered a casino with a small sum of money and he had no idea how the game worked. He had walked up to the wheel and placed a wager. He won. He just left the money there. And won again and again. I mean, he left the chips there, you know. He still left them there when he went to the men's room, and when he came back he had won an enormous sum: $19,000. Does this seem possible? Or maybe I don't have it quite right. I remember the sum, though: $19,000. Cosmos went to the cage to collect and they asked him if he wanted a check or cash. He took the cash.

There was a very handsome woman about that night and Steve mentioned to somebody that he wanted that woman. That somebody told him that that was impossible, that that simply was not that kind of woman. He told this somebody that he would give this woman $2,000 for her favors. They went up to a room in the casino and that was that. Steve was hooked. He hung around casinos. He met some con artists. They went from casino to casino doing their tricks. Cosmos told me many of them which I don't have the freedom to divulge here. Except one. They had an electronically controlled roulette ball which they could make drop into any number. The button was operated from a fake package of cigarettes. All they had to do was switch balls, which was easy enough to do with a screen of distraction and fast hands. The ball was very delicate, however, and one night during a good run it exploded. They left their winnings there for a quick exit.

The gang went from city to city around the world. They became known and had to wear disguises. At times they got enough money, wearied of it, split, only to meet and start up again.

In between times, my friend Steve learned other tricks. Besides passing bad checks with fake I.D.'s, he had a little camera, and with this little camera he walked up to expensive cars, put the little camera against the door lock and snapped the shutter. When the film was developed it showed the inside grooves of the lock. A key was made from this. Then

Cosmos would go back to the car, open the door, jump-start the car and drive it off. He stole a great many cars this way. A steering-wheel lock meant nothing: he could break one down on an average of one minute and 15 seconds.

And he lived for free in the finest of hotels. He ran up huge sums and merely walked out, leaving an empty suitcase in the room with a note:

"Thank you so much for everything."

A man like that could never consider an eight-hour job.

And there I had had him pulling weeds out of my garden . . .

And there was no way I could ever write about him because then the law would have me for harboring a criminal and the French Mafia would be after my ass, but I sat around thinking about the whole thing. I could present it as a work of fiction and then in the fiction I could say it was real. It was too long for a short story and not long enough for a novel. Well, shit.

I had just finished my fourth novel and my favorite cat had died, a real tough son of a bitch, and Cristina and I were having our problems, but the racetrack was still there. I really loved that place, all those places, Anita, Hollywood Park, Los Alamitos. Del Mar and Pomona you could have. But the track was the best shrink I could ever have. It taught me about myself, the others, everything. It was the open lesson of balance and chance, it was a flash of lighting and it was the durability of the gods. It was the place for me.

I drove into valet and the guy who handed me the yellow stub said, "You been sick, champ?"

And I said, "No, what makes you ask?"

"Didn't see you yesterday," he said.

"How's your wife and family?" I asked.

"Fine," he said.

"That's great," I said.

I walked on in and checked the program. Lots of maiden races. Good. My favorite play. Very little public information. But I had a method of detecting where my solid money was going.

By the fourth race I was $225 ahead, sitting there, checking my program against the racing form and the board action when I sensed somebody sitting behind me. I could feel him there, looking over my shoulder. I didn't like anybody near me. I moved on down. I felt this same figure following me, sitting down behind me again. I am one who is not too fond of humanity, even those who we are told are great, even those sicken me, so, you see, I didn't like anybody around, so I turned and I said, "Hey, look, you son of a bitch—"

And, you guessed it, it was Steve Cosmos.

"Ank—" he said.

"Well, baby," I said, "all I can let you have is a twenty—"

"Don't worry, my friend," he said. He pulled out a huge roll of money, very green, very fat, very legal.

"What are you doing here?" I asked.

"I could ask you the same. How about a drink?"

"Fine."

We walked up to the bar. Steve had a double whiskey and water. I ordered a vodka tonic.

"Who do you like in this race?" he asked.

"Well, if the board doesn't change too much I like Blue Fire."

"Far Dream will win," he said.

"You ought to lay off those big closers," I said. "I keep telling you that over and over but you won't listen."

"Far Dream will win. There will be a fast pace."

"The old textbook approach. The game is different now. Nowadays the speed of the speed usually wins."

"Winner buys dinner?" Cosmos asked.

"Winner buys dinner," I said.

We raised our drinks, clicked them, drained them off.

SOURCES

Open City, June 23–29, 1967

Open City, July 7–13, 1967

Open City, December 29, 1967–January 4, 1968

Open City, October 25–31, 1968

Open City, January 24–30, 1969

NOLA Express, December 31, 1971– January 13, 1972

NOLA Express, February 25, 1972

Los Angeles Free Press, July 7, 1972

Los Angeles Free Press, February 9, 1973

Los Angeles Free Press, February 23, 1973

Los Angeles Free Press, June 15, 1973

"Bukowski Takes a Trip: No Nudie Bars," *Los Angeles Free Press*, August 3 and August 10, 1973

Los Angeles Free Press, September 28, 1973

NOLA Express, November 2–15, 1973

Open City, June 16–22, 1967

Los Angeles Free Press, January 18, 1974

Los Angeles Free Press, August 2, 1974

Los Angeles Free Press, September 6, 1974

Los Angeles Free Press, October 4, 1974

Los Angeles Free Press, December 13, 1974

Los Angeles Free Press, March 7, 1975

Los Angeles Free Press, April 4, 1975

Los Angeles Free Press, May 16 and May 23, 1975

Los Angeles Free Press, July 11, 1975

Los Angeles Free Press, July 18, 1975

Smoke Signals, Vol 2. No. 4, 1982

"Ecce Hetero: Bukowski's Thoughts to Live By," *High Times*, February 1983

"Night on the Town," *High Times*, December 1983

"My Friend, The Gambler," *High Times*, October 1984

AFTERWORD

by David Stephen Calonne

Nineteen sixty-nine was Charles Bukowski's *annus mirabilis*: *Penguin Modern Poets 13* (Bukowski, Lamantia, Norse), a volume in the distinguished British series devoted to contemporary poets edited by Nikos Stangos in London, *A Bukowski Sampler*, and *The Days Run Away Like Wild Horses Over the Hills* were published. And, perhaps most significantly for his transformation from a largely unknown "underground" writer to a literary figure with an international reputation, *Notes of a Dirty Old Man* appeared on January 24, 1969, from Essex House, a small North Hollywood publisher specializing in erotica, in an edition of approximately 28,000 copies.[1] The genesis of the book was aided by the efforts of an indefatigable editor named John Bryan. Bukowski had appeared previously in several Bryan publications: as early as July 1961 in *Renaissance*, with his poem "The Way to Review a Play"; in 1962, again in *Renaissance*, with his essay "Peace, Baby, Is Hard Sell"; and in 1964, in the magazine *Notes from Underground*, with his story "A Murder." In San Francisco in November 1964, Bryan started *Open City*, then known as *San Francisco Open City Press*, which continued for fifteen issues. Bukowski's brief story "If I Could Only Be Asleep" appeared in the January 1966 issue.[2] Bryan had been in San Francisco when the owner of the *Los Angeles Free Press* asked him to move to Los Angeles to help with the newly inaugurated newspaper: he became managing editor and was responsible for significantly increasing its circulation.

Then in 1967, Bryan decided to start his own newspaper

in Los Angeles—*Open City*—and asked Bukowski to contribute, agreeing to pay him $10 a week. Bukowski claims in his autobiographical essay "Dirty Old Man Confesses" that it was he who invented the title (echoing one of his favorite books, Dostoyevsky's *Notes from Underground*): "one day John Bryan decided to start an Underground newspaper called *Open City*. I was asked to contribute a column a week. I called the column 'Notes of A Dirty Old Man.'"[3] The debut installment appeared in the May 12–18, 1967, issue.[4] Bryan would publish 93 issues, ending in March 1969, with Bukowski appearing in 89 of them.[5] In his Foreword to *Notes of A Dirty Old Man*, Bukowski described the ease and pleasure of his new assignment:

> Then one day after the races, I sat down and wrote the heading, NOTES OF A DIRTY OLD MAN, opened a beer, and the writing got done by itself. There was not the tenseness or the careful carving with a bit of a dull blade, that was needed to write something for the *Atlantic Monthly*. . . . There seemed to be no pressures. Just sit by the window, lift the beer and let it come. Anything that wanted to arrive, arrived.[6]

Bukowski went on to describe the *Sturm und Drang* involved with writing and publishing poetry—sometimes he would wait two to five years to see a poem in print after it was accepted—but "with NOTES, sit down with a beer and hit the typer on a Friday or a Saturday or a Sunday and by Wednesday the thing is all over the city."[7]

Bukowski was thrilled by the birth of his first volume of prose and dashed off a happy self-review for *Open City*:

How many times can a man go through the thresh-
er and still keep his blood, the Summer sun inside
his head? How many bad jails, how many bad
women, how many sundry cancers, how many
flat tires, how many this or that or what or what
or what? . . .

Frankly I read my own stories in easy wonder-
ment, forgetting who I was, almost almost, and I
thought: Ummm, ummm, this son of a bitch can
really write.[8]

The offer from Bryan actually came just at the right
time, because Bukowski had already been composing prose
for the past few years. In 1965, Douglas Blazek published
Confessions of a Man Insane Enough to Live with Beasts—a story in nine sections dealing with Bukowski's life from childhood through his marriage to and divorce from Barbara
Frye—and in the following year *All the Assholes in the World
and Mine*, a hilarious account of his hemorrhoid operation.
Now he had contracted to produce a weekly column: the
discipline of the deadline opened the creative floodgates.
Open City, and subsequently *NOLA Express* and the *Los Angeles Free Press*, gave Bukowski the opportunity to mine his
past experiences and to try out various treatments of material which he would later transform in his novels *Post Office*,
Factotum, *Women*, and *Ham on Rye*.

Notes of A Dirty Old Man was reprinted in 1973 by City
Lights and since then has been continuously in print. The
series became a forum where Bukowski presented stories,
essays, poems, interviews, even several cartoons (now more
elegantly christened "graphic fiction"). However, the original book contained only forty of the hundreds of works he
submitted under the "Dirty Old Man" rubric: other columns

would later be collected in *Erections, Ejaculations and Other Tales of Ordinary Madness* (1972), *South of No North* (1974), and *Hot Water Music* (1983), as well as in the posthumous volumes *Portions from a Wine-Stained Notebook* (2008) and *Absence of the Hero* (2010). *Notes of a Dirty Old Man* met with international success: Bukowski had broken through into new territory in American literature. He was a strange, compelling creature: a "drop out" from the mainstream, a "working-class" artist in love with "high culture"—Beethoven, Mahler, Sibelius, Stravinsky, Catullus, Li Po, Céline, and Dostoyevsky—and composing a hip, direct, swiftly moving prose, a new American argot: "vulgarity" punctuated by sudden, exquisite flights of lyrical sensitivity.[9]

Bukowski first read Dostoyevsky in the early forties in the El Paso Public Library.[10] And on the opening page of *Notes of a Dirty Old Man*, the narrator tells us that he was "a student of Dostoevski and listened to Mahler in the dark."[11] Like Dostoyevsky's character in *Notes from Underground*, many of Bukowski's Dionysian poets, dreamers, and misfits are half-mad, angry, impetuous, inspired, ecstatic. The title precisely describes Bukowski's aim: he combines Dostoyevskian "notes" with the American slang expression "dirty old man," thus mixing the Eastern European tradition of dark psyches at war with themselves and others with a cool, subversive American style informed by all the countercultural themes and obsessions of the sixties and seventies.

For example, in the story depicting his trip to New Orleans, his wit and verve can be seen in the abrupt, telegraphic opening: "Going east. In the barcar. They had sent me money for the barcar. Of course, I had a pint getting on and had stopped for a pint at El Paso. I was the world's greatest poet and he was the world's greatest editor and bookmaker (and I'm not talking about horses)." The repetition of the primarily mono- and disyllabic words—"barcar," "pint," "greatest poet," "greatest editor"—and stop-and-go syntax mirror the sound of the chugging and clattering train as it sets out on its journey. The narrative then grows organically, one element of plot added to another in a natural, effortless way. This skill was the product of years of labor, although what was new in Bukowski's style of the sixties was this rapid movement of a shrewd, tough intelligence under the influence of the new, heady, casual openness of the Age of Aquarius.

The compulsive eroticism of the series was at once a clever way to attract attention to his writing (as well as to sell newspapers) and an exploration of sex and love as the ultimate arena in which the frequently comic struggle for selfhood takes place. Bukowski often sees the sexual drama as an insane farce:

> So, to some writers, including the gloriously im-
> pertinent Bukowski, sex is obviously the tragi-
> comedy. I don't write about it as an instrument
> of obsession. I write about it as a stage play laugh
> where you have to cry about it, a bit, between acts.
> Giovanni Boccaccio wrote it much better. He had
> the distance and the style. I am still too near the
> target to effect total grace. People simply think I'm
> dirty. If you haven't read Boccaccio, do. You might
> begin with *The Decameron*.[12]

Interestingly, Pasolini's film version of *The Decameron* (1970) appeared the year following the publication of *Notes of a Dirty Old Man*, and Boccaccio (1313–1375) served as Bukowski's thematic and structural model for his novel *Women*: *The Decameron* has 101 chapters, *Women*, 104. The other great Italian (Roman) writer to whom Bukowski was most devoted was Gaius Valerius Catullus (ca. 84–54 B.C.), to whom he wrote several homages, including the humorous poem "what have I seen" in which he imagines seeing Catullus at the race track bar in the company of a lady of questionable virtue: "I like your way, Catullus, talking plainly about the / whore who claims you owe her money, or about / that guy who smiled too much—who cleaned / his teeth with horse piss, / or about how the young poets / come with their blameless tame verse, or about / how this or that guy married a slut."[13] Although he played brilliantly the role of an anti-intellectual primitive, Bukowski would bring his considerable knowledge of world literature to bear in his portrayal of the human sexual comedy.

Bukowski explores a good deal of taboo territory, every form of sexual expression, "perversion," or "deviancy." We are introduced to a gallery of characters worthy of Wilhelm Stekel, or Krafft-Ebing's *Psychopathia Sexualis*. Although he surely did not intend in a conscious way to present such an encyclopedic summary of paraphiliae, "Notes of a Dirty Old Man," over the course of the column's lengthy run, would provide portrayals of child rape, castration, anal intercourse, three females picking up and ravishing a man, intercourse with a high-heeled shoe, voyeurism, bestiality, sexual role playing (in which a man is treated as a child by a middle-aged woman), fetishism, onanism, necrophilia, and violent sadism. Surely part of the success of the series was due to the fact that Bukowski said things that many people would have liked to say but lacked the courage to express. He took the lid off the id; he is "unrepressed" in his insistent uncovering of the submerged activity of the libido in the unconscious.

As Michel Foucault asserts in *The History of Sexuality*:

The legitimate couple, with its regular sexuality, had a right to more discretion. It tended to function as a norm, one that was stricter, but quieter. On the other hand, what came under scrutiny was the sexuality of children, mad men and women, and criminals; the sensuality of those who did not like the opposite sex; reveries, obsessions, petty manias, of great transports of rage. It was time for all these figures, scarcely noticed in the past, to step forward and speak, to make the difficult confession of what they were. No doubt they were condemned all the same; but they were listened to; and if regular sexuality happened to be questioned once again, it was through a reflux movement, originating in these peripheral sexualities.[14]

Bukowski provides an often humorous opportunity—as if to lessen the pain of the revelation—for these various characters to make a "confession of what they were." And even "the legitimate couple"—in, for example, the story of the couple in bed in which the wife is dreaming of intercourse with another man and the husband confesses to incestuous longings—is exposed in Bukowski as harboring dark secrets lurking beneath the surface of conscious awareness.

Yet Bukowski, like D.H. Lawrence, sought a more natural expression of sexuality which was constantly frustrated by our alienating, cold, technocratic society. He writes in his NOLA essay of December 31, 1971–January 13, 1972 about

all these people, the love-lost, the sex-lost, the suicide-driven . . . somewhere in the structure of our society it is impossible for these people to contact each other. Churches, dances, parties only seem to push them further apart, and the dating clubs, the Computer Love Machines only destroy more and more a naturalness that should have been: a naturalness that has somehow been crushed and seems to remain crushed forever in our present method of living (dying). See them put on their bright clothes and get into their new cars and roar off to NOWHERE. It's all an outside maneuver and the contact is missed.

It is possible to read Bukowski's elaboration of all the varieties of sexual behavior as a kind of diagnosis of the ills of our culture, of the ways this "naturalness" has been subverted. The inhibition of this need to make "contact" with one another is precisely what has led to the frequently frenetic efforts of the caged human animal to break out of its traps in whatever ways it can devise—even if this means amputating parts of itself as it attempts to break free from the manacles.

Bukowski's column would also appear in *NOLA Express* edited by Darlene Fife and her husband Robert Head. Fife explains in her memoir *Portraits from Memory: New Orleans in the Sixties* that her husband

had read Bukowski in one of the mimeo mags and wrote asking him for submissions. We published him from late '68 [the first "Dirty Old Man" column was actually August 15–28, 1969] to the end of *Nola Express* in January, 1974. He sent us poems or, most often short stories every two weeks; always clean copy, always on time. He took his responsibilities to his editors seriously. His writings elicited more letters to the editor both for and against than any other. Bukowski occasionally responded to the letters with his own letter to the editor. We paid him $25 for each published piece. As little as this is, Bukowski told us it was this money that gave him the courage to quit his job in the post office.[15]

Bukowski never met the couple and they spoke only once by phone, but he sent a letter of support when *NOLA* encountered censorship difficulties: it appeared in issue #53 of April, 1970 in the typical, mainly lower-case style he favored during this period:

> you are the liveliest thing happening in the U.S. right now. you've always layed your guts right on the line without laying on this juvenile hippy Romanticism which destroys papers like the *Berkeley Tribe*. don't put me down as anti-hip or yip or whatever, but somehow building those paper heroes has destroyed the force of what really needs to be said. each issue of NOLA is a thing I read over and over. it's magic . . . Wrote *Evergreen* about you people, hoping they can break the back of whatever is trying to break you. your courage is the quietest poem of all. you make me feel good when very few things do.[16]

By this time, Bukowski had experienced difficulties of his own with the "authorities": in 1968 the FBI began to investigate him. He would eventually leave the Post Office— not only because John Martin offered him a monthly stipend to quit and write full time, but most likely because he was about to be dismissed, not for supposed "absenteeism" but due to his work for *Open City*, a clear violation of his right to free speech. Bukowski's FBI file also indicates that they began to investigate his "common law wife"—this was clearly Frances Smith, although her name has been redacted from the file—who "has been reported to have attended a number of Communist Party meetings in the Los Angeles area." The file indicates "that one Charles Bukowski, poet, was the author of an article appearing on page 43 of the June, 1963, issue of 'Mainstream.'" This essay, which Bukowski had submitted about the "little magazines," contained some X-ed out language which the editor, Felix Singer, saw fit to censor. The report continues:

> The March, (1968) edition of the "Underground Digest, The Best of the Underground Press," Volume I, published by the Underground Communications, Inc., P.O. Box 211, Village Station, New York, New York 10014, telephone WI 7-6900, contains an article by Charles Bukowski on pages 76-79 entitled "Notes of a Dirty Old Man." Page 79 indicates that the writer's name may be Henry Charles Bukowski. The publication indicates at the end of the article on page 79 that the article may have originally appeared in "Open City" 5420 Carlton Way, Los Angeles, California 90027; $5 per year. Single copies of the article "Notes of a Dirty Old Man" together with a copy of the masthead of the Underground Digest are enclosed for New York and Los Angeles under obscene cover.
>
> New York and Los Angeles should make discreet efforts to resolve whether this article and the item appearing in the June, 1963, issue of "Mainstream" were written by the employee. If

employee's authorship is indicated copies of the articles should be designated as exhibits.[17]

It is clear that the FBI was conducting surveillance in the attempt to fathom Bukowski's political commitments during this time as well as to build a dossier against him in which his "obscene" writings for the underground press would be cited as evidence. Four "exhibits" were included at the end of the FBI report: (A) an essay about Leroi Jones from *Open City*, Dec. 8–14, 1967;[18] (B) a column about a sexual encounter with a woman with red hair from *Open City*, Dec. 29–Jan. 4 1969, which is included in this volume; (C) a column from *Open City*, January 12–17 1968 collected in *Erections* as "Great Poets Die in Steaming Pots of Shit";[19] and (D) a March, 1968 column beginning "when Henry's mother died it wasn't bad" from *Underground Digest*, which appeared originally in *Open City*, October 18–24, 1967, and was included in *Notes of A Dirty Old Man*.[20]

The final newspaper carrying the series (and the place where it had the longest run—February 1972–September 1976) was the *Los Angeles Free Press*. This incarnation was more artistically oriented, with a special "Dirty Old Man" logo appearing at the beginning of each installment depicting a comically mustachioed man with a bemused visage, a stubble beard, floppy hat, very large shoes, cigar in mouth, pen in hand making notes in a spiral notebook. "The Dirty Old Man" was now a recognizable brand. In addition, many of the installments were accompanied by Bukowski's entertaining, Thurberesque drawings, placed at strategic points in the narrative. He even submitted a series of cartoons, "The Adventures of Clarence H. Sweetmeat," which appeared in the September 19–25, 1975, and October 24–30, 1975, issues. The editor, Art Kunkin, continued the policy of

Open City and *NOLA Express* of allowing Bukowski virtual carte blanche in terms of language, style, and subject matter.

The late sixties and early seventies were a volatile time in the gender wars. Kate Millett's *Sexual Politics* (1970), Norman Mailer's *The Prisoner of Sex* (1971), Germaine Greer's *The Female Eunuch* (1971), and Erica Jong's *Fear of Flying* (1973) (the novel on the nightstand of the travel agent ravished in one of Bukowski's columns) were all summary statements of the sexual revolution. The racial, political, social, and military convulsions of the times are also represented in Bukowski's prescient commentary on current events such as gas rationing, as in the January 18, 1974, column: "Americans have cheated and lied for so long, have become so decayed under the great moral Bob Hope front that I wonder why justice hasn't arrived and all our streets and boulevards do not have Chinese names. We babies, you and I, have been saved by our atomic stockpiles, not our ingeniousness, our guts, our souls, our courage." And in another column he considered the oil crisis: "Who could have believed that the Arabs and their near–monopoly on oil could have caused massive layoffs here?" The story about the survivor Robert Grissom—a holdout in between the two forces of Revolutionaries and Government in a post-apocalyptic America—presages the plot of a famous recent novel, Cormac McCarthy's *The Road*. Grissom has many characteristics in common with his creator: he listens to Mahler and Stravinsky, he is solitary, and he has gotten in trouble for his writings. This is clearly a reference to the period in 1968 when Bukowski began to be investigated by the FBI. And, in a later, 1982 incarnation of the column in *Smoke Signals*, Norman Mailer's involvement in the Jack Abbot case is wittily observed.[21]

Bukowski chronicled the sixties and seventies counterculture in his own inimitable fashion, and in some ways considered himself to have been the first "hippie" back in the thirties and forties. Bukowski had defended the hippies from the attacks of his publisher, Jon Webb: "Why not let your hair grow and smoke a bit of grass? Relax. Take each moment as a miracle gift. I was that way before the invention of the Bomb. I was hip on the premise born before the hips—if a man is going to die, why stockpile useless human possessions?"[22] And during World War II, Bukowski was a pacifist:

> I was anti-war in a time of pro-war. I couldn't tell a good war from a bad one—I still can't. I was a hippie when there weren't any hippies; I was a beat before the beats.
>
> I was a protest march, alone.
>
> I was in some Underground like a blind mole and no other moles even existed.
>
> This is why I couldn't adjust my sights, make sense of it. I had already done it all. And when Tim Leary advised "drop out" twenty-five years after I had already dropped out, I couldn't get excited. Leary's big "drop out" was a loss of a professorship somewhere (Harvard?)
>
> I was the Underground when there wasn't any Underground.[23]

This attitude is reflected in the story recounting his irritation with his co-worker's attitude toward the counterculture, which he contrasts with his own more accepting stance. However, as we saw above, this did not mean that Bukowski was uncritical of the youth movement. As he wrote to Darlene Fife, he objected to "this juvenile hippie

Romanticism which destroys papers like the *Berkeley Tribe*." Bukowski wanted perhaps a bit of *Realitätsprinzip*—a bit of German toughness and backbone to accompany all the peace and love. Like Robert Grissom, Bukowski ultimately identified with neither side of the cultural conflict, rejecting conformity with mainstream American society even as he remained skeptical of the counterculture's attempts to revolutionize it.

Notes of A Dirty Old Man also allowed Bukowski the opportunity to explore his experiences from childhood to the present and to transform them into thinly veiled autobiographical fiction. The series became a kind of extended *roman à clef* in which the events of Bukowski's life were treated in a variety of imaginative ways. For example, his traumatic childhood is portrayed in the tale concerning Petey, a 13-year-old boy with "strict parents." At the close the narrative veers into the fantastic as his abusive parents meet their deserved terrible fate. In one column, Bukowski interviews his publisher Jon Webb and discusses the art of book-making: Webb and his wife Gypsy Lou published *The Outsider* magazine as well as Bukowski's *It Catches My Heart in Its Hands* (1963); in another narrative, he describes a rollicking journey by train to New Orleans to visit the Webbs in order to work on the second, lavishly produced book of his poetry, *Crucifix in a Deathhand* (1965). Yet another story, describing a trip with his daughter to the beach at Venice, packs a good deal of Bukowski's life *aetatis* 52 into a brief space: his separation from Frances Smith, the tension between the estranged couple, his love for their daughter Marina, and his struggle to preserve a balance in his own life between destruction and creativity, between hate and love. The swift narrative movement, deft dialogue, and terse descriptive style poignantly reveal the tender connection between father and daughter as adult ugliness and violence threaten the sand castle she has constructed, symbolic of the fragile innocent world of childhood.

A love triangle involving Bukowski's then-girlfriend Linda King becomes a tale of an evening watching the fights with "Patricia" at the Olympic Auditorium. And in July 1973, Bukowski went with King on a trip to Utah and got lost in the woods, which is reflected in an extended comic sequence which was later partially used in his novel *Women*, yet with significant passages omitted: for example, the lovely scene of his encounter with the brown eyes of the squirrel, which so moved him that he refrained from committing suicide. His burgeoning fame as a reader of his poetry is humorously sketched in a tale of his trip to Detroit. And we are given a portrait of the artist as an older man in "My Friend, the Gambler," which describes the preliminary stages of the creation of the film *Barfly*. Now Bukowski is sixty-five, suddenly immersed in the Hollywood whirl (which he would satirize in his 1987 novel *Hollywood*) along with the film director Barbet Schroeder ("Jean Sasoon") and Bukowski's wife Linda Lee Beighle ("Cristina").

From January 1983 to December 1984, Bukowski contributed "Notes of a Dirty Old Man" to *High Times* magazine. In addition to the long story "My Friend, the Gambler," he also composed a lively set of aphorisms entitled "Ecce Hetero." Like La Rochefoucauld, Nietzsche (the title is a play on Nietzsche's book *Ecce Homo*), and E.M. Cioran, he was especially fond of the form, examples of which are scattered throughout his work. In *Notes of A Dirty Old Man*, some of the finest are: "The difference between Art and Life is that Art is more bearable" (a variation on Nietzsche's "We have Art so we will not perish from Truth"); "I'd rather hear about a live American bum than a dead Greek God"; "There is nothing more boring than the truth"; "The well balanced individual is insane"; "Sexual intercourse is kicking death in the ass while singing"; "An intellectual is a man who says a simple thing in a difficult way; an artist is a man who says a difficult thing in a simple way." Other Bukowskian wisdoms include: "The problem with women is that they are problems" and "I like dogs better than men and cats better than dogs and myself best of all, drunk in my underwear looking out the window." Thus we see in his *High Times* column his continued affection for the form.

Notes of A Dirty Old Man—the book as well as uncollected columns—would have an impact on other artists. They would be read attentively by a young musician named Tom Waits: "I just thought this was remarkable . . . This guy's the writer of the century and he's being published in this kind of street rag, which seemed kind of poetic and perfect . . . and of course you felt much more like you had discovered him as well—that he wasn't being brought to you but you had to dig and find *him*."[24] And Raymond Carver's biographer notes that "*Open City*, the city's alternative paper, ran a weekly screed of stories and opinion called 'Notes of A Dirty Old Man,' by Charles Bukowski, then a middle-aged postal worker and little-known poet. Ray liked Southern California so well for a couple of weeks that he thought of settling there."[25] Carver said that Bukowski had been "a kind of hero" to him.[26] Bukowski's "new journalism" was a creative and imaginative use of all his genius as a writer to inspire and shock his readers into a new engagement with the truths of intractable reality. And more than forty years after the Dirty Old Man was born, he will surely find new fans among those hungering for alternatives to the trivia offered by what still passes for American culture today.

NOTES

1. Aaron Krumhansl, *A Descriptive Bibliography of the Primary Publications of Charles Bukowski.* Santa Rosa: Black Sparrow Press, 1999, p. 41.

2. "If I Only Could Be Asleep," in *Absence of the Hero: Uncollected Stories and Essays Vol. 2, 1946–1992,* ed. David Stephen Calonne. San Francisco: City Lights, 2010, pp. 42–43.

3. Bukowski, "Dirty Old Man Confesses," in *Portions from a Wine-Stained Notebook,* ed. David Stephen Calonne. San Francisco: City Lights, 2008, p. 102. On the *LA Free Press,* see John McMillian, *Smoking Typewriters: The Sixties Underground Press and the Rise of Alternative Media in America* (New York: Oxford University Press, 2011), pp. 37–46. According to McMillian: "In 1967, one irate staffer, John Bryan, left the Freep to start a rival paper (*Open City*) after Kunkin refused to print a photograph of a disfigured napalm victim (apparently for fear of offending advertisers)," p. 239, no. 84.

4. Bukowski had published a review of the *Artaud Anthology* in the *Los Angeles Free Press* on April 22, 1966. See *Portions,* pp. 49–53. A week before the debut of the first "Notes of a Dirty Old Man" column, Bukowski's review of A.E. Hotchner's biography of Ernest Hemingway, "An Old Drunk Who Ran Out of Luck," appeared in the May 5–11 issue of *Open City.* See *Portions,* pp. 54–56.

5. Scott Harrison, former proprietor of the Abandoned Planet bookstore in San Francisco, kindly supplied me with information about John Bryan and *Open City.*

6. Bukowski, "Foreword," *Notes of A Dirty Old Man.* San Francisco: City Lights, 1973, p. 6.

7. *Ibid.* p. 6.

8. "Bukowski on Bukowski," *Absence of the Hero,* p. 57.

9. On the "working class" and literature, see *The Columbia Companion to the Twentieth-Century American Short Story,* ed. Blanche H. Gelfant (New York: Columbia University Press, 2000); Larry Smith, "The American Working-Class Short Story," pp. 81–93.

10. See Howard Sounes, *Charles Bukowski: Locked in the Arms of a Crazy Life* (Edinburgh: Canongate, 2010), p. 21; Dostoevsky was also a major influence on the Beats as well as on Henry Miller. See Maria Bloshteyn, *The Making of a Counterculture Icon: Henry Miller's Dostoevsky* (Toronto: University of Toronto Press, 2007). On Bukowski and Dostoevsky, see *Charles Bukowski: Sunlight Here I Am/Interviews & Encounters 1963–1993*, ed. David Stephen Calonne (Northville: Sundog Press, 2003), pp. 41, 74, 139, 180–81, 198, 243, 267, 269, 275.

11. Bukowski, *Notes of A Dirty Old Man*, p. 9.

12. *Ibid.*, p. 132.

13. Bukowski, "what have I seen," in *The Continual Condition: Poems*, ed. John Martin (New York: Ecco, 2009), p. 110.

14. Michel Foucault, "The Repressive Hypothesis" from *The History of Sexuality, Volume I*, in *The Foucault Reader*, ed. Paul Rabinow (New York: Pantheon Books, 1984), pp. 318–19. Bukowski's work has been included in several anthologies of erotic literature. See *Fetish: An Anthology of Fetish Fiction*, ed. John Yau (New York: Four Walls Eight Windows, 1998), "Love for $17.50," pp. 23–28; *Love Is Strange*, ed. Richard Glyn Jones (London: Indigo, 1998), "The Copulating Mermaid of Venice, California," pp. 143–153; *The Best American Erotic Poems: From 1800 to the Present*, ed. David Lehman (New York: Scribner Poetry, 2008), "Hunk of Rock," pp. 67–74.

15. Darlene Fife, *Portraits from Memory: New Orleans in the Sixties* (New Orleans: Surregional Press, 2000), p. 4. On Bukowski, NOLA, and an account of the "persistent harassment" the paper experienced, see Laurence Leamer, *The Paper Revolutionaries: The Rise of the Underground Press* (New York: Simon and Schuster, 1972), pp. 146–52.

16. *Ibid.*, p. 15. On Francisco McBride's artwork, which illustrated Bukowski's column, see p. 26. On Bukowski and New Orleans, see Jeff Weddle, *Bohemian New Orleans: The Story of* The Outsider *and Loujon Press* (Jackson: University of Mississippi Press, 2007); "Writing New Orleans" by Andrei Codrescu in Greil Marcus and Werner Sollors, *A New Literary History of America* (Cambridge: Harvard University Press, 2009), p. 405.

17. *Federal Bureau of Investigation File #140-35907, 1957–1970. Henry Charles Bukowski, Jr. (a.k.a. "Charles Bukowski").*

18. *Absence of the Hero*, pp. 59–63.

19. Bukowski, *Tales of Ordinary Madness* (San Francisco: City Lights, 1983), pp. 77–82. The original *Erections, Ejaculations and Other Tales of Ordinary Madness* has been subsequently divided into two titles and republished as *The Most Beautiful Woman in Town* (San Francisco: City Lights, 1983), and *Tales of Ordinary Madness* (San Francisco: City Lights, 1983).

20. *Notes of A Dirty Old Man*, "When Henry's mother died it wasn't bad," pp. 112–115.

21. Mailer admired Bukowski's poetry, writing in a letter to Al Fogel that "he spits his words out like nails" (personal communication from Al Fogel, July 19, 2010). Hank Chinaski comments on "Victor Norman" (Mailer) in *Hollywood*: "What I liked best about him was that he had no fear of the Feminists. He was one of the last defenders of maleness and balls in the U.S. I wasn't always pleased with his literary output but I wasn't always pleased with mine either." See Bukowski, *Hollywood* (Santa Rosa: Black Sparrow, 1989), p. 107. For Bukowski on Mailer, also see *Sunlight Here I Am*, pp. 54, 121, 150, 162, 224. The two men met at the Chateau Marmont in Hollywood during the making of *Barfly*. See Sounes, pp. 210–212.

22. "Dirty Old Man Confesses," p. 101.

23. *Ibid.*, p. 92.

24. Barry Hoskyns, *Lowside of the Road: A Life of Tom Waits* (New York: Broadway Books, 2009), p. 73. Waits's poem beginning "diamonds on my windshield, tears from heaven" appeared together with drawings by Bukowski in the magazine *The Sunset Palms Hotel*, vol. 2, Spring 1974, no. 4.

25. Carol Sklenicka, *Raymond Carver: A Writer's Life* (New York: Scribner, 2009), pp. 168. Also see pp. 207–9, 210, 448.

26. *Conversations with Raymond Carver*, eds. Marshall Bruce Gentry and William L. Stull (Jackson: University of Mississippi Press, 1990), pp. 36. Also see pp. 192, 226. For Carver's poem on Bukowski, "You Don't Know What Love Is (an evening with Charles Bukowski)," see *Fires: Essays, Poems, Stories* (New York: Vintage Books, 1984), pp. 57–61.

ACKNOWLEDGMENTS

More Notes of a Dirty Old Man—like my earlier book of Bukowski interviews, *Sunlight Here I Am: Interviews & Encounters 1963–1993*, and the two previous volumes I have edited
for City Lights, *Portions from a Wine-Stained Notebook* and *Absence of the Hero*—has had a long genesis. Back in the nine-
ties, Jamie Boran sent me an anthology of Bukowski's work
that he had compiled from the *Los Angeles Free Press*. This
was one of the catalysts that set in motion my fifteen-year
quest for unpublished and uncollected Bukowski writings. I
included a selection of the *Notes of a Dirty Old Man* columns
in *Portions* and *Absence*, but it became clear to me that there
remained a still unknown cornucopia of wonderful stories,
essays, interviews, cartoons, poems, and aphorisms. At City
Lights, Garrett Caples—who like T.S. Eliot is both poet and
editor—shared my enthusiasm. He imagined this book as
a sequel to the first and famous *Notes of a Dirty Old Man*,
and I would like to thank him for his dedication to this project during a time when he has been working hard on his
own groundbreaking edition of Philip Lamantia. I would
also like to thank Julie Herrada, Head of the Labadie Collection, Special Collections at the University of Michigan, Ann
Arbor. This is a treasure trove of anarchist literature, and I
spent many happy hours in that seventh-floor room with a
view. Thanks to Roger Myers of the University of Arizona
Library, Special Collections and to Ed Fields, University of
California at Santa Barbara, Department of Special Collections, Davidson Library. Thanks Scott Harrison, former proprietor of the Abandoned Planet bookstore in San Francisco
for information about John Bryan as well as to Al Fogel for

his exchange of letters with Norman Mailer. I am grateful to Roni, head of the *Charles Bukowski Gesellschaft* in Germany and editor of a splendid series of *Jahrbücher* devoted to Bukowski scholarship published by the Society. Roni, at the very last moment of the book's production, alerted me to the existence of the extremely cool photograph by Michael Montfort that graces the cover. My thanks to Daisy Montfort for granting permission. Gratitude as always for everything to Maria Beye. *Muchas gracias* to Abel Debritto—*il maestro di che sanno*—who helped with his encyclopaedic knowledge of all things Bukowski. To my 90-year-old father, Pierre Calonne, who during this past year showed me the meaning of the word courage. To the memory of my mother Mariam. To my brother Ariel, his wife Pat, my nephews Alexander, Nicholas, and Michael. Deepest thanks to E.M. Cioran, for keeping me up, bright, and sublime. And finally, my gratitude to Linda Lee Bukowski whom I had the pleasure of meeting for the first time in October 2010 at the Huntington Library's *Charles Bukowski: Poet on the Edge* celebration in San Marino, California, and whose unflagging energy and passion continue to inspire me: thank you, Linda.

Charles Bukowski was born in Andernach, Germany, in 1920 and brought to California at age three. Although Bukowski spent two years at Los Angeles City College, he was largely self-educated as a writer. He spent much time in his youth in the Los Angeles Public Library, where he encountered some of the writers whose work would influence his own: Dostoevsky, Turgenev, Nietzsche, D. H. Lawrence, Céline, e. e. cummings, Pound, Fante, and Saroyan. He was a prolific poet and prose writer, publishing more than fifty volumes. City Lights has published several Bukowski titles including *Tales of Ordinary Madness, Notes of a Dirty Old Man, The Most Beautiful Woman in Town, Portions from a Wine-Stained Notebook: Uncollected Stories and Essays, 1944–1990*, and *Absence of the Hero: Uncollected Stories and Essays Vol. 2. 1946–1992* (2010). Charles Bukowski died in San Pedro, California, on March 9, 1994.

David Stephen Calonne is the author of *William Saroyan: My Real Work Is Being, The Colossus of Armenia: G.I. Gurdjieff and Henry Miller*, and most recently *Bebop Buddhist Ecstasy: Saroyan's Influence on Kerouac and the Beats with an Introduction by Lawrence Ferlinghetti* (San Francisco: Sore Dove Press, 2010). He has edited *Charles Bukowski: Sunlight Here I Am/Interviews & Encounters 1963–1993*. For City Lights, he has previously edited *Portions from a Wine-Stained Notebook: Uncollected Stories and Essays, 1944–1990* (2008), and *Absence of the Hero*. He has lectured in Paris and at many universities including UCLA, the University of Chicago, the University of Pennsylvania, Columbia University, UC Berkeley, the European University Institute in Florence, the University of London, Harvard, and Oxford. He has taught at the University of Texas at Austin and the University of Michigan. During Spring Term 2009, he taught a seminar on William Saroyan at the University of Chicago. Presently he teaches at Eastern Michigan University.